YESTERDAY 9

YESTERDAY 9

AAKASH V SHIVACH

INVINCIBLE PUBLISHERS

Published by
Invincible Publishers
201A, SAS Tower, Sector 38, Gurugram – 122003
Phone: +91-124-4034247, +91 9355675555
Web: www.invinciblepublishers.com

This book is a work of fiction. Names, characters, places and incidents are either the product of the author's imagination or are used fictitiously. Any resemblance to real persons, living or dead, or actual events or locations, is purely coincidental and the publisher does not hold responsibility for the same.

First Published in 2020

ISBN: 978-93-89600-51-3

Acknowledgement

I would like to express my gratitude to all people at my work place and the girl who established peace in my life, healed me to help me build and secure myself. Above all, through the friendship that she nourished me with and by calling me 'Sky', she helped me trace a life that everyone adores.

My satisfactory travels which gave me a chance to taste my sprouted emotions well and pen them down in this book.

My parents, who are everything to me, but always deny to accept it.

To my sister, who is not in this world but carries her dreams in me.

Lastly and more strongly, to all my travel buddies.

Thank you everyone who helped me turn this dream to reality.

Contents

Prologue

And the light was set in,

For getting those eyes to shut to a slumber.

Sun rose quite late. Must have got covered by dark clouds.

Mrs. Charles couldn't help but feel mesmerized by the environment. She set the messy room in order. Her child, Mark, was pretty naughty. It became her routine that downcast her enthusiasm and made her hit rock bottom.

Her eyes were filled with tears. She went to the window. Her hands trembled to remove the curtains. They covered the glass wall fitted to the wooden frame of her backyard. Mark—the chain to her routine, stayed with Mr. and Mrs. Charles, his parents.

They lived in a cozy sea-facing house which had wilderness behind it. Mr. Charles was grateful to the US federal agency, NASA, for accommodating the couple as caretakers. His services to the agency bore ingenuity and workmanship. He was hired for a project to work round the clock. It was 8 am, things moved at a slow pace. Mrs. Charles couldn't brace herself up against the poor sunshine. She ran swiftly towards the window pane to set her emotions free. Tears rolled down her cheeks. Something was bothering her. The environment made her pensive. Her feet trembled. She felt melancholic but could do nothing to throttle her uneasiness.

Somebody knocked at the door.

"Who is it?" asked Mrs. Charles.

Half-heartedly she opened the door, gazing at the stranger.

"It's me Aunty, Maunik," replied Maunik, her son's friend.

"Oh yes. Come in," Mrs. Charles said while wrapping her stole over her shoulders and taking a deep breath.

"How's Mark now? Has the doctor gone?" enquired Maunik hesitatingly as she held the door ajar.

"Yes, he has left but Mark is still unconscious."

"How can it be?" wondered Mrs. Charles, eyeing the boy with sympathy.

"Doctor said that he will keep Mark under surveillance for 24 hours and then say something."

Mrs. Charles poured water into the glass from a flask nearby.

"I wish to enquire about your predicament, Aunty." Maunik occupied the rearmost couch.

"Who could it be? Have you told your neighbour about the accident last night?" Maunik asked.

"No, I haven't. Why would I? You asked me not to share it." Mrs. Charles looked sullen.

Mrs. Charles gave her one look and worriedly asked, "Why are you trembling, dear? Is it necessary?"

There was a knock at the door. Mrs. Charles jumped to see who it was.

"Wait, I shall see." Maunik was at the door before her.

"Is Mrs. Charles in?" enquired Mrs. Sinha. She stayed next door. Maunik let her in with a smile.

"Why won't you pick up the phone, Mrs. Charles?"

"A neurologist from the Apollo hospital in Delhi called me on my Landline and informed me about Mr. Charles ill health. I think you gave them my number as an alternate contact number," Mrs. Sinha said.

"What?" shouted Maunik.

"Relax," said Mrs. Charles, calming him down.

"Tell me what happened, Mrs. Sinha?" intervened Mrs. Charles, putting her hand over Mrs. Sinha's shoulder.

"I received a call from Mr. Charles' neurologist. She wasn't picking up. He narrated about queer changes within Mr. Charles' body. The doctor said he has been trying to talk to you since last night," said Mrs. Sinha.

"Aah, has he intimated about any solution?"

"He asked someone to accompany him," replied Mrs. Sinha.

"Why did he say so? Is he not aware of the fact that Mr. Charles never makes things worsen in the hospital," said Mrs. Charles and moved into her room to take out her stuff from her cupboard.

"Mr. Charles has lost his senses," replied Mrs. Sinha.

Mrs. Charles was disheartened. She started stuffing her things in a suitcase to leave for Delhi.

"I am still bewildered. Will somebody explain?" asked Maunik, on hearing the ambiguous conversation.

"I didn't tell you or Maunik this because your exams are due next month," said Mrs. Charles.

"What shall I say to Mark?" wondered Maunik aloud.

"See, I am not wrong. Things were pretty unclear, it didn't allow me to share anything with you," replied Mrs. Charles.

She continued towards Mrs. Sinha with her suitcase.

"For now, let us pray for Mark to get conscious. Everything else can wait," declared Mrs. Charles.

"Will you come with me?" asked Mrs. Charles to Mrs. Sinha.

"Sure," replied Mrs. Sinha.

"I still don't know the answers, Aunty," said Maunik, looking at the women.

"How can you? You failed to convey what happened with you both last night on your way back from Delhi," replied Mrs. Charles.

"I swear, it was an accident." Maunik was hesitant.

"It wasn't and you know it very well." Mrs. Charles was sure.

"About your privacy, please uphold my onus," said Mrs. Charles, moving towards his stood to pick up her inhaler.

Two stories stayed undisclosed,
Trying to grab the knowledge of what was left behind the door which was still closed.
Intense desires are in favour of producing helping hand,
Wanting to know what's lying underneath every band.
Every other person is trying to capture the instinct of each other,
Wanting to know the hidden reality which is not willing to open its feather.

"I understand," smiled Maunik.

"Thanks, hope you will take care of everything. I can't share things with you right now, hope you understand," said Mrs. Charles, closing her eyes.

"Don't bother. I understand. Please look after Uncle Charles," said Maunik, approaching the door.

Anticipation Of Survival

Six hours passed by without any improvement in Mark's health. This was becoming a source of emotional strain for Maunik. He moved from one room to another swiftly. His numerous calls to the doctor to enquire whether there was any improvement in Mark's health were answered in negative. He felt exhausted by the burden of the uncertainty that the situation posed. He went mad trying to accept the reality of Mark's health. He prayed every second for betterment in Mark's health.

Silence reigned over Mark's home. The feelings of agony and distress could be felt in every nook and corner of the house.

Maunik sat cross-legged against the wall, with his elbows placed over his knees, and his palms holding his forehead. It rolled on to many answers uncalled for. Underneath the reality, many cubes overlap. Asking for generalisation in return. The entire house was enveloped in silence. Eight hours had passed by but there was still no positive news regarding Mark's health. Maunik's stress increased rapidly with the passage of each minute. His anxiety was clashing with his past. The papers kept on Mark's study table began to fly in the air like some storm had moved them. Having been scattered in the whole room, they covered every little space there. Maunik did not react strangely on noticing the papers having moved on their own. He got up from his seat and simply went on collecting the papers one after the other.

"Get up my boy. This is not what we want. I can't look at you like this," Maunik said, restoring those papers.

A glass filled with water which was placed on the table fell down making a loud noise. The glass broke into many pieces and scattered on the floor. Maunik rushed to Mark's bed and bent down to uncover. His eyes were focusing on the darkness somewhere in the distance. It went on to encounter something left off. Maunik stood up and began to collect the broken pieces at one place. He was lost wondering about the exhaustive events that had recently been taking place.

"God, why my intense dedication finds frustrated? What's wrong with this place?" Maunik said, caressing Mark's forehead with his hand.

Maunik turned his back towards the wall to find out what was going on over the door. His feet felt warm as they rubbed against the ground. His hands shook due to some unknown feeling. His pulse was low. He was unable to feel any force or thrust. His weary face kept him compressed even after ecstatic moments.

"Nothing is abnormal; I've realized from my discomfort," said Maunik as he returned to the room, throwing veils harshly on either side.

"See, it's because of you. Why don't you come out?" said Maunik, looking at Mark.

The atmosphere was locked with asylum. Maunik took place over rope swings kept in the drawing room. He swung back facing the wall with his eyes shut. Something surrounded moisture spreading those lively breath. A few hours rolled by without any news about Mark's welfare. Maunik stayed quiet, holding many hidden facts within him. Whatever helped him think practically facilitated him to sift through time. Everything he inhaled was exhaled quietly.

"Umm…" A sound echoed out of Mark's room.

"What is it?" asked Maunik as he woke up and rushed into Mark's room.

"Mark…Mark!" exclaimed Maunik.

"Is it you?" Maunik asked, his hand on the door knob as he stared at Mark.

"I believe the sound I just heard was made by you," he said while entering the room, noticing Mark's body to still be still.

"Oh! You don't know the state I am in. I believed you to have returned to your senses," he said.

He sat next to Mark's feet. His eyes searched Mark's face for any sign of innocence.

***

Mark returned to normalcy, and like always, became the hero of the day. Maunik wondered about the charm that he had. Mark praised people in an artistic way and added a certain flavour to it that people cherished. He knew how to make people happy and at times, he did it through his creativity. Mark was an IT professional. He had inherited skills from his father, Mr. Charles–the great scientist. Interestingly, he was also a fictional story writer and a great dancer. His style of writing was appreciated by many of his readers. But he did not very well understand what people meant when they used the word "natural" in their compliments. His stories were continuously recognized by the media and were debated on. He was in Delhi the past one year and came back home that very morning. He found travelling extremely strenuous.

As per information he had attained, Mrs. Charles met with an accident back home. Maunik gave Mark's mother, Mrs. Charles, assurance that he would take care of her boy. She believed that her son would be alright very soon. The pressure of many things hauled Mark. His persistent prayers remained unanswered. Maunik's control over Mark yield it no return. His wish for Mark's wellness was still positive. The warm water of broken aspirations was awash. Maunik's identity was hung in balance. His breath sounded heavy as though it was being reflected off the wall.

***

"Aah… Tamanna!" Mark exhaled.

"Yeah, yeah. Come again." A smile floated on Maunik's face as it spread over his cheeks.

He instantly called the doctor and informed him about Mark's response.

"Hey, yeah. Mark spoke a word; he's back, Doctor. He's back," said Maunik loudly.

"Oh, that's wonderful! God takes care of his pure souls," the doctor said, exhaling.

"Yes... he just said someone's name."

"Is it? Then let's check how he is doing." The doctor began to examine Mark.

"I am getting a positive sign from his pulse," he added.

"Huh, I can't tell you how much this means to me, doctor. Thank you. Thank you. Thank you everyone," Maunik said as he began to breathe in excitement.

"It all depends on you now," the doctor said his last word before he slammed the call.

After having heard the doctor's last word, Maunik put down the phone and a beaming smile spread over his cheeks, covering every pain that previously prevailed. He wiped his tears as he walked towards Mark.

"I am on the top of this world. It feels like I've got one more life to live," uttered Maunik.

Maunik gently wiped Mark's face and moved aside the strands of hair that were falling on his forehead, to look at his face.

"Speak up, brother! Speak something," insisted Maunik.

"Tamanna," said Mark, with a husky voice and closed eyes.

Maunik understood nothing coming out of his lips. His eyes peered helplessly towards Mark.

***

Tamanna was the girl who met Mark while he was in Delhi. Mark, Tamanna, and Maunik had come from Delhi to Mark's home yesterday. It was then when they encountered a deadly accident. Maunik was driving the car as Mark was never interested in driving. Mark and Tamanna were sitting on the back seat. During the past few months that he spent in Delhi, Mark and Tamanna fell in love. She was everything he had ever wished to see in the girl he would be in love with. Mark did not fall in love with Tamanna intentionally. Every power in this cosmos had magically worked to make Mark and Tamanna fall in love. Mark, a guy who has a pleasant personality, was not even interested to get involved with anyone in a way to allow them to unnecessarily occupy his time. But after meeting Tamanna, he began to fall more in love with her with every passing day. She became an important part of his life.

***

"I asked you something; where is she?" Mark tried to get up with extreme difficulty and in tormenting pain. With his slightly opened eyes, he asked Maunik this question, who was holding his head with his right hand.

"You aren't fine yet… your health. Please don't get up," insisted Maunik.

"I want my answer," Mark said loudly as he tried to gather his energy.

"And I want you to heal soon," replied Maunik.

"I will be. Answer my question," Mark said while bearing excruciating pain.

Maunik got up from his place. He went towards the rearmost bench to get water for Mark. There were tears in his eyes and he was barely able to keep them from being noticed by Mark.

"What are you doing there? Where is Tamanna? I want to see her. Can't you understand?" Mark said while pain ran through his body.

"Wait, I am bringing water for you," Maunik said while hiding his face, wiping the tears off his face.

"Not required! Just answer me," said Mark, as he tried to get out of bed rather unsuccessfully as he partially fell down the bed.

"What are you doing!" Maunik placed the glass filled with water aside and hurriedly moved towards Mark.

"I am doing nothing. I just want you to answer my question."

"She is completely fine. Are you listening? She is all right."

"Where is she? I can't see her."

"She got injured a little and was taken back home to Delhi by her father."

"Home? But you and I were well informed in Delhi that Sinha Aunty is the one who is her mother," Mark said.

Maunik did not reply to anything Mark said. He tried to stay busy organizing and fidgeting with things present in the room. He started to check the medical instruments attached to Mark's body that were monitoring his progress.

"What home, Maunik! Her home is here only. Aunty, Mrs. Sinha, lives right next to us," Mark said again, after giving it a thought.

"But her father lives in Delhi."

"So, they took her? But why?"

"How do I explain it to you?" replied Maunik.

***

Tamanna, the girl Mark met in Delhi, was the daughter of his neighbouring Aunty 'Mrs. Sinha'. Mrs. Sinha had been living close to their home since many years. Mrs. Sinha earlier lived in her parental house and built her own house only a few years ago. Mark met Tamanna by luck and then their mutual attraction and similarities brought them close. In the beginning, Mark wasn't aware of Mrs. Sinha and Tamanna's relationship. The passage of time brought them close enough to discuss their families. Tamanna took the initiative and conveyed to Mark about her family and her lineage. Mark being peppy knowing everything. After impish this relation, he felt the same concerns his book story speaks, which came in front of him. 'This world is very small and circular; good people meet other good people with some strange force moving around.' So Mark's perception of life became stronger after this:

"Why do they say that this generation's people aren't good?

Just maintain your goodness, kindness, and your generous nature all along,

and you will come across good people just like you."

These three decided to surprise their families with their amazing discovery. And so, they left Delhi that night.

***

"What? She isn't here?" asked Mark while putting his feet down on the floor and removing the medical instruments attached to his body.

"Don't do that. The doctor has asked that strict precautions be taken. You are under observation," said Maunik, rushing towards Mark.

"Don't worry, I don't require these. You said she's not here but I am getting a strong hunch of her being around us," said Mark as he stood up and walked around his room.

"How come this bedsheet moved on its own?" asked Maunik, pointing towards Mark's bed.

"It's true, I can perceive her in this air," said Mark, with his eyes lost, looking around for her unknowingly.

"Can you first listen to my words? There are many strange things happening around here," Maunik said, urging Mark to listen to him.

"But I can feel her around me," Mark said, with a smile on his face.

"There are many other things in life that you need to be concerned about," said Maunik as he moved towards Mark.

"I never mask my feelings. I can feel her around me… believe me," said Mark, as he turned towards Maunik, held him by his shoulder and gazed into his eyes with confidence.

"How can it be?" Maunik looked into Mark's eyes searching for an answer.

"See, her favourite song is being played right now. Can you hear it?" said Mark, as he pointed his index finger towards the window on his left.

"It's coming from outside; somebody must be playing it." The second he uttered those words, he was himself caught in confusion.

"Who decorated the space next to my pillow with her crafts?" asked Mark, pointing towards his bed.

"These designed cards and decorated sheets with colourful paper balls; how can you forget those wool-covered artistic bottles. She made them that day, remember that day I shared the images with you?

Look at those designed seasonal plates; she crafted them so well that its complete picture could be kept framed in everyone's mind after just one look. She is the one and the only one. She has taken my heart and I am proud to say that."

Maunik wasn't able to respond to a single word Mark said. He was extremely stunned to learn about all the things happening in that room.

"Who kept those things there, I don't know. Please understand this, Tamanna isn't here." Maunik's throat dried and his eyes widened to learn about all the strange happenings in that room.

"Okay! Ok, I agree that she's not here at present. I think about her the whole day. I cannot think of anything else except for her. She has left her mark on me to last forever," said Mark, moving towards the living room with Maunik's help.

"Your perilous reactions makes me hard to control," said Maunik, rubbing his right palm over Mark's mouth.

"Whatever it be, I am happy that nothing went wrong yesterday 9," said Mark.

"Yesterday 9?" Maunik starred at Mark for answers.

"Oh yea… I haven't told you anything about it? Those mysterious words of our astrologer Divyansh..." Mark said, lost in the words the astrologer said.

"Now, who's Divyansh?" Maunik asked.

"Divyansh is an astrologer friend of mine whom I recently met. He is kind and generous, and has a pure heart."

"He joined our organisation some time ago," he added.

"Ok, could you please clarify what you meant when you said Yesterday 9?" Maunik asked anxiously.

"Wait, I'm coming to that. Was first telling you who this person is. So, everything between me and Tamanna is pretty good. But you know, I don't believe in those astrological predictions that some people make about your future. That is the only thing which is very different between both of us," Mark said.

"I want to know what happened yesterday at 9. You're making it seem worthlessly deep," Maunik said, exasperated.

"Or I am trying to give you the exact picture."Aren't you too feeling something crawl underneath this carpet?" asked Mark, with wrinkles forming on his forehead.

"Hmm, there is something wrong with your room today," said Maunik, with a puzzled look on his face.

"What's wrong? Everything is just as it was," Mark said.

"Leave, let's not divert the topic. Continue with what you were telling me," said Maunik, standing on the carpet.

"Yes, he spoke to me on that day that we left Delhi which was yesterday," said Mark.

"What did he convey?"

"He asked me not to travel on that care day, as it would be harmful to me in some strange way," Mark said, still puzzled.

"What? And why didn't you consider it?" shouted Maunik, as he looked at Mark limping to move towards him.

"You know that I don't believe in these future myths and predictions. So, why would you even ask that to me," replied Mark

"Do you need something?" asked Maunik.

"No, I'm just thinking of how your come back to India was planned months ago. You came back from Australia last afternoon, right?" Mark began to breathe heavily as he spoke.

"Wait, you need water," Maunik said, stepping back to get some for Mark.

"I don't," said Mark, grasping Maunik's wrist tightly.

"Help me a little here," said Mark, and moved out of the room, holding onto Maunik's shoulder.

"Now see, what you are doing again! You still haven't told me what all he said exactly," said Maunik as he followed Mark who was heading towards the kitchen.

"Uff, such an untidy kitchen," said Mark, irritated.

"Wow, now you care about the kitchen," replied Maunik, throwing his hand above his head in the air in annoyance.

"I want to cook. You don't know it; Tamanna loves the way I make food. You should have seen her face when she had those meat rolls of mine," said Mark, as he dusted the shelf with a red cloth that was lying around.

"You are still thinking about her? What about your own health?" Maunik said, irritatingly.

"Still thinking about her... What do you mean? I haven't allowed my soul to think of anyone else apart from her. Oh, let this be. Give me her father's number; let me check on her," said Mark, pushing his feet moving towards Maunik carrying rag.

"Can't you understand this! The doctor has given strict instructions for you to rest." Maunik snatched the rag out of his hand.

"Do you see the condition in which the kitchen is? How can I tolerate this!"

"It is not untidy, Mark. See, it is well-aligned and decorated," said Maunik, making Mark face the kitchen.

"Umm...Yeah... But how did this happen?" Mark looked at every corner of the kitchen.

"What happened? The kitchen is as it was."

"No... No."

"Look, you are coming with me to go back to your room," said Maunik, holding Mark's hand tightly, making him move towards his room.

"Wait...wait... please."

"Why can't we sit here only, come! Come on! See… let's sit here." Mark pulled Maunik's hand with his complete strength to make him sit on the wooden bench that was present in the middle of the kitchen.

"What are you trying to do?"

"I will tell you the story you kept asking me while you were in Australia," said Mark, as he pulled Maunik to sit next to him on the bench.

"Wait, let me bring you coffee as I am sure you want to have it," said Maunik, opening a shelf in which the coffee container was kept.

"Yes, brother. While you make coffee, I will take you to a beautiful land of love," said Mark.

"But remember that everything around here is proving my point, and making me know that she's here only," shouted Mark, with a smile on his cheeks.

Over To Metro

It's Monday, which has arrived after two relaxing weekends. The day is quite the same as every other working day of the week. Now the mind needs to get attentive to again begin the struggle to complete the work which was kept on hold during the weekend.

Mark's morning starts pretty early. He wakes up at 4:30 a.m. and begins his day exercising, followed by a full breakfast for a healthy start. Professionally, Mark is an IT technocrat working in a renowned company. The company takes care of all of his expenses for staying in Delhi. Mark isn't from Delhi and works from home. Presently, due to work, he needs to stay in Delhi for a longer period of time. The company requires him to deliver their latest project which they attained recently from a crucial client. Mark inherited his technical knowledge from his father, Mr. Charles. His passion for literature made him move into writing fictional stories and become a successful author. He recently released his second novel through a famous publishing house last month in Delhi.

Though Mark had all the amenities for living an easy and good life in Delhi, he preferred to live with his Aunt, Mrs. Shivach.

Mrs Shivach had been living in Delhi for 30 years with her husband, Mr. Shivach. They don't have a child, so take care of Mark as their very own. Mark loves to spend his free time with them and stays with them in North Delhi. He needs to travel for two hours every day to reach his office but this hardly matters to him as long as he can stay with people he loves.

It was 7:30 a.m. and Mark was rushing to get ready to reach office on time. He left home at 8:00 a.m. to reach office on time.

"So, how many days has it been since you've met Sayoni?" Mrs.

Shivach asked Mark, standing in the kitchen while he was busy tying his shoelaces.

"Ah, Sayoni. Good question. I haven't met her since some time," replied Mark, after having given some thought about the matter.

Sayoni was a very good friend of Mark. They built a wonderful bond of friendship when Mark went on his previous solo trip to Tartan Valley. Sayoni has a kind heart and a pure soul and whenever Mark interacted with her, he felt her gentle words heal all his negative emotions. Sayoni belonged to Delhi which is what made Mrs. Shivach interested in keeping an update on her status.

"Means you haven't been concerned about your best friend since the time you've come from Delhi," Mrs. Shivach said, handing a glass of milk to him.

"No, it isn't like that. I speak to her on the phone. Whenever I try to leave office early to meet her, some or the other thing comes up," replied Mark, looking at Mrs. Shivach while taking the milk glass.

"It depends on you; how you want to manage your personal life over your professional one," said Mrs. Shivach, going back to the kitchen.

"It looks like you have given your life to your stories and the rest of it to your everyday work," added Mrs. Shivach.

"Oh… It's 7:50," said Mark, looking at his watch and realizing he needs to hurry to reach office on time.

"Don't forget anything in a rush," Mrs. Shivach said and left to go downstairs to the ground floor.

Mark rushed to keep his laptop and other documents in his baggage, took his helmet and went straight to the drawing room on the ground floor to pick his packed lunch made by Mrs. Shivach. Finally, he went to the main door where Mrs. Shivach was waiting for him with sandalwood powder in a small bowl in her hand.

"Wait, stop; else in your hurry, it will again not be placed how you want it and you will stand to correct it in front of the mirror," said Mrs. Shivach while applying the auspicious powder on his forehead.

“Yes, today it’s perfect,” said Mark, looking at his face in the mirror near the exit door.

“Take care, *bacha*,” said Mrs. Shivach, placing the helmet in his hand.

“You know Maa! My busy mind with all its thoughts does not let me think of driving safely,” said Mark, smiling at his aunt.

“Yea… you and your thoughts… Leave your mind to stay free sometimes,” said Mrs. Shivach, putting her hand over Mark’s head.

“I can’t,” said Mark, smiling, and headed towards his bike and started it.

On reaching the metro, Mark thought: “I should walk faster, I feel there is going to be a long queue at the metro’s check-in,” as he left his bike in the metro’s parking area and rushed towards the check-in.

“God, nobody’s here and it’s Monday. I must be blessed that there is no rush today,” he thought, looking up as he checked-in easily.

Mark stood at the platform with both his arms folded, eyes closed, and his hands rubbing his eyes. He held his bag tightly which was hanging over his right shoulder. He heard the sound of the train approaching.

“She hasn’t come yet it seems. Yesterday she was reading some motivational book. Who was the writer. I wasn’t able to check,” Mark murmured, looking at the time on his watch.

“Will she come or do I leave?” Mark thought, his feet moving towards the opened gate of the metro but his eyes were fixed at the stairs.

“If God wants, I will see her again someday,” Mark said as he stepped inside the metro.

Mark had to change his metro in between. There was no direct metro to reach his destination. He changed his metro and boarded the other one. The minute he entered the train, he felt a sensation and a glow spread across Mark’s face. At his left, he saw the person he had been wanting to see since the start of his journey.

There was a soft smile on her face; a smile that made Mark feel numb within. He gazed at her beautiful eyes. She was beautiful, he knew it without a doubt. He could not resist looking at her and kept gazing at her. But simply gazing at her would not help him with anything, so Mark found the courage in him and approached the girl to begin a conversation with her.

"Heavy crowd… A bit hectic, isn't it?" Mark said, facing her. She looked at him and greeted him with a smile.

"Hey, hi…" he said after a break.

"Umm… Yes?" the girl said, with her eyebrows raised, removing her earphones out of her ears.

"I saw you yesterday; you were reading some motivational book," said Mark shyly.

"Oh yea... that one! Yes, I was just going through it," she answered.

"I noticed the title, so know its genre," he replied.

"Seems you know a lot about these things. Interesting," she said.

"No, I understand a little about it as I am an author myself," he said.

"Oh…Is it? I see! What is your book about?" she asked with a smile on her cheeks.

"Oh, wonderful! Somebody just gave me a chance to promote my book," he said, taking a deep breath with a bright smile.

"I write fictional stories. My latest book was released some time ago," he conveyed.

"What's the name of your book?" She asked with a lot of curiosity and a craze in her eyes.

"It's called 'Steps Taking Backward'–an unpredictable romantic venture of mine where the protagonist is trying to uncover the true factor of love and life which aren't the same as the delight produced when one is in love," Mark said. He was lost in the same beautiful realm in which his story existed.

"I have tried to bring out emotions in a healthy way. Trying to touch every desire without any bad influence on the reader," added Mark.

"That's superb to hear," she said with cheerfulness, conveying the truth of her joy through her sweet eyes.

"Is it something you have taken form your real-life story?" she asked with her eyebrows raised.

"No, there's nothing I have taken from my real life. But yea, some early chapters can be related to my adolescent age. I have squeezed in the best parts of my story in this," he replied.

"Everyone first asks me this question only." Mark laughed.

"Your short summary has filled me with questions. I want to know more now," she said with a smile while tucking the loose strands of her hair behind her ear.

"Yea... It means a lot to me. I carry a copy of my book all the time," he said.

"Cool! Can I see it?" She asked for the book with a genuine smile.

"Yes. Why not!" he said while bringing the book out of his bag.

"Wow... It is so nice to see this. And may I ask why do you carry one copy of your book all the time with you?"

"So that I can always show my book to someone like you when they ask me about it," Mark answered quickly, his left hand scratching his head.

"Oh. Can I take this one?" she asked sweetly.

No one had shown such sweet craving in front of Mark for his book before. He wanted others to give the same love to his book that he himself gave to it every day. This new girl had already made herself a space in his heart with her craze for his book.

"Aah... yea, you can," said Mark after a little thought. He had never before let anyone take the book which he carried with himself.

"Will love to hear any critics that you have if you find any after going through it," he said, handing her the book.

"Yea... sure, I will."

"Well, writing came into my life at a later age. Music has been my first love since birth," Mark added.

"Oh. So you must be a guitar player?" she asked while giving an impression of holding a guitar in her hands.

"What? How do you know this?" he asked.

"I once saw you listening to a song and playing the tune virtually with your hands," she said.

"Is it?" He giggled.

After thinking for a second, he said, "My family gets to easily understand my entire day's status each night when I begin to play my guitar."

"That's sweet… Your emotions get known without being told," Tamanna said. "I only know how to play the piano. My mother pushed me to learn it."

"Wow. I wonder if I should also try it," Mark replied.

"You know, books mean a lot to me. At home, we have a complete library with a collection of the best books," she said.

"So that means, I have given my book to the right one. God only knows how I gained the courage to talk to you," he said.

"Why so?"

"Leave that. So what's your name?" Mark asked.

"Tamanna," she said in a whisper. A vibration passed through Mark's body as he heard it and went silent for a few seconds.

"Like a desire," Mark said, staring at Tamanna's face.

"And my name is… you just read it on the book. It's Mark."

"Yes," replied Tamanna, closing her mouth, moving her brows up, and raising her chin.

"Where do you work?" Mark asked.

"I am working with an apparel company which designs only for US brands," she said with her beautiful smile.

"I am working with an IT company and struggling with IT since the last 5 years," he replied.

"Oh… are you an engineer or so?" she questioned with a natural reaction.

"Yea… I did my engineering and then, all of this started; after that, I completed my MBA as well," he replied.

"Ok... It was good to know and interact with you. My station is here, I have to go," she said and stepped towards the exit door when she heard a sound from her back.

"I'll be waiting to hear from you again after you go through this book," he replied, with a big, elongated smile which captured his face.

"Do you want that book you asked for at first?" asked Tamanna.

"Yea, I would. If you can bring that," he replied swiftly.

"Will carry that the next time," she added, with excitement in her voice.

"It's really nice to meet you," she replied, looking back at Mark with a smile on her face as she stood in front of the door to get out.

"Aah, same here!" said Mark, as he smiled back at her.

"Your destination came," said Mark, pointing his finger towards the platform's notice board.

"Yea…" said Tamanna before she turned to step out.

Mark was left behind curious to know many things about her.

"Why do I want to know about her more? I haven't cared for such things before," Mark said to himself.

The day passed by. Mark walked everywhere without any knowledge about anything; he felt like he was walking without wearing slippers. He was lost in his thoughts. He wasn't able to give his best to anything whether it was his morning meetings or his presentations, and he couldn't even concentrate on his client meetings.

"Can we also know what's happened in your life?" asked Geetanjali at evening when she found him extremely at unease in the entirety of his day.

Geetanjali, Mark's office colleague, had been working with him on the same project for the last two years. They carried a strong bond of understanding between them. Geetanjali stayed concerned about him when she didn't see his ever-present smile. She wanted him to always be happy. Mark lovingly called her 'Geet'.

"Aah. Nothing happened, Geet," replied Mark, while placing down his black coffee mug on his desk.

"Oh please, don't make me begin now. You haven't ever given a presentation the way you did today," replied Geet.

"You really want to know?"

"Of course, Mark. I can't see you like this.," She held Mark's hand and dragged him from his place, pulling him into the meeting room.

"Oh man… I can't say what it is. I cannot erase her from my mind," said Mark, letting his hand off Geet, as soon as they entered.

"Who's this? What happened to you?"

"I met her today; I told you before about her. I don't know how it happened but huh... it happened," said Mark in despair.

"Which girl? That one with the red hair you saw on over way?" she asked.

"Yea… about whom I had spoken to you before?"

"Woah! Tell me what happened? So did you speak to her?" she asked with elation to sprout silence of his face.

"Her name is Tamanna. An inkling of her that I had before speaking to her is now unfurling like a sweet chemical in my entire body," he said and took a deep breath, gazing at the roof.

"After I interacted today with her," he added.

"Oh… is it?" she questioned, with an open mouth.

"So now, over this event, you are stuck whole day long," she added.

"What name I should give this thing? I really don't know what it is," he said, scratching his head with his fingers.

"You know well, I am not in favour of being a part of such things," added Mark.

"Why do you even try to stop your emotions when you know that you can't defend them?" she asked him.

"Then what should I do?" he asked with desperation in his tone.

"Try interacting with her; first figure out what it is that's going on in your mind and soul. As bonding with her can only be done after you'll get more time to link with her," Geet said.

"Geet, can you come here once? Mr. Kumar is calling you," a colleague of their team said after peeping inside the room.

"You go, I'll take care of these things. Don't worry, I will be normal soon," said Mark.

Mark sat down on a chair thinking about all that had happened. At times, he stood up and again got mixed in the previous hunch that he had.

Conversation started like those buds inclined towards the wind flow,
Mark tried to step over this track very slow.
Someone whispered some words that he was waiting for,
Those attempts had unintentionally knocked at his door.
Whether these sweetest impressions he generated or not,
But these actions had started to bring together
inside him those left far elongated dots.

Floating Stream

Morning never came with such a surprise,

One feeling that has been felt before, now wanting to open its sprite.

God had whistled to give someone a beginning,

He asked to bless and make that smile of the other like anything.

Mark always tried to make his mornings stay calm and give him pleasure. By making them stay in one place, Mark learnt how to handle his emotions for making things a beautiful treasure. This new morning had also to bring him delight of thought that inspires his soul. Nothing changed, things were constant. His day kick-started at its usual time at 04:30 a.m. in the darkness of the morning.

Whether it be jogging or while he was at the gym, those thoughts of her could be easily sensed around the place by his smile. His full cheeks, his smile and his joy had already been felt by nature as the wind began to flow softly. Mark's ever-present smile which he generally found to be unwanted behaviour was becoming a reason of surprise for everyone. Mark's willingness to do everything said by Mrs. Shivach was noticeable. He never before listened to her with such obedience. This change caught her attention.

"Why are you in a hurry? It's just 7:40 a.m.?" asked Mrs. Shivach.

"Aah… Not in a hurry. Trying to do things a little before time so I won't be in a hurry at the time of driving," Mark said while folding back his shirt sleeves.

"Your lunch isn't ready. It will take time," she said.

"I am not feeling hungry enough to have lunch today; my stomach isn't happy," he replied.

"Ok, so take something or the other from there itself," she said, carrying breakfast for Mark.

"Will surely do," he said, before he went into the washroom.

"Well, how's Sayoni these days?" she asked, heading back to the kitchen.

"Huh, shit! How did I forget to call her? Thanks Maa, for reminding me," he said, checking something on the screen of his phone. Mrs. Shivach smiled looking at him.

"Yea… she shows a generous gratitude towards friendship; how can I miss to do the same… Will surely call her today," Mark said while rushing down the stairs to exit his home, carrying his office bag.

"Ride safely," said Mrs. Shivach, looking out from the window.

"I never do that. You perceive it," replied Mark, giving her a wink while wearing his helmet.

"I should reach before time as I don't know what time she reaches," Mark thought while riding his bike.

Every step Mark made to move towards the metro station was very quick. Every step he took gave the glimpse of that auspicious wonder stepping over heaven's white belching smoke. His eyes glanced around; that was something he hadn't done ever before on his way. The warmth of the sun started touching his body in such a way that it made him feel blessed. His lavish expressions and good beliefs started making him feel this aura of love at every instant.

"It's been time now, I think I have been late already," said Mark, looking at his watch while moving around the same spot.

"Let me wait for her a little more, she might be coming in a while," Mark said to himself.

After half an hour, "Oh God, what is it? I guess I should leave now," said Mark, looking up.

"Why has she not come? Sometimes things remain unpredictable," he smiled, stepping inside the metro as he pressed his palm on his forehead.

"I shouldn't think much about it," Mark pleaded himself to concentrate on the morning meeting to be held at office.

Don't feel, it would be functional, so what it evoked from your pure heart,
Trying hard to spare that feeling from everything, still, it gets stuck with worthless dirt.
I try to realise the positive part of it ever,
But I feel people are much clever.
I ever praise my true intention,
As they ever want to stay away from negative fact retention.

Heading to Office:

"Hope you will be fine today and not make a mess?" asked Geet.

"What are you hinting at?" queried Mark, raising his brows.

"Umm... why are you taking my buffs in a serious way?" she asked.

"I am not," said Mark and got up to make his coffee from the machine.

"So, how are you holding up? Met her today?" she asked, moving in front of Mark.

"Nah... nothing happened, I waited but she didn't come," he said, turning to move out of the cafeteria.

"Oh man, what happened?" Geet rushed to clench his hand and asked him to sit there only.

"Now tell me, what happened?" she asked, full of anxiety and curiosity.

"How do I know?" he replied with grief on his face.

"Maybe she was late to reach home. Are you aware of her timings?"

"No, not really."

"Then how can you assume or predict anything with this

perspective!" said Geet, moving his chin up to face her.

"Look, you haven't done anything and you are making it an issue," she told.

"What should I do?" he asked.

"Give me your phone," she said, before she pulled Mark's cell phone from his hand.

"What are you up to now?" asked Mark.

"See, here she is; I guess this one is Tamanna. Am I correct?" she asked while scrolling photos on a Facebook profile named Tamanna.

"Aah yes… Yes, she is the one. How you did this?" Mark stared at her with shocked eyes.

"Hey, would you just stop thinking all this and talk to her once?" she asked.

"Ok, leave my cell phone. Come, time for our call," Mark snatched his phone and pointed his finger at the clock.

"That's ok, but what about my words?" asked Geet, walking along with Mark towards the board room.

"Let's start this now, will think about it later," he said, picking up his mac and moving towards the projector.

Within minutes, the room got filled with many people. They all settled around the table and without entertaining any spectator, Mark picked up his pen and kept it in his pocket and began his presentation. Mark's eyes were repeatedly glancing at the light of his cell phone which he left on the middle of the table. After giving many irregular answers to all the queries raised by everyone, he became the victim of Geet's crippling questions. At last, Mark was able to finish the whole presentation without any output.

Mark finished his presentation and thanked all the members for patiently listening to him from the time he had started. Geet was still staring at Mark with her hostile eyes and Mark seemed not to worry about the crap he just delivered, which was very effectively noticed by Geet. Internal superiors and visitors started to leave the room after Mark winded up. Everyone indulged in small talk post-meeting. Mark's face wasn't cherishing the moment as the smile he had seemed to act like a swank.

All of this was noticed by Geet. She was suppressing her shoddy affection towards Mark. Her twitching eyes and lip-biting showed anxiety in her thoughts. Words she was holding back to throw at Mark over time.

Mark was waiting for everyone to depart the room so that he could move aside and pick up his cell phone. After a couple of minutes, he made way towards his phone. Mark gently picked it up within a second after the last person went out, and quickly glanced at his cell phone screen.

"Hey, listen... Listen Mark!" clamoured Geet.

"What's so important that made you ruin this presentation as well?" she said swiftly, looking at him as he was going away.

"No one can find me out here," he said, leaving his floor and sitting on the corner most staircase of his building.

"Geet found her in just one go. So sharp she is," he said while looking at the Facebook profile of Tamanna.

"Should I send her a request first? This much I can do, I guess," he said, pressing his head in stress.

"But what if she accepts the request; then how would I proceed?" he crooned, rising from the staircase and moving towards his ODC.

"What a confused person I am!" said Mark on reaching his cabin and picked up his blazer that he had kept behind his chair.

"So you're leaving?" asked Geet, as her steps followed him.

"Yea, endeavour of the day got completed so I felt it to be best," he replied, carrying his bag over his right shoulder.

"Yes, they have been accomplished, as who can tell it well about the way it went," she said, scoffing him.

"Oh... please drop it, I guess you know me better than anyone else. And you already imagined my moves since morning. You know it all," he said, stepping his right foot towards the exit.

"What about the way I asked you to take?" she asked from behind him.

"I will think about it. Bye, you take care," Mark said and left.

From the time of office till he covered his metro's way,
Those feeling juggled back and forth inside him, making it hard to stay.
He guzzles water till his stomach gets filled,
But couldn't cease his emotions from the way they drilled.
He looked at his palm which unfolds sweltering and shivering,
Seems like his every struggle to disregard wants to increase his willing.
Lastly, Mark gets dropped to his station,
Those hands weren't able to stop and pursued to click the friend invitation.
His heart sensed to push a wave over messenger,
And his hand became an organ, picking at words passed through blood by his heart like a passenger.
Heart won at the emotional track once again,
Which made Mark's heart syrupy and spiritual as he had always remained.

Chat over Facebook messenger:

"Hey, hi Tamanna, Mark here… Are you a designer?" Mark pinged, once he was out of the station and trudging towards the street.

It took a few seconds for him to stroll a little and get in front of the road which he had to cross when his phone's notification bell rang.

"Let me check it once," he said, shifting his blazer from one hand to the other.

"Hello. Wassup? I was carrying that book today but anyways," the message from Tamanna said.

The grin it brought over his face could be easily noticed by the way it decorated happiness on his face. He moved aside to a peaceful place from the zebra-crossing while his fingers ran over the screen to reply.

"You brought that along with you today? Aww! I was really not aware of this. I waited for you but then left… thinking you won't be coming today," replied Mark.

"Ahh ok ok, no prob…

Yea, I design for mass or brands basically," she replied.

"Well, I am feeling really impressed and happy to meet a designer. (An Artist) Creative, haan?" he said.

"Haha kind of… Maybe hehe. Yea and I read the book today. It is nice, a decent one. claps," she said.

"Yeah. But I would love to listen about its flaws if you found any… Thanks a lot for your praise… it really means a lot to me," he replied.

"Yea surely I would love to tell you more…

And yes, you know what I was thinking," she added.

"Yes please I would love to hear."

"Day before yesterday was my birthday, so I had a gift from your side as well."

"Aww, I am the happiest person to know that I gave you that," he said.

"Yea, even in my company we exchange our books," she informed.

"Good people get the best things in the world as God wants them to be with the goodness like they themselves contain so that their goodness can stay alive," he said.

"Yea, so true and deep; must say Mr. Novelist ☒," she said.

Those small talks enlarged, as one after the other, words left their spark.
The day came to its end, and life felt a beautiful trend.
Emotions that were written before, now were in front of life to

adore.

Steps not wanting to move much,
as they want to stand still and get lost in its feel so much.
Their chat ended but the words were still alive,
That lovely scooter wants them to sit on it and drive.

Mark commenced his walk to go home. All of a sudden, his phone rang. Mark's feet stopped on hearing the sound, breaking that solitary mood he had gotten himself into.

"Yeah Geet, say," he said, picking the call with a weird facial reaction before he could express it with a smile.

"See, you either forgot or don't care that I am flying to Australia tonight," said Geet.

"What's the date today? Oh, it's 7th September. Oh sorry! How can I forget that?"

"You can, the same way you are forgetting many things these days. God knows what happened with you!" she replied.

"Why did you not tell me at the time I was leaving?" he asked with his heavy voice, scratching his chin with his hand.

"I thought you might be reaching the airport in evening," she replied with ease.

"Ok… you don't think much. Try settling your mind and take care," she added before putting down her phone.

"Yea, I will and you too," replied Mark.

Next Recall

After a few days, Mark was flowing with that same unstoppable stream of life. He was scuffling with his notion to start writing again. To write, he wanted to feel all those leftover emotions which he had collected in some container over his life's journey. He wanted to get all those emotions back. Leaving home at morning gave him the sensation that he would be meeting someone, so he thought he would try to get his things cooked before time.

"Don't be in such a hurry," said Mrs. Shivach.

"Nah, I am just trying to tender all in time, for not hassling in the last moment," he replied while brushing his teeth with heavy smacks.

"I said it because if you got ready soon, even your breakfast will have to be made quicker," said Mrs. Shivach and giggled.

"Hahaha.... No, no, please you don't do things in a rush. Else you'll harm yourself Maa," he said to Mrs. Shivach.

"Well, your cheeks are retaining some glow from the past few days," asked Mrs. Shivach, while scooping some vegetables inside the embroidery.

"Aah... what did you say?" he asked, carrying his towel and moving towards the bathroom.

"You haven't shared anything about Sayoni from many days. How's she?" she asked, changing the tone in her voice.

"She... Sayoni... sky girl," he shouted while taking a bath, glee spread all over his cheeks.

"What? Why did you say Sky girl? "

"Yes... my Sky girl, she's the one in my life who calls me 'Sky',"

Mark said.

"Why so?" she shouted from the kitchen.

"She says that 'Sky is the limit' and being with me, limits end as she finds me limitless," said Mark, before getting lost in a glimpse of her smile.

"Oh… she feels to be someone who thinks really deep, and what do you feel about her?"

"I feel she is an angelic friend I have in my life whom I can't afford to lose."

"I guess, we shouldn't talk like this, otherwise you'll get late," Mark said while getting into his room, rubbing his body with a towel.

"Is there any good hope between you both?" she asked, getting anxious as she came into Mark's room.

"Nah… nothing, and you again are getting late," he said while wearing his watch.

"I know how time scurries and how I make things before I run out of time," she said going towards the kitchen.

"Well, I'll be meeting her in the coming days," he replied humorously.

"But why you asked me if I like her?" he asked, being nosy with his brows raised.

"Maa, I am ready, and leaving now," he said, tightening his bag over his shoulder while standing in front of her.

"What about breakfast, can't you wait for two minutes?" she asked, insisting him to eat.

"I can but my stomach is not hungry," he said having carried his lunch and kissed Mrs. Shivach forehead, and then ran towards his bike.

With a hanging bag and his dancing feet,
He rode his bike with the desire to meet.
His scattering cardigan pointing towards the track,
Someone is breathing far apart, making him feel an attract.

Taking quick steps to reach the metro platform and his eyes lost in her thoughts, he did not notice her. Mark checked in and commenced to walk when he sees her. As words of that solitary bird were forging sensation over nature for him.

Mark isn't able to identify which one it is, as someone carries her hair and another movement whispers the way she is.

A wave flown across right turned to check if he wasn't missing her sight.

He went to the place they met before, stood there to do what he did never before.

One question repeatedly rose to his mind?

Why everyone seems just like her

Starting from the top, the way she handles her hair,

To the bottom, the way she carries her footwear.

"She has a hush over her face, spreading freedom in her surrounding air to flow independently," he murmers while gaping towards distant folks who were descending the stairs.

"She's wearing yellow today… Ah, it's Thursday, maybe that's why," he queries to himself.

Eyes had defined the colour of his fellow,

Today is Thursday and she would be wearing something in yellow.

"Am I willing to meet her today or not?" he asked himself as his feet were fidgeting to settle.

"She's carrying my book," he crooned, with his heart full of joy and enlightened eyes.

"I shouldn't disturb her; she would be at some story. Will look at her from a distance," he thought and got out of her way and sight.

Standing couple of meters away from her, they were inside the metro. Mark's eyes were fixated on her. Her eyes lost in the book were finding some space of comfort to stand inside the metro. She found one and stood over there, and went back to the page which she read last. Her eyes turned back to the story, giving the sensation of someone going astray into a different world.

"I wouldn't be able to say anything to her now," Mark crooned.

"I guess; I saw her today, this has already filled my happiness jar. Let me leave now," Mark murmured, making his way towards the next coach while sparing himself from getting perceived.

He moved away with a smile,
His face, his feet, his developed charm were
Speaking of intentions of making her mine.
He hadn't felt this ever before, where he can find himself more secure.
Though his desires were high, he wanted to make her all dreams to fly.

"Guess this is cool, being in a different coach. She wouldn't spot me here," he said, taking a deep breath.

"Wow, what a climate!" he said looking out from the metro's glass.

"Yes, it is," A voice spoke from behind him.

"Aah… you! How come… see," he said as he turned and noticed Sayoni gaping at him.

"Hey. Let me first ask, where have you been lost the last few days?" she asked.

"I was lost in my own world."

"Your world! I see, full of thoughts and stories," she said, pointing her finger towards him.

"But presently, it's workload… I have been dumb with no thoughts for a long time."

"Oh… Are you Mark? You are saying you're lacking thoughts? Strange," she said, touching his shirt sleeve with her hand.

"What's there? What are you looking for in that coach? Is someone there? Since the time I have been talking to you, your whole attention has been there," she said, looking intently into Mark's eyes.

"Sayoni, it isn't good," Mark said.

"See, again you've started to think something… Can I know what is it you're dealing with?"

"Hey, you know everything about me. You already know your importance in my life. In fact, I was talking in the morning to 'Maa' about you," he said.

"Oh… is it? What did Aunty say about me?" asked Sayoni.

"She was asking how long has it been since we both have met."

"Who?"

"Me and you," replied Mark.

"See, how worried she stays about me and you aren't even concerned about your friends," she said.

"I have to tell you about a recent epic change in my life; let's meet in the evening today."

"Oh… My dear, sorry, not today. You know I have a big project to finish in the next two days," she replied.

"It has never before happened that you ask for my time and I deny, has it? Please make it next week if possible," she asked with puppy eyes and her eyebrows raised.

"How can I, a hill of beans, say something!" he replied, adjusting the strap of his bag hanging over his shoulder.

"Please, next week?" Sayoni said, coming closer to him, looking into his eyes and ran her fingers through Mark's hair.

"Well, then let's make it someday next week," he said.

"Yes… That's perfect."

"I really want to discuss some emotion stuff with you, but not now. We will do it later."

"Can't you tell me about it now?" she asked with concern in her voice.

"Nah… I can't share it with you in any other way without a proper face-to-face meeting," he said and moved towards a vacant space in the coach.

"Then, we'll discuss it soon," she said, bowing her head.

"Your stop has come," she pointed outside.

"Yes, and what about you? Where are you heading towards today?"

"I am heading towards the 'head office' today," she replied with grace.

"Ok then, leaving for now. Will catch you later." Mark left, waving at Sayoni while the metro moved.

That day passed in those convictions of an internal love belief,

Trying to bare those hidden emotions, to give the heart some relief.

Seems like eyes have found their source of relaxation,

Time for love to come out of its barren land for its manifestation.

The day went in hoarding words, now they need to be said tomorrow,

He knows that it's love, not a materialistic thing, then how can I borrow.

Breathe without any instinct or awareness will take their height,

Being confident and futuristic–it's somehow become hard for him to fight.

The best answer he got for every question he raised to his heart.

Was that it will check and get you engulfed in its adventure before it starts.

Carrom Board

Striker is trying to place the small pieces into the corner holes.
And the little roughness on those corners makes it stop to reach the poles.
Next hard stroke hits the corner and returns to the playground with other folks.
Not asking whether it wants to continue with those, or else what it wants.

It was the next morning and the last working day of the week. Mark left home early like every other day To reach the metro station half an hour before time.

He carefully took his steps to not step on someone else. Still confused, sad, and exhausted, Mark was trying to avoid his feelings. The sun was shining brightly on his face as he crossed the outer lane to reach his destination. As he climbed down the stairs to reach the platform check-in, his eyes crossed someone giving him a hunch that she was not in there but somewhere outside.

"God, save me from these strange feelings," he murmured, looking at the space in front of him.

"I've never been like this before."

"I am either really sweating, or something is wrong. What is it?" He thought noticing the sweat.

Mark stepped ahead trying to avoid the emotions he was going through.

"I can't feel this as I am not meant for this."

Somehow with those bundles of questions in his mind, Mark

began to walk to the location where he saw her last time. He did not board the metro whose gates were open in front of him. He wanted to look at her once properly and feel this thing called 'love' which was being felt by others.

"I have to not board this metro too," he said as the third metro arrived in front of his eyes.

"This is something I haven't done for anyone before. I am always on time to teach everyone the importance of time.

But today, why am I delaying? Why am I not able to move on? What's her intention? I am oblivious to it. These soft feelings that I have are so strange; they are making me do things I never thought I would do."

Hearing the blare of the oncoming train, Mark looked towards the stairs with desire in his eyes hoping to see her arrive this time. The hope he had was withering inside as he began to count every passing second.

Mark turned the other side apprehensive of the surrounding crowd. He plugged in his earphones and switched on the music on his phone. He believed that even if she were to come, she wouldn't think that he was waiting for her.

His feet tapped to the beat of the music. Mark now frisked his favourite tracks on Bluetooth. He began to register the passing time which was crossing his convention of maintaining time punctuality at work.

"I am trying to lessen my stress by doing all this," Mark said to himself and looked for the person whose presence his soul was asking for repeatedly.

Tamanna began to walk towards the platform taking one step after the other leading her closer towards him. A bright smile spread across her cheeks.

"Has she seen me? Her smile says so," Mark thought, looking down at the floor.

The metro arrived within a few seconds and Tamanna walked in carrying the same novel that she was reading earlier. Her inquisitive eyes and innocent face were fixed on the book pages.

She snuggled in a little space inside the coach. Mark took his place a little away from her, not wanting to disturb her in the ending of his book. Mark wanted an answer as to why he was doing things that didn't make sense to him.

The way he' s waiting,
The way he thinking,
The way he's bending his rules and
The way he's breaking his schedules.

There were a lot of changes happening in his life. Mark's reactions could be easily noticed. He had now begun to stay in his very own world, lost in Tamanna's thoughts all the time.

Mark began to collect strength from every piece of his soul to approach Tamanna, speak to her, and tell her of his heart's desire. Mark began to step closer to Tamanna very leisurely with innocence and a sense of truth in his eyes.

Within a second, the station arrived where they both had to interchange and board the next train. Mark had to stop momentarily as a swarm of people started to push through to get inside. As Tamanna looked around and began to move towards the exit door, Mark froze for a moment believing she was about to leave.

But she detoured to move towards the platform and Mark again followed her into the coach she boarded. He wanted to be with her. He was only looking for some strength within him and a chance to approach her.

Walking behind her, he isn't feeling humiliated,
As his mind was polished and needs are not fascinated.
He desired to touch the smile that she retains,
Knowing it's beautiful, but the heart knows these smiles are fancy and he will attain.
The same standard is built inside the next train,
as she's lost in story and Mark is standing away from her notice,

a distance he's trying to maintain.
In a while, he tried and went closer,
as he felt it's the time of exposure.

"So, what do you think of it now that you have read it," a voice approached Tamanna.

"Oh… You! What's up?" Tamanna gazed at him. She held a big smile on her face which made Mark's mind forget everything else.

"This is beyond anything; her smile set me blank," Mark thought to himself.

"I am good, was looking at you from a distance for quite some time," he said, as they both shake their hands.

"Aah… Surprising! I am still surprised as to how you came from back and…," she said.

"Its life, things happen suddenly here every day," he replied.

"But you know well how much effort writing a book takes certainly," Mark said.

"Yeah, the story is going fantastically well," she replied with a wide smile.

"So, how did you find the chemistry between the characters? I hope you loved the beautiful climate of Kolkata I created inside the book!" he asked while thinking about something.

"Yes, yes… I loved it."

"And Darjeeling?" he asked quickly.

"I can see from where you are holding the book that you have reached the climax of the story that takes place in Darjeeling," he added with a gentle smile.

"Oh… Yes, that beautiful," she said.

"I went to Darjeeling before writing this chapter," Mark replied with a gleam in his eyes.

"Such a nice setting you have built and above all, such a beautiful story. It makes the book more worthy," she replied, bringing the book closer to her lips.

“Hey, what happened to your toe? It’s wounded,” he asked, as he looked at her feet and moved back enough that there was enough space for a person to pass.

“Yea, I hurt my toe yesterday morning while gymming,” she replied.

“What were you doing that caused this?” he asked, worried about her.

“I was pulling a chain with weight and I couldn’t handle that and so, this happened,” she replied innocently.

“My nail is broken and I am scared to pull it out,” she added.

“Huh…I don’t know what to say. You should have consulted a doctor till now. He would have done what is required.”

“Yes, but I am scared that he’ll pull this nail out and it will hurt a lot.”

“But.” Mark stopped midway while speaking.

“Yeah, I know. No if’s and buts, let’s wait a little for it to get healed on its own. Meanwhile, tell me, what else is going on at work and in your life?” she asked.

“Work stays ever the same and I do it easily,” replied Mark, looking for something in his bag.

“What are you looking for?” she queried.

“Nothing, it’s all there.”

“Many things keep on going in your mind,” said Tamanna smiling.

“Nah, it’s like as you asked about work, I looked inside to check whether I’ve brought something important or not,” Mark replied.

“So, I am right. Many things keep going on in your mind,” she giggled.

“I can’t imagine how you correlated these two things,” he replied, looking outside.

“What are you looking at outside now?” she asked.

“Looking at how much time I have with you before your station arrives," Mark flashed a gentle smile while looking at Tamanna.

"Oh, forget that. It will come when it has to come… You cannot control it," she replied.

"Yes, as it's the next one, you should find yourself some space near the door to get off," he said, giving space for her to move out.

"Ok, then… Loved to see you. It was a surprise today," she said with a smile.

"But go carefully as your toe doesn't seem that good. And I am sure it must be hurting still," he said, looking down at her toe.

"Yes, and we can't help it," said Tamanna with a blush on her face.

She passed like winter and shove along her way,
Memories she gave, stayed close all day.
The wait for her glimpse stretches itself and becomes long,
Questions arising back and forth in my heart keel over like a bomb.

Triangle

The one whom you love and the one who loves you,
Why we make love a difficult standard of living, as in the end it won't be understood by either one of you.
Emotions should be cared for; desires should be met.
Things are so clear, but you still ask for something in return yet.

A day later that night, Mark's phone rang.

"Uh… I kept it on charging it in the other room and now it's ringing. Man, it's 11:30 p.m." said Mark, annoyed. He put down the pen and his notepad on the bed.

"No one will check it; I only have to go," he said.

"Mark, are you there?" shouted Mrs. Shivach from her room.

"Yes Maa….here only, about to pick up the phone," he replied, leaving his room and walking in the corridor.

"Heat your milk as well before drinking, don't drink it cold," she said.

"Yes, Maa."

"I don't know why is drinking cold milk a crime!" he murmured.

"Oh… Who's calling me over and over again; must be something serious," said Mark, as he picked his phone and looked at its screen.

"Sayoni's calling! Oh Man, I should have called her. I again forgot," said Mark. He called her back.

"Hey… Hey… Hi Sayoni. What's up?" Mark started fumbling.

"Hi Sky, can I know why are you fumbling? What are you scared of?" asked Sayoni laughing.

"Sorry I know, I know. I had to call you today evening but…"

"But Sky got lost in many things and forgot the other unimportant things," she said swiftly with her kindness.

"How can your Sky forget a commitment he made to a person who means a lot to him," said Mark locking the room.

"Where were you busy?" she asked.

"I don't know what's happening with me these days," he replied.

"What is bothering you?"

"Leave it. Just confirm, are we meeting tomorrow?" he asked.

"Yes, we will but where?"

"As tomorrow is a Monday, let's meet at Central Delhi in the evening; our old meeting spot," he replied.

"Is there any issue, Sayoni?" asked Mark.

"It is far from my place and we won't get much time to be with each other cause I will have to rush in half an hour from there," she answered.

"Hey, I'll get my car tomorrow and will drop you at your place once we wind up," he added anxiously.

"Is it a yes now?" Mark pity goi.

"You always have my yes Mark, and you know it," she replied.

"Oh… You don't know, how calm your words make me feel," he replied.

"Ok, it's late now. I was worried about you so I called cause you looked disturbed when we met," she asked.

"I didn't know I said something that got you worried. I'm sorry. I am blessed to have you in my life," he replied.

"No, it's like I am blessed to have you," she said and the call disconnected due to network interruption.

"You are such a masterpiece for me, you don't know," said Mark, moving towards the kitchen.

"Let me meet you tomorrow. I have so much to tell you," he said while pouring milk into his glass after heating it.

Some people spread immense shine in your life.
They step uninformed and play a beautiful song with their generous strike.
Their kindness starts spreading over your life in such a way,
You want to listen to them, setting your heart in peace at least once every day.
They work to design a beautiful track in your life,
Walking with them you never feel alone, no matter how long you ride.
Their care is unbeatable from anyone else's kind word,
As they fill your life with satisfaction, more than any other bird.

Next Morning came. Mark stretched his limbs and with a big yawn he shouted, 'Sayoni'.

"What happened?" Mrs. Shivach ran towards Mark's room.

"Nothing, Maa. I just woke up."

"Well, I saw you wake up early at 4:30 a.m. and workout."

"Yes, Maa…I did. Afterwards, I don't know how I ended up falling asleep," he said while wearing his cardigan and moving towards his washroom.

"Happy to see you seem better now."

"Yes Maa, I had a word with Sayoni last night," he replied.

"So this is what she did. I am anxious to know what exactly happened?" she asked while folding Mark's blanket that was lying on his bed.

"Nothing Maa, she didn't do anything," said Mark, getting out of the washroom, picking up his comb and combing his hair.

"But you know, I heard you shout when you woke up," she said before going quiet.

"You first tell me, why were you up so late last night? You were up at 1:00 am," asked Mark.

"Ok, so you didn't sleep until that time either," Mrs. Shivach said.

"And this doesn't answer my question," he replied.

"You know, I don't get what construction is taking place in our neighbour's house. There is a loud noise of drilling and hammering all the time. 24/7. Seems like the labour is always working," said Mrs. Shivach, looking at Mark with a confused look.

"Do they start working anytime?" he asked.

"Yes, it's one uncertain construction I have ever seen in my life. They have been making a commotion for quite some days and then, they stay silent for weeks or even months. There is a mysterious sort of work going on there," she said.

"Huh, what's that? I'll be in your room tonight and we'll investigate what is it that disturbs you," he said standing tall and touching her cheeks with his finger.

"And by what time you'll come tonight?" she asked, pushing away his hand aside.

"I am meeting Sayoni tonight, so can't predict when," he said.

"Understood, not tonight then. No worries!" said Mrs. Shivach, leaving the room to go to the kitchen to finish her pending work.

"It's after a long time we are meeting." He raised his voice to be audible from a distance to Mrs. Shivach.

"I will be going to the market. Is there anything you need?" he asked Mrs. Shivach.

"Nothing, you meet her first," she said, washing vegetables under a running tap. Mrs. Shivach loved to cook.

"I smell you making my favourite dish," Mark said.

"What happened Maa, why aren't you responding, you know I can't see you like that," Mark said.

"You have no time for me. Today, after a long time, you said you'll give me time and that also, the other second you said you can't," she replied.

"Maa, you know nah, every other thing except you becomes secondary to me," said Mark standing in front of Mrs. Shivach.

"Then what is primary?" she asked.

"It's you. My ladybird, my God," he conveyed.

"You have loved me since I was born. I love you, Maa," he added with content on his face.

"Ok, Ok! Complete your work, else you'll make me cry with your words again," she replied with a smile on her face.

Mark picked up the towel that slipped from his hand and moved to finish his shower, singing a song dedicated to his Mother.

At office:

Mark got delayed in finishing his official work cause he was worried about Sayoni. He knew that getting late would delay Sayoni's timing of reaching home.

"Mark, are you leaving to go somewhere?" John, his colleague, asked.

"She won't tell me anything or complain to me, but reaching late would make her feel tired," Mark answered abruptly, as soon he heard John speak, placing his things inside his baggage.

"She... but whom?" asked John, staring at Mark.

"Oh... leave, I just said something unknowingly," replied Mark.

"You can share it with me, Mark," conveyed John.

"I am just leaving to meet my friend Sayoni," he said, hanging his bag on his shoulder.

"Sayoni... your friend?" asked John, with a smile.

John was aware that Sayoni was Mark's friend whom Mark met when he left for his solo trip, and on that trip, this less interactive person attained his lost smile after meeting such a generous and understanding person as Sayoni.

Sayoni had the magical sense of knowing every unsaid word by the people around her.

"Run, man. I guess you are late already," John added as Mark ran towards the exit.

Your time punctuality adds pride to a relation,
When you are waiting on a platform before the train reaches its station.
Needs might differ from person to person
But your commitment of devotion can't be erased by any creation.
To get this thing understood crisp and clear
You need to be responsible for your devotion, making yourself someone without fear.

"Sky! A punctual guy," said Sayoni when she saw Mark already at their meeting spot.

"Tired?" asked Sayoni, placing her hand over Mark's hand.

"Hey, you came!" Mark said.

"I am sorry," she said.

"But for what?"

"You came before time as ever and I got late again."

"You are asking me something whose answer you already know," Mark said.

"Yes, your those philosophical talks," Sayoni said, smiling while spinning her fingers in his hair.

"Ok, come on, let's get in," said Mark, pulling her hand taking her into their famous street bar and cafe, the best place they always hung out on.

"The same?" she asked, without letting her joy capturing her face.

Reconciling after sitting on a bench :

"Now, what you'll take, Miss?" he asked.

"No... not today," she replied.

"What would a couple of drinks do to you?" Mark said.

"It wouldn't, but why today? Anything special?" she asked, with her eyebrows raised.

"You just think that it's for me to float out those newly developed emotions in a beautiful way," he requested.

"Amazed to hear such lines from a person like you, way beyond my imagination," she said, taking a sip from a glass of water which was just served.

"A person must feel a different sensation for delivering something divine," said Mark, before leaving his bench and conveyed something to the bartender with his fingers.

"Well, what did you just tell him?" she asked with curiosity.

"Asked for two glasses of wine, with your ideal flavoured bottle," he informed, with innocence in his eyes while looking at her anxious face.

"Let me listen to you, Mark! What's so tough you are dealing with?" she asked, gazing into Mark's eyes, placing her chin on her palm and her elbow balancing the weight of her body on the table.

"Yes I will, I am altogether fraught to convey to you how things are with me. First, please take the honour," he said, as drinks were served on the table.

Sayoni smiled and filled both the glasses partially by pouring wine swiftly into the glasses while staring into Mark's eyes like she never did before.

"That looks amazing, I can't tell you how it has taken half of my worries away," he said, passing such a smile that Sayoni fell in love with him.

"Aah... just like before, you are avoiding saying things," she said.

"Why?" Mark asked.

"We came to talk on a topic of your concern, Mark!" she replied, with her same notching tone like how a teacher scolds a student.

"Huh. don't you have any emotion of love in your heart?" he asked, with a beaming smile while rubbing his forehead.

"How did you think of this now?" Sayoni said while taking her first sip of the wine.

"There is a lot Mark, you won't understand," Sayoni murmurs.

"So you want to listen to what I have to say?" he said, keeping his empty glass aside after finishing his first drink.

"Easy, Mark. Why do you treat every alcoholic beverage with the same standard?" she asked.

"Let's not get into this, I am starting to tell you now," he said, tucking his shirt back into his jeans, and keeping back the pen in his hand into his shirt's pocket.

"Is all good, Mark?"

"Yes, why? Why did you ask such a question?"

"After seeing so many actions in few seconds," Sayoni said with a shocked face.

"I am just getting ready to start," he replied, rubbing his face with his palm.

"Desperate to listen. Yes please, go on," said Sayoni, with complete consciousness.

"I met a girl in the metro," said Mark, slowly.

"Oh!" Sayoni exclaimed.

"I don't know why, but I am not able to forget thinking about her," said Mark, with the same intense feeling in his eyes as he starred at Sayoni.

After a couple of seconds, the silence was evoking impassive emotions over Sayoni's face.

They both stared at each other in search of something.
Desires might differ, but for one another, they're desperate to do anything.
One's breath waits to hear something.
Other one's breath gave so much importance to it, not focusing on anything.

"I see... Sky... Your eyes are telling me many things," she said, with her glazed face.

"When did you meet her?" she queried.

"I met her last week, but I noticed her much before," he informed.

"I can understand every bit of the thing you are undergoing," she said as she ended her last word with a soulless voice.

"What?" he asked Sayoni with his eyebrows raised.

"So our Sky… is in the world's most beautiful feeling," she said, with a graceful face and smoky eyes.

"No… I don't know what is it and what to call it. Don't want to give it any name till the time I understand it," he said.

"Her words sound in my ears whole day long. I don't know why!" he said.

"I am getting you completely," she replied, with her peaceful eyes.

"And it's not all, I seem to be becoming a fan of all the things that she does," he said, with hand movements demonstrating his feelings.

"Calmness she wears on her face and the way she is as free as the ocean. This all shows the standard of her heart that she carries on her face," he added.

"My heart gets dissolved just by looking at the smile on her face at the time when she greets me. Seems like that is the smile I am in search of," he said.

"My heart gives me many ways to interpret her. What's this strange feeling?" he added.

"Control yourself, Mark, these ways of love are not easy. I am getting scared, I don't know why," she replied.

"Nah, Sayoni, things wouldn't be wrong ever. I know about the voids in your heart for these feelings," he said, taking his face closer to her face, to look into her lost eyes, and to move away the fringe that fell on her face.

"I think I should be a lost person, not you!" he said very swiftly into Sayoni's ear.

"No, no. I am just praying to get these priceless feelings of yours to settle down with good results," she said.

"Yes, they will. Spot my fingers, they are all crossed," he rejoiced, with a glow capturing his face.

"Of your feet too," she giggled.

"Tell me about when you both had your first interaction," she interrupted Mark to make him say some words.

"Last week," he said, being all excited.

"So quick, you developed such intense feelings?" she said, being awestruck.

"Quick, you think it is quick? I can sense a year to have elapsed in this much interaction only," he replied, pouring some wine into his empty glass.

"Complete up your first drink fast, see I am already on the second," said Mark, raising the next toast.

"No, I don't want to have much," she responded.

"Walk safely on this track, Mark, I know your heart's purity," added Sayoni, with anxiety.

"Yes dear, you are such a nice soul. Your every blessing means a lot to me."

"So tell me, how's everything going on now?" she asked.

"Going on as God wants," said Mark.

"And what does God want?"

"We share some personal fortunes," he said.

"So you meet every day?" she queried.

"No, it's when God sets a timing for us to meet."

"Mark! Is it God or you, who has feelings for her?" she said, raising the pitch in her voice.

"But how can I approach her? You know me well," he said, getting up from his place to walk around.

"It's a matter to make it finer," she replied, joining Mark's footsteps for a walk.

"In these assorted feelings, I don't want to make any idea or prediction," he said, gazing at her face.

"But you are the one who will settle this down."

"Yeah…I know," Mark's reactions intensified, getting lost in a notion while walking.

Those steps they stroll
are dipped in the brood of each other.
They desire the other one to fly higher to kiss the sky
without giving any attention to their feather.
The much they walked, aegis increased for each other,
They found a blockage in achieving happiness
as now it involved some other creature.

The Way We Met

Some meetings ensue so instant
that they linger away, giving realisation of their occurrence.
The road they designed shows creativity of its master,
Who makes to touch your belief in every aspiring way under his presence.

"What happened? Why you seem so stressed? " asked Divyansh (Mark's Office colleague) while exiting the company's premises in the evening.

"Nothing, things seems fine," replied Mark.

"Then why these strain lines are on your forehead," said Divyansh, taking Mark's bag from his hand.

"No, I can carry it," Mark said hesitatingly.

"You surely can, but not with this stress," intervened Divyansh.

"Don't you understand, I can't smile all the time," screamed Mark, getting annoyed and taking his bag off from Divyansh's hand.

"So is it so that you will grin only for making other people happy? Then in aloneness, you'll bear pain all alone?" Divyansh queried being indignant.

"No. Why are you stretching this conversation? I don't know," he said.

"I noticed you the whole day today," replied Divyansh.

"It's a matter of some other thoughts going through my intellect."

"Ohh I see, some other! That you can't share with me?" said Divyansh.

"Don't make me stand somewhere where I don't want to be," said Mark, tightening up Divyansh's coat from the front.

"Please be normal, don't make such faces. Your smile is what I love, maintain that," said Mark.

"Let's walk Mark, I believe you are getting late," replied Divyansh.

"Me getting late, not you?"

"I reach in a short time while you have a long way to travel," said Divyansh.

"Well, and I am coming with you today," added Divyansh.

"Why? What happened?" asked Mark.

"I have some work on the way," replied Divyansh.

"What work? Oh Divyansh, please don't be worried. I am alright," he insisted.

"No, I have some work for sure, it's important," replied Divyansh.

"So, you want to come with me. But I already said, it's of no use," said Mark.

"Come fast then, let's board," said Mark walking towards the metro escalator.

"Nothing is normal with you and you're saying..." said Divyansh, standing below Mark on the escalator.

"Sorry, you said something?" Mark turned to ask.

"Nothing, you heard anything?" reiterated Divyansh.

"Question above question and answers stays still unsaid," Mark said, laughing out loud.

"Happy seeing you happy like this, after all, no matter if it's on my helplessness," said Divyansh.

"But you aren't pictured," laughed Mark.

"Whatever it is, I am happy that you are out of that sorrowful face of yours," said Divyansh.

"Oh my astrologer, you're ever such a delightful champ for me," said Mark, placing his hands on his shoulders, and peering at his face.

"It's all your generous ways that makes everyone yours," said Divyansh, stepping forth and punching in his card.

"Ok, let me tell you," said Mark.

"What?" screeched Divyansh.

"Yes, first get out of that door thing," said Mark.

Moving towards the platform, while looking inside his bag, Divyansh heard Mark's voice:

"Someone has become like a poem to me."

"What?" asked Divyansh.

"Yes."

"Is this the season building the blush on your face?" asked Divyansh.

"Have you both conveyed it to each other?" he asked Mark, discerning silence over Mark's face except his slight smile.

"What both, it's just me presently," said Mark.

"Oh... It's one-sided."

"But something tells me that she loves me through her responses," said Mark.

"A guy like you, living a normal life, and is into those emotions," said Divyansh.

"I don't know why everyone is trying to give it a name," replied Mark swiftly.

"Means you'll stay like this only?"

"What difference did you feel? I am not getting you," said Mark.

"You won't get that either," said Divyansh.

"We have to board the train," said Mark pointing at the oncoming train.

"Oh... I just remembered an important work," said Divyansh.

"No," Mark laughed loudly while saying that.

"Why are you so happy?" asked Divyansh.

"As it came true, what I thought you were trying to do," replied

Mark.

"Ok, don't miss the train, get in before the door shuts," said Divyansh, treading back towards the stairs.

Mark stood there facing the black glass.

"All seems natural. Then why did he say so?" Mark asked himself.

Rubbing his brows with his fingers, he said:

"Maybe these larger going dark eye curvature be the difference."

"Or maybe, my cheeks seem dull."

"I can't carry such a low personality if he's right."

"Or... something else is there. What do these things have to do with my character?" crooned Mark, gazing out of the door.

"But what?" he said loudly before a hand tapped his shoulder.

"Is it really you?" said Mark.

"Yes it's me, did I scare you? I was wondering what you were thinking of so intently," said Tamanna, who found Mark in the same coach that she just boarded.

"Was into you only," crooned Mark from his soul.

"What? You said something?" she asked.

"Umm I..."

"Forget it…So, how come you left so early today?" she asked. "As I said, our timings are never set. It starts late in the morning, though people stretch hours into the evening to wind up," he said.

"My actual time of leaving is when you reach home and have your food…haha," Mark giggled.

"But at least, you don't have fixed timings," she said slowly.

"Yeah, can rely on that only," he said, before beginning to laugh.

"Seems like you've completed reading the story?" he asked.

"And how did you know that?" she smiled and queried.

"Just a guess, as you were reading the climax when we met last," he replied.

"Umm… You noticed that?" she said with broadened eyes.

"Yes… words and phrases are like my God," he said, staring into her eyes.

"You write so beautifully," she replied, with a slight smile over her cheeks.

"I got an indirect appreciation," said Mark.

"Yes, it's overall fantastic. Many twists in the story," she said.

"Grab a seat first as it's vacant right there," he said, pointing at a seat that just got vacant.

"I don't sit while travelling in the metro generally," she replied, with her pretty lips which smiled.

"We have to change at the next station," she added after listening to the announcement.

"Time passes quicker than ever with you," Mark said, moving closer to the exit door.

They both moved swiftly finding spaces within the crowd towards the downstairs platform. Mark's eyes often tried to catch a glimpse of her face. His steady steps wanted to match her speed. Often he smiled, once his eyes caught a glimpse of her. The way she walked and maintained a calmness around her had sprouted something in Mark's heart already. Millions of bubbles were bursting inside him spreading a sense of sweetness. Time passed so quickly when she was around him. Observing happiness in the silence between the two of them, he walked behind her and observed her moves making him feel everything much comfortable and divine about her.

Love is never a mission, it's a sense containing valid reasons.
But why those reasons are still away from realisations.
It never asks for a picture to be specially decorated.
To frame those emotions that aren't yet stated.

"So what time do you usually have your dinner?" asked Tamanna breaking the silence between them while they both waited at the platform.

"As soon I reach," replied Mark.

"What about your workout?" asked Mark.

"Only thing I can't leave any-day," replied Tamanna with a glow on her face.

"You can leave food?" said Mark asked while giggling.

"No…don't say that, I am such a foodie," she replied, scolding Mark with her eyes.

"So is it flexible for you to maintain food and workout?" he asked.

"Man, everything I eat gets to be shown all over my body," she replied.

"You are asking me such questions when you yourself are a fitness freak," she said.

"Aah... You saw my status?" he asked.

"Oh, come on!" she said.

"So you also have a physique like me?" said Mark.

"And I also do eat a lot being a '*Bhraman*,'" she said.

The metro came :

"Not there, this one," she said, holding Mark's hand and pulling him towards another coach as she observed his feet stepping towards another coach.

"Aah yeah, it would be crowded," he said, pointing at the coach he was about to enter.

"That's why I pulled you… understood?"

"Smart princess," said Mark, swiftly walking into the metro.

"Yes… I am."

"I read someone's post," said Mark, giving a break between his words.

"What?"

"That red-haired people are genetic superheroes," he replied laughing.

"Aww…You read my Facebook posts," she said with a smile on

her face.

“Yes, superhero! ,” replied Mark.

Words of one another had scrolled inside out.
Those entangled feelings are about to sprout.
Nothing has been said.
Emotions need to be felt before any other harsh feeling tears every thread.

“So, superhero, I don’t have your number,” he said, bringing out his phone.

“Oh…yea, that is it. Ring me once,” she said, after giving him her number.

“What about your toe?” he asked, looking down at her toe.

“It’s healing now, nothing to worry,” she replied.

“See our stop came,” she spoke, after an interim silence of seconds.

“And again, time flew too fast converting my minutes into seconds,” crooned Mark.

“What? I didn’t hear you,” she said abruptly.

“First time I’ve seen a man with such a blush on his face,” she said, stepping closer to the door, walking ahead of Mark.

“Nothing like that, I wonder what you noticed,” he said, rubbing his right eyebrow with his right hand’s fingers.

“It’s not just about your writing. You have many things inside you that people could observe and make note of,” she said.

“Don’t observe me like this,” he said, blushing.

“Hmm yeah, yes.”

“Our stop has at last come,” he said looking outside.

“Yes... come, we have to move out,” she said, holding Mark’s hand as they walked out of the exit door.

“You’ll be exiting from which gate?” he asked.

“Gate No. 1,” she said, pointing her finger at a board that said ‘Gate no. 1’.

"Aah... our exit is also common," he said.

"I'll drop you. Where do you stay?" he asked.

"Oh... I am thankful, but my home is only a few meters away," she replied.

"Got it, then will see you later... take care! Be blessed," he said and left.

That last smile they gave to each other
Had an aura with blessings and beauty like none another.
Respect has already built its own space,
Like it's the beginning of a love bonanza and not a race.
The summon tenderness started going away of being worried.
As these superior invoked feelings, are out after staying long buried.
It wasn't said the way it was felt,
But they attempted to use the glow of light before it did melt.

Those Interactions

Look of days and nights had changed.
Something got lost while something else they gained.

Words trying to settle to reach one another. Feelings of both started getting shared by texting each other. Between sunrise and the time it took for the sun to set, that period became very difficult to cover, and any gap in conversation made it even hard to breathe for both of them.

Mark and Tamanna had interacted over messages. Still, they hadn't settled their everyday travel time to compliment each other. Mark didn't want to ask the time at which she came in the morning.

Those conversations that they had made Mark feel a sensation he hadn't felt yet. Streams of oceans never tried to raise themselves to that height yet.

Emotions of their true heart had begun to come out. Seemed like he found a creature with whom he could walk, with whom he can feel silence even when many people shout. His covers were getting uncovered.

Nothing is necessary, nothing is compulsory.
But still any single thought of detachment from her makes him get worried.

Light and smoulder captured his face waiting for him to get free and take its place.

He never asked anything and was about to give his all.

Without knowing the pain felt in this feeling, forgetting stories of many who did fall.

They both were having fruitful reciprocity of emotions. The way Mark received replies from Tamanna was full of generous reactions. Her reactions to her feelings were very obvious. The emotion she felt got delivered by her words. Her messages carried such a flavour of state attached to them.

The sand started to fly in the air.
Settling down with all desired emotions, mixed in its flair.

They began to share internal family talks to help them realise the analogy between both to walk. Habitual obliging had moved Mark bringing out a fire from a tiny spark. Generalisation was trying to go yonder, picturing future. As it was the first time, such emotion had made Mark think ahead of those feelings he found miniature.

The soul is to worship God.
God built relations for everyone to hold.
Identities are not admired when you try to rule someone.
As it waits for you to generalise and bend for the one.

After some days, it was Friday.

Briskly stepping ahead, Tamanna settled at the place where she waited at the platform. Her eyes looked around trying to find someone.

Standing at the place where they met first, she found that someone whom her eyes were looking for. She smiled, with a feeling inside her that today she'll break the crust.

She walked towards him with her smile getting broader.

"He's listening to songs," she thought.

She moved closer to him and tapped his shoulder with her right-hand palm.

"Hey," said Tamanna.

"Yes?" the guy turned around and asked.

"Oh…I am sorry, I thought you to be someone else," she said, stunned.

“Ok… No worries.”

Tamanna stepped back and stayed awestruck with this impression. She never encountered this before. She was finding herself uneasy. Her unsettled impression was not allowing her feet to stay calm. Within seconds, the sound of the metro’s arrival filled the platform. Tamanna was still trying to get away from what just happened.

Metro halted and its doo opened. She was the last one to get into the metro this time which was something she never before did. She asked herself why all of it happened this way. A very self-esteemed girl confronted something loony. Dealing with all of that, she found herself a place and stood still as if her mind was lost in solving some unresolved puzzle.

Tamanna brought out her cell phone and moved her finger over to the pad. And then, she typed :

“Where were you?”

Mark, who was busy in his writing, saw a light elicit out of his cell. Without considering to respond anything, he roamed astray in his wanders. To stay away from distraction, he did not pick up his phone. Suddenly after a couple of minutes, he thought:

“Why am I feeling so restless to give importance to this message,” Mark crooned.

“Who’s this?” said Mark, picking his phone up.

“Tamanna… oh, let me see,” said Mark.

“Am at home today…I took leave for a day,” Mark replied to her text.

“Oh… Great, you’ve got a leave,” texted Tamanna.

“Yeah wanting to finish some work,” texted Mark.

“You know what happened today?” she said.

“Yes, please tell me?” he asked.

“I tapped some other guy thinking that it was you,” texted Tamanna, with a sad face emoji.

"Oh… is it?" replied Mark.

"Yes…That's super embarrassing," she texted.

"Hey… Please don't worry about that… It happens," texted Mark.

"But really, something like that," she said.

"No… No, don't worry, you know one thing," said Mark.

"I felt you many times to be around me even when you weren't there. Felt like you were walking ahead or aside or standing at some distance from me," texted Mark.

"Hmmm," she texted back.

"So, don't think about it much, please!" texted Mark.

"Well, you say… you got a big weekend now," she asked.

"Yes, this Friday and continuation."

"Lucky you, enjoy it."

"Nothing like that. I've already worked very hard for the company," he texted.

"Yea… don't think about it. Just have your best time," she texted.

"Hmm… I'll try to," he replied.

"Wait… Are you going to office on Monday?" asked Mark.

"Yea… I will be."

"Then, let's meet on Monday," he texted back.

"Yea… Sure," she replied in her text.

Some words remain ever unsaid.
Like emotions ever contain very sleek thread.
Those long hours, that were shortening but still behind the dark.
Feelings are still numb, being scared of beginning a spark.
Moisture developed to protect it from dust.
As this needs to be given attention first.

Monday

Mark reached the spot before time. Starting a week with this meet would make his day divine. His feet were dancing on the beats of a song he was hearing through his Bluetooth. This hadn't happened for a long time. Feet tapping in excitement. His soul was peeping out for joy from ever door.

Today, he was not edgy about how many metros left as his desires were committed to the wish of meeting someone.

"She is cute," said Mark, blushing.

He left himself to wander in his song again without any brood this time and a conviction of meeting Tamanna today. Getting into his music and moves, he walked in a relaxed manner. Wondering about the meet, he looked at his watch to know the time. He confined himself to reaching office at a defined time, and that too, at present, he didn't want to worry about.

While listening to a song, someone came from the right side wearing a sky blue top, blue shaggy jeans, and a bag over her shoulders. The time his eyes were facing the floor.

"Aah... Hey, Good Morning," said Tamanna as she saw Mark.

"Oh... You came," said Mark, removing his Bluetooth buds from his ears.

"Yes...and what are you up to?" she asked.

"Listen to this song... Amazing background track," he said, passing on his Bluetooth to her.

"Hmm, interesting," said Tamanna, after listening to the song for a few seconds.

"I get goosebumps listening to the track," he said.

"That I already noticed," she said, smiling, and keeping her hand over her mouth.

"You noticed?" he asked.

"Yea... Well, it's a nice track with lyrics," she added.

"I listen to one song repeatedly if I like it," he said.

"Same here," she replied.

"Great... Wow... Music is an other life to me. I asked myself many times: what if I was left with music only, would I be able to live?" he said.

"And what answer did you get?"

"I can live."

"Let's go," said Tamanna.

"Hey… what about cooking?" asked Mark.

"That's a very strange query," she said, after a second's silence, looking at Mark while boarding the metro.

They boarded and stood inside the metro:

"You feeling comfortable, na? While standing here!" asked Mark, noticing the crowd inside.

"Yea… I am totally in comfort," replied Tamanna.

"Hope, you've also got used to all of this," he said.

"Yes, I have… even I don't try to grab a seat," she replied.

"Even an empty seat doesn't make you want to be seated… Hahahaha," he said.

"Yes, true, true… but you do get settled, I noticed once," she replied, giggling.

"When did you notice it?" he asked, being surprised.

"Oh… Leave that, say what you just asked… yes, cooking," she said, tapping her hand on Mark's chest.

"Yes, do you cook?" he asked curiously.

"I and cooking are like partial things together," she said giggling.

"Means?"

"Means I am learning cooking actually. So, whenever I feel like it, I cook."

"Sometimes, it's so bad but papa is always supportive and says '*arey, haan haan, bahot ache bana hai, very good*'," she said, engrossed in her thoughts.

"And what does mom say about it?" he asked, chuckling louder.

"Mumma gives me actual feedback. Then I do not like it," she said, before laughing ceaselessly.

"My yesterday went away cooking," said Mark.

"Cooking provides relaxation to my mind," he added.

"Huh… you do cooking as well?" she asked.

"Yea… but that depends on my mood only," replied Mark, tightening his bag strap that was lying on his shoulder.

"Oh… I am excited to know what all things you do," she said, staring at him.

Mark lost himself again but this time by the way she stared at him for those few seconds. There was just one cute, evoking desire on their faces.

"What is this feeling called, I still don't know," Mark thought.

"Yes… say, I want to listen," said Mark, after a few seconds.

"Nothing, dear, let things come out slowly," she said.

"On time, you mean?" she asked.

"Oh… gosh, you are such a mysterious guy," added Tamanna.

"But I am really passionate about your profession. I wanted to try it but my family didn't allow me to even try attempting it," he said.

"Is it?"

"Yes, I tried to apply to NIFT (National Institute of Fashion Technology) but you know na, family have other plans," he said being solemn.

"Oh, I see," said Tamanna.

"It's really interesting… Hmm, yeah," said Mark.

"Now don't do this as well," said Tamanna while boasting, broadening her eyes and moving her chin.

"Oh… Yeah, I wouldn't do that," he said before he let himself loose to laugh.

"Will give you a surprise after doing something creative around it," crooned Mark to himself.

"And at last! Like always, your stop has come," he said.

"Yea… it came, our new day of work has started," she said and raised her palm to hi-fi Mark's palm.

"The day has already partially got over," said Mark.

"What?"

"On meeting you 'My half of the day gets completed', and you asked to start the day," he said, lost in his thoughts.

Tamanna smiled looking at Mark for a while. She showed him gratitude through her eyes through the way her lids supported her smile. That stiffly beating heart had now found a boon. Like a moon crossing the sky after a sunshine gloom. Mark wasn't clear of his heart's immediate reactions. He was not clear of how he said that quotation '*My half of the day gets completed*'.

He followed her towards the door and said :

"Are you late?" whispered Mark into her ears.

"No… I am not. Actually, I can reach until 10:30, no compulsion for me," replied Tamanna.

"Ok… that's good to know," he said, standing amidst a crowd which was about to move.

"I'll be coming with you," he uttered, as the exit door opened.

"Oh…really?" she asked while getting out of the door.

"Yes, I am out already… God! This rush," he said, getting out at the same stop.

"I still can't believe that you got down here," she said.

"Yes, I have plenty of time to reach office. Come, let's stand there," said Mark, pointing to a space at the platform.

"I am truly amazed," she said, walking along with Mark.

"My heart asked me to talk to you more, so I came out," he said.

"You… I wonder," she said.

"So, hmm… now, let me know," added Tamanna, looking at Mark's face.

"Huh… Don't know, I have time and my mind is set to talk to you more," he said.

"Ok…ok! Tell me how you manage to do all these things that you do?" she asked.

"I just have a small lesson in my mind," he replied and stopped.

"And what is that?" she asked.

"Whatever you do at a particular time, do it with all of your heart."

"And how does this make you do all the things that you do so beautifully?" she insisted again.

"I love doing what I do and then, the finest piece comes out."

"Great," she said, exhaling heavily.

"Nothing great, yet," said Mark, being intense.

"The journey has just started, I wish my weakness never breaks me down," he added.

"And what is that?"

"My emotions," he said.

"Aww...you're an emotional one," she replied.

"Ok, what exactly is your aim?" asked Tamanna, after a break, to gather Mark's attention back who was again lost in his wanders.

"You really want to know?" asked Mark.

"Yes."

"This question hasn't been asked by any person in my life," said Mark.

"Come on...say nah."

"I want to become a moviemaker with all my tools used in it," said Mark, slowly and sensibly with credence in his voice and esteem in his eyes.

"You will one day, I am sure," she replied.

"Aah... what did we get into? Say, how many metro's passed after ours?" asked Mark.

"I guess, two," he added.

"Hahahaha... It's around five metro's that have passed after the one we left," she replied with a broad smile.

"Aah... see I told you that time passes very quickly when I'm with you," he said with an unbroken smile with its flavour of joy on his face.

“It’s getting late for you,” he said, looking at the lift aside.

“Yea… let me go now. I had a really nice time,” said Tamanna.

“I did too,” said Mark as Tamanna began to leave.

The way she turned over my last word,
I wonder, have I ever before seen such a bird.
The delight drooping from her eyes,
Had known until now, but my heart still asked for its price.
Every single step she took to get away from me.
Stuck those feeling to give them rise, whom I kept away as I don’t want to be.

Mark stood at his place for the next 15 minutes. Like today someone took his brood of starting work on time. He sat in a space, enjoying the sound of the train’s arrival and listening to it as it passed through. He smiled at every person who passed by him that day as his life wanted to mingle in some other tune for the day.

“Oh God! How am I going to go to work today?”

staring

“He said and stood up.
Trying to start from where he left taking sips from his coffee cup.
Taking forward the next step in his way, he found it difficult.
The way he’s dealing with this precious emotions, he didn’t found feasible.
Wanting to settle this down by making clear what he wants
By measuring the sentiment, forgetting how hard it counts.
The heart is scared of getting missed,
the way it previously misunderstood other bonds.”

Thursday

“Eyes defined a colour to find in many my fellow
As today’s Thursday and she would be wearing something yellow.”

"I won't have breakfast," said Mark.

"But I already served it on the table," replied Mrs. Shivach.

"Oh... is it so?"

"Yes, keep your lunch and have your breakfast properly," instructed Mrs. Shivach.

"Maa, please understand. I am getting late," he said abruptly, picking up his lunch and placing his bag over his shoulder.

"Wait, Mark. What is this?" asked Mrs. Shivach.

"What?" he replied, opening the door.

"You know what I am asking about," said Mrs. Shivach.

"Aah... Maa, you know I share with you everything," he said.

"But this time you are hiding something," replied Mrs. Shivach.

"Ok... Ok... let me say... but you know it already," he replied.

"What? And what do I know?" asked Mrs. Shivach, sitting on the rearmost chair.

"Good you sat down, let me also sit now," he said, pulling a chair to settle.

"You aren't getting late now?" asked Mrs. Shivach.

"You know nothing is more important than you are to me," he replied.

"Now just tell me what happened, my child," asked Mrs. Shivach, passing her sweetest smile like every other time.

"Maa, this is about that girl 'Tamanna' I told you about that night," he said.

"Couple of days before," he added.

"Aah, I just remembered. Are you so intensely into her?" Mrs. Shivach asked.

"I am, Maa…" he replied.

"I have only mornings when I can meet her," he said.

"I thought that you like Sayoni," queried Mrs. Shivach.

"So said that is why you were avoiding what I said the last time," added Mrs. Shivach, with a hush over her face.

“Maa, I agree that Sayoni is a wonderful mate for my life but my feelings towards her aren’t like that,” he said, bringing his chair closer to her.

“I believe you agree to what you’re saying. Yes?” said Mrs. Shivach.

“Yes, Maa,” replied Mark.

“It’s even hard for your Maa too to pick the right one for you,” said Mrs. Shivach.

“But you perfectly know of my heart’s desire, Maa,” said Mark.

“Yes, I do.”

“Then why are you taking unwanted stress?” he asked.

“You are a soft-hearted person, you won’t understand, Mark,” instructed Mrs. Shivach.

“And your hassle was for this reason?” asked Mrs. Shivach.

“Mark, it’s been said by you. See you,” said Mrs. Shivach and got up to step back towards the gallery.

“Yeah… It sounds weird, that’s why I am controlling my expressions from being revealed,” he said loudly.

“Yes, though I know you never keep a secret about your feelings for anyone, whatever you feel,” said Mrs. Shivach.

“Don’t be shy like this… my child! Go, you are getting late,” told Mrs. Shivach.

“You are the sweetest, Maa,” he said and ran to kiss her cheeks before leaving.

“He traced his emotions for what’s he’s desiring to.
Found it difficult to interpret, to prove his soul.
For which his moves are fighting too.
Breathing was easier before.
As they never stuck with such emotions that were so hard to cure.
The way from home to metro too have become pleasant like heaven’s vibe.

Heart raised a request for making working days more than five.
The mind heals even without succeeding now.
It's in love with the present feeling, forgetting all other's who once wore it down.
Height is not meant to be conquered.
Why make it so hard, that you will get an inkling of not achieving it for sure."

She's on her way to reach the metro. Mark's feelings are unique, that's what he's trying to tell himself.

Wanting to know, what is more alluring. Lend ever over the same persona where he found it more fruitful.

He was directed towards her like a sailor.
She is a designer and he wants to be her tailor.

"Why do my feet feel so light while stepping on this floor. Have I lost weight? Or after such a long, did God feel to open my happiness door," crooned Mark.

"She will be wearing yellow today," he murmurs while stepping down the stairs to the platform.

"And if she doesn't?" he asked.

"Then also my eyes will identify her easily in this crowd," crooned Mark.

"As eyes had already defined the colour to find her in a crowd, my fellow.

As today is Thursday and as always she will wear something yellow," said Mark little aloud.

"Hey, where are you going?" said Tamanna, moving closer to him from his left side.

"And finally I found whom I was looking for," said Mark with a beckon and pointing a finger towards her.

"Are you ok?"

"Why?" replied Mark.

"Never saw you greeting me like this," she said, laughing.

"But I play many characters in life," he said.

"Is it?"

"To judge and adjust according to the climate is very important," he answered.

"One more thing of yours," she said, stepping inside the metro that just arrived.

"You tell me, how's the health of your Maa now?" she asked.

"She's good, happy to hear your treat for her," he replied.

"I share my life's every good part with her," added Mark, to answer the question raised on her face.

"What do you mix in your every word that your every stanza brings delight?" she asked, with innocence on her face.

"I just say the truth wrapped with commitments," he said.

"You again said something, the same way," she said.

"They both had discussed a lot over social chats.
Knowing about each other's likes, they build their stats.
That knowledge of knowing became so essential
That they started making each other's point very crucial.
Breath ever stayed slow while delivering.
Like it's also asking a favour for current wills in those words its retaining."

"Commitments… hmm," said Tamanna, nodding her head.

"Yea… Well, I don't find myself worthy for so much trust that people have on me. But it's a person's responsibility to prove them right when anyone trusts them," said Tamanna.

"Yes, a true cycle of commitment," added Mark.

"Huh… it's all like an other world," she replied, with her wandering eyes.

"Yes?" asked Mark, raising his eyebrows.

"Nothing, you keep on saying. I am a good listener," she said softly.

"Time to change our metro," he said, giving her way to step out first.

"You stay on, don't bother about these changes," she said, stepping ahead to move out, with a smile.

"His words stayed on.
Letting the light of that glow over her red cheeks to stay on.
Her every reaction he stored beneath his eyes.
Nourished them in a way that they stayed without any price.
Her every attempted look made his feelings to flow intense.
And such an attitude he could build, just in her presence.
He had never seen himself conveying so much to anyone before.
No one knocked and asked those things, standing in such a way at his door.
Light started becoming powerful then dark.
He was not waiting, but somehow it was set on fire with her spark."

"What have you started thinking?" she asked.

"Access smile sometimes get shun with a single dark cloud," he replied.

"Oh… What, I again started this philosophy!" he added.

"Yes, silence isn't meant for you," she said, giggling.

"Huh… And you have conquered how to smile," Mark replied, saluting her and stepping ahead to gaze outside through the glass pane.

"How beautiful it feels to see the silent water of Yamuna flow everyday on the way, isn't it?" he said, staring out of the glass pane.

"Yes…such peaceful aura is what is the present requirement of everyone," said Tamanna, looking intact just like him.

"You are a single child, right?" she asked.

"Yes."

"You once spoke about a sister. She's your sibling?" she asked.

"Hmm," prompted Mark, with his lips pressing each other.

"What? You didn't say anything," she said.

"She was my elder sister. I have not been a single child since birth," he said, with silent grief.

"Oh, sorry… I wasn't aware," she replied.

"Yes you aren't, I haven't conveyed it to you."

"She is such a nice person and God took her away from our lives four years ago," he added.

"I can understand it completely," she insisted.

"I wouldn't have told this to you even now," he said, looking back at the Yamuna that flowed.

"Look, this is her," Mark said, opening her pic in his cell phone.

"Aww, she is such a beauty… Love," said Tamanna.

"Yes, an angel," he replied.

"The extent of humanity she had was above many saints, I believe," added Mark.

"Surely, she is beautiful and her face clearly says it all. The good deeds she was into and meant so much to a person like you, her brother. Right?" she replied.

"I can't say how great I feel when I talk about her," he said.

"Aah, it's so beautiful to see you tackling God's decision and maintaining your livelihood so calmly with cheer. Surely, if she can see you and your family now, she would be definitely happy seeing you excel and doing great," she said, with soberness on her face.

"Let's not talk more about it," said Mark,

"You tell, how was your weekend? Mine went mostly with family only," he said.

"Mine, as well, went away being with my family. I like to be with them while they cook and stuff," she replied, with her cheeks conveying the joy behind her words.

"They need our time and we should be responsibly giving that to them," he replied.

"Time passed, like it had stopped, to show the beauty of its place," he said, looking outside.

"Yes, Mr. Novelist, you and your words," she said, raising her hand for a high five.

"And you noticed their depth," said Mark, looking into her eyes.

"Yes, I have started getting some flavour of yours in me now," she said while stepping closer towards the exit.

"Yea," replied Mark.

Coming to office

"Someone's smile isn't stopping, can we know the reason behind it?" said Nita, Tamanna's colleague.

"Nothing dear, let me get settled," said Tamanna, keeping her bag on her desk and switching on her system.

"This smile–I never before observed it on you. Something surely happened," said Nita, while playing with a pen's cap which Tamanna just kept on her desk, having brought it out from her bag.

"Nothing happened, what are you so curious to know?" said Tamanna, stepping towards the pantry to fill her water glass.

"It's not just today, I've noticed this change in you since quite some days," said Nita.

"You are such a stalker," replied Tamanna, getting back to her desk.

"Tell me nah," said Nita.

"What?" she replied, keeping her chin on her palm and her elbow on the desk.

"You are my bestie, you know everything about me," said Tamanna.

"That's why I am asking. Let me also be happy for you," she replied.

"Aah, means you won't leave without knowing?"

"Hmm."

"Ok.... Listen. I met a wonderful guy. That book I was reading is his only," said Tamanna.

"Is his only means? You borrowed that book from him?" asked Nita.

"He's the author of the book. He wrote it," replied Tamanna, with a craze and pitch in her voice.

"You met him where?" asked Nita, with her same unsettled curiosity.

"Now that wasn't your question," replied Tamanna, getting lost in her phone, seeing images to find something.

"But what's his name?" she asked.

"Could you stop checking the images on your phone and answer me," added Nita, snatching the phone from her hand.

"Give it back. I have to share something to him now," said Tamanna loudly.

"Oh ho... What will you share with him? Let me also have a look?" said Nita.

"See, this one," said Tamanna, showing a Goddess 'Lord Krishna's' feet image with a message written over it.

"This one?" Nita asked, with a weird expression on her face.

"It's God's message, dear. Why this?" added Nita.

"He wasn't feeling good today and I raised a topic," said Tamanna.

"What topic?"

"You want to know every bit about this, don't you?" she replied, staring at her.

"Let's cut this off, I am sending it to him. Hope he feels better," said Tamanna.

"Hey, what message you'll attach along with it?" said Nita, gazing at the phone's screen.

"You don't need to worry," said Tamanna, with a smile on her face.

"Don't panic! I am going to my desk..." said Nita stepping

backwards.

"Let me share this and start working," said Tamanna, taking a sip of water from her glass.

"Hope you attached a nice message," Nita shouted, as she headed back to her seat.

"Oh, yes. I'll do," replied Tamanna, turning back to look at her smile.

"And here it goes," said Tamanna, after pressing the send button.

One leniency has been packed to deliver with a Goddess's message.
This flight has been booked with the emotional package.
Some unsaid desirous waves are yet to flow towards the ocean shore.
The way those small bricks of emotions are kept secure in a single store.

Stepping Ahead

Mesmerisations were turning pages to unlock reality.
Things received are ever sweet in love as they are not due to any charity.
Those beautiful gestures and the way they move over each other's mind.
Their intellect can observe this changing aura as it's not blind.
Nothing is too late, nothing can be built in a hurry.
A relation for its longer being should be recognised before you carry.

Next day:

"Hey, why did you change your profile portrait to this one?" asked Uzeeta, an office colleague of Mark.

"Isn't it good?"

"It's good... but never seen you being holistic, so," replied Uzeeta.

"I'm not being holistic now either. It's just about the message it contains," said Mark.

"Oh... So now, Mark is concerned about spreading such a message," said Uzeeta.

"A person who hardly cares of these things," added Uzeeta, with a very intrinsic reaction.

"What are you trying to find out?" said Mark, smiling as he looked at her confused face.

"Oho! Wait, I'll convey," added Mark, after staring at Uzeeta for a few seconds.

"Could you once read the message?" said Mark, pointing his finger over his phone's screen.

"Yes,"

"Let your thoughts flow past you, calmly. Keep me near at every moment, trust me with your life, because I am you, more than you yourself are.

Lord Krishna," read Uzeeta, very patiently.

"Aah, you both are here," said Divyansh, breathing heavily, trying to settle down.

"Anything important? All good?" asked Mark.

"Yes... all good," Divyansh replied.

"So Uzeeta, hope you felt motivation in its every word," said Mark.

"Hmm," replied Uzeeta.

"Uzeeta, Manisha is calling you over to your seat," said Divyansh, in a rush.

Manisha was the manager of Mark's team. She majorly worked from home. Today, she had come to office and the first thing she meant to ask for was her core member–"Uzeeta".

"So, Manisha is the reason for this discomfort?" asked Mark giggling.

"No, that wasn't my concern; I am afraid of what you are about to tell Uzeeta," replied Divyansh.

"Yes, but how could you know this?" asked Mark.

"I saw your profile image has been changed, so," said Divyansh, looking from the glass pane.

"And you assumed the present story?" asked Mark.

"Yes."

"How come your intellect works that strong?" asked Mark.

"You know that?" said Divyansh, smiling, picking up the water glass which was closed with a lid.

"And what wrong would happen if I tell her?" asked Mark.

"Your heart is clean, you wouldn't understand this," replied Divyansh.

"Oh... please... say," Mark queried.

"It isn't good for you to share it with everyone," said Divyansh.

"Man, true feelings should be told to receive the blessings of everyone."

"But everywhere, they won't receive it."

"She's a supportive girl," Mark said.

"Ok. But why... why everyone?" said Divyansh.

"I am not trying to prove you wrong, please understand my concern. I am saying this having considered your stars," reiterated Divyansh deliberately.

"Ok, my astrologer... Ok," said Mark.

"Well, nice profile pic," said Divyansh.

"This is such a precious thing she gave..." said Mark, before getting silent for a while.

"I can see your attitude towards it," said Divyansh.

"You already have made it superior," added Mark.

"How much ever I say about this pic would be less," said Mark, kissing the pic on his phone's screen.

"More precious is the message she has attached along with it," said Mark, losing himself in thoughts.

"Don't look at the roof and get lost again. Tell me please, what is it?" asked Divyansh.

"Why would I tell you?" said Mark, teasing Divyansh.

"What can I say! That you should be knowing," replied Divyansh.

"Listen, she wrote with it 'Read this one whenever you feel low. Like I keep it close to me with trust that it will make me feel better. You will find yourself healed and strong.'" said Mark, while getting lost in thoughts of her.

"She seems to be a true soul," said Divyansh.

"I know," replied Mark.

"My tracks are directed towards hers now," said Mark, looking out of the door.

"See, she's coming back," said Mark, noticing Uzeeta walking towards the room.

"Oh."

"Hey, Manisha is calling everyone... come," said Uzeeta, spying inside.

"Yes, Mark. Come," said Divyansh walking towards the door.

"Well, that gig of sending me out was interesting," whispered Uzeeta, staring at Divyansh while walking.

Those impressions took their lead over mind after heart.
Something beautifully got conveyed, before anyone feels it to be just a flirt.
No one is there whom you can blame.
He's the one, who meant her to be his code final variable name.

Everyone took their place inside the meeting room and noticed Manisha's smile missing from her cheeks with which she starts her everyday. It had already developed goosebumps on everyone except Mark. Mark was still adrift somewhere.

"Who wrote this code?" asked Manisha.

"I am asking something, who wrote it?" she again iterated, turning her screen for everyone to see what she was talking about.

"Manisha," said Uzeeta, with her eyes directing her towards Mark.

"Mark, are you listening to me?" Manisha raised her pitch.

"Yes, what happened?" he replied, startled.

"I asked who wrote this code."

"Oh, this one, I did. You forgot?" he answered, bringing the screen closer to him.

"Who takes such long variable names to store value in codes," she said.

"And now you all see what it is: 'Taaa maa nnaa,'" Manisha read slowly, cracking it out.

"Aah, it's Tamanna," said Mark.

"Yes, I know well. It's a person's name," she said.

"You are looking in the test environment. Please check the production one. It's with accurate variable," he justified.

"Let me check it now only. This could be a blunder, you know that Mark," she said.

"You already know how much I am concerned about these things," he replied.

"I understand, Mark. Yeah, I saw things were fine in production," she replied with relief in her breath.

"I told you."

"Please correct that in our test environment as well," she reiterated, while picking up her laptop's pad, and moving out of the room hurriedly.

"After this instance, I am getting at what you did not me," said Uzeeta, whispering in Mark's ears. And Mark peered at Divyansh in anger.

He conveyed his impression moving towards his desk.
With what he's living, remembering its back and forth, forgetting rest.
Those deep breaths he's taking
And the way he's repeatedly drinking sips of water.
His words aren't getting proved today,
Which he says that one-sided emotions in heart, he hardly bother.

Phone bell rang :

"Hey... hi," said Sayoni, from the other side of the call.

"Uff... yeah hi..." replied Mark.

"Why this 'Uff'?" asked Sayoni, with her same smile that she wore for Mark.

"Uff... is for missing to talk to you from a long time," answered Mark.

"You know well, your call is ever wished and expected with love," said Sayoni.

"Yeah that's all on me, then who else got lost," said Mark.

"What happened, Mark?" she asked.

"Someone seems lost," she replied, after waiting for a few seconds for him to answer.

"Lost... you can say," he replied.

"And is it because of Tamanna?" she asked.

"Can't say anything, my mind seems lost and blank," he replied.

"Don't worry, everything will fall into place," she said, settling down her voice.

"I don't know why I am reacting like this this time," he said.

"Because of things going on in your mind, especially those you aren't able to reveal," she replied.

"No, not like that. You know I say everything in a much clearer way to you. But what and why is this... I don't know," he said.

"Mark, life contains something good for you too… Believe me! You have to be strong for maintaining your stand."

"Don't know... why am I scared of giving a hug to my wishes," he replied.

"Now you please stop picking up such low words," she said.

"I know you. You contain a valour to overcome every challenge," she added.

"But I become feeble in front of my feelings and emotions," he said, scrubbing his feet on the grass carpet while sitting on a swing.

"Mark, is it you who is speaking all this?" she asked.

"Yes, I don't know how come I am saying these words today," he said, standing on the floor having jumped from the swing.

"Hey, forget this, you tell me how's everything at your end?" he asked.

"You're again turning things," said Sayoni.

"Mark, I need to talk to you and have been wanting to since a long time over this," she said, being intense.

"I am being called now. Will catch you soon. But please don't allow anything to bother you," she said and left towards her manager who was calling her.

"Yes... but it never happens," said Mark, after hanging up.

"Hope you are aware of the post-lunch conclave by Mr. Tiger?" asked Mr. Pradeep.

Mr. Pradeep was one of the senior-most members on his floor and was the person whom Mark respected and shared his life twists with.

Mark was lost in his thoughts.

"What? You're coming or not?" asked Mr. Pradeep.

"I am," said Mark, before he quickly went to his desk.

My eyes would be staring at you.
Till the time someone doesn't interrupt and lets me wonder.
It wouldn't be physical.
But fortunately or unfortunately, it's making everything musical.
I am not afraid of the tone it plays repeatedly.
But I am scared of the way it's rising rapidly.

Striker

When things are felt and meant from the heart.
They set themselves free from all useless dirt.
Your heart is pure with those auspicious feelings flowing through.
I understand you are the one to handle this ship without any crew.
Secure every love sprouted feeling, by being its doorkeeper.
Because the world might not be aware and swipe it like a sweeper.

Today, the bird seemed to be in a different mood at Mark's home courtyard. Mark was on his way back home from his morning jog. The street dogs were licking Mark's feet. Mark was enjoying their dancing tails and their jumping feet. Today they didn't seem to be hungry. There was a difference in his walk as his smile on every step whispered something to his aura.

"This relief after a jog wasn't as thrilling before," said Mark.

can'tThe mist that rose from the ground, settled back, and decorated the climate in such a way that it started to take his breath away. Unable to realise the reason for this, he crossed the street with a smile on his face. Reaching closer to home didn't make him feel good. He observed the beauty of nature from the place he stood.

"Mark, Shubhash bhaiya hasn't come yet. Charlie is getting jittery. Can you take him for a walk?" Mr. Shivach shouted from the first floor.

Shubhash : He was the caretaker of Mr. Shivach's pet. They had a dog of a Siberian breed. And his name was Charlie. Mark's family loved him a lot.

"Yes Maa...I will go," shouted Mark, standing on the pedestrian track.

He was happy for that extra time he gained to spare in this environment. He took Charlie along with him towards the field. he too started running with him, enjoying the breeze.

He can't count anything
That can beat his present feeling.
His time is running,
Asking him to take the warmth from the fire that's still burning.
The day shone,
letting him know it was all mine.
Getting scared of the night,
whoever destroys him with an excuse of having no light.

The day started asking its devotion from him for work.

He asked God to work in favour of his luck.

Mark and Tamanna met again in that same way of devotion,

Building their uncertain sensation to a certain emotion.

"Hey... I was waiting for you over there," said Tamanna on noticing Mark.

"And I was waiting here," replied Mark, turning towards her.

"Why? We always meet there only. So?" she asked.

"I felt it to be a little crowded and..." he replied, with a stammering voice.

"Ok, I read your status that you put up today morning," said Tamanna.

"Wait... I'll read it out once :

'#DelayInReply

Amazing world...

And it doesn't matter whatever you are.

To whatever extent of happiness you can deliver.

There are people whose message replies you wait for but they delay in their every reply.

For making you realize of how it feels when you delay in replying to others.' read Tamanna.

"Is it?" she said, with her raised eyebrows and eyes staring at his face.

"Hmm," he said, with a bowed head and slight smile.

"No, please. I don't want to make you realise anything. It's just as I said–I am not close to my phone always. As I feel it kills your own time," she replied, with her same broad smile.

"I thought I was unable to reply to many messages. As they leave to stay unread," she added.

"Hey, no worries. I understand it," he said with laughter.

"You are as free as an ocean," added Mark.

"From where did you read this?" she asked with her opened mouth.

"I read it somewhere, leave that," he said while boarding the metro.

"Ok, wait, let me read your last text," she said, bringing out her phone from the bag she was carrying.

"Oh... such a nice quote," she said, staying adrift in thoughts while reading from her phone screen.

"Hmm… and a very nice display picture," she added, facing Mark.

"Yes, it touched my heart," he responded.

"You keep your emotions well packed in your quotes. That is so bewitchingly," she said, noticing Mark back in his joyous flavour.

"I don't talk to a lot of people, but the ones I do, it is this way in which I do... now you know this well," he said.

"Belongingness isn't just an affection for me. It's a matter of commitment to bring a smile on someone's face," he said and took a deep breath.

"Aww... forget it now," she uttered, punching his shoulder with her right hand's fist.

"I already have," he said, rubbing the spot that she touched.

"My bestie once pinged me 'Hi'. I also replied back with a 'Hi' and left my phone," she explained, with her face covered in laughter.

"Got it, I am getting it now. You don't need to explain to me more," he said.

"So how's aunties health?" she asked, her tone getting slower.

Without knowing her, he's getting mad over her kindness.
The way she asks first about his mother's health.
Forgetting all other factors.
That will play with his emotions by keeping them ever melt.

"'Maa is feeling good these days," replied Mark.

"Hey which song were you listening to when I saw you?" asked Tamanna.

"I was listening to one holistic song with the best music direction I have ever heard. Listen," said Mark, giving his earphones to her.

"Yes, that's seriously beautiful," she replied, after she heard the song for a minute.

"You love it?" he asked with a craze.

"Yess... Of course!"

"I hear one song back to back instead of changing a song one after the other," he said while taking the buds from her.

"Same I do," she replied in elation.

"Music seems to be my first love. I can live just with it, if not given anything else," he said, with a glow on his face.

"Wow... That shows your endearment clearly," she uttered.

"You know I adore music like anything and the way you said implies the same to me," she added.

"Similarities," he said, with a smile.

"Yea...," she added, with a beautiful gleam in her left eye.

The way she agreed over our similarities.
Mind stopped asking the heart about any clarities.
Now heart became superior to feel as it needs
Soul prayed to get a sappy fruit this time, from heart newborn seeds.

"Hey, I observed you started using 'yea'... in place of general 'yeah'?" she asked with a smile.

"When did you observe?" he said.

"In your text. Don't you know?" she replied.

"Yes... I felt it to be good, so I opted for it," he replied.

"And you opted this from whom?" she asked.

"From someone."

"It's from someone, or it's from me?" she asked.

"So what, it's you. You must have also opted it from somewhere," he said while facing her.

"Yes, I understand," she spoke, with a cherish smile.

"I have observed that you miss out one or the other question of mine when I ask two-three questions to you over chat," he said.

"Oh, that."

"Why do you leave them unanswered?" he asked.

"I feel you to be asking them too early," she replied.

"I asked you yesterday about your timing of reaching the metro in the morning. It's just that," he said, with intent eyes and an innocent face.

"Yea. But... Ok, leave this, can't we talk about something else?" she said.

"Leave... to go where," he said slowly.

"Yes, you just speak anything?" she asked.

"Aah…Nah," he replied.

"Don't think too much and take stress, heal your mind… relax!" she said.

"See, that seat is vacant. Have it," she said.

"No need, you know it," he said.

"Yes, I know, we both don't sit while travelling," she said, giving a break between her every word.

"Say, any new wonderful thing in your life 'wonder boy'?" she spoke.

"Nothing as such, all practical practices going on," he replied.

"What?" she asked.

"Trying to make good music and composition with my guys," he said.

"Aiming to reach for a big crowd," he said.

"You read my interview for my first book?" he asked, settling his curiosity.

"Yes, you don't need to worry about these. It's just the start, there are too many things to come," she said, with her fingers touching her face.

Your blessings bend me more towards you.
Making you get packed with all those things which are found in very few.
Your crossed fingers over my wishes and shine over your cheek.
Gives way for blessings to come closer, so they can meet.
This sweet quantitative mixture of all your features together.
Makes my excitement to reach good heights opening all my feathers.

"Oh... your crossed fingers," said Mark with a blush.

"Yes, for your words to come true and stay free from others vision," she answered.

"And our words asked for an end,

As they saw that we have the same destination as our trend," said Mark.

"You are a master of rhyming, Mr. Novelist," she smiled and came closer to Mark with her sensitive eyes.

"Are you feeling warm?" she said while looking to Mark's palm.

"Why so?"

"Look at yourself, you're sweating," she uttered.

"Is it?"

"Hmm... take this," she said, handing a napkin from her bag to him.

"No, I have one. Ok, give," he said, placing his hands inside his pocket.

"Everything is alright nah?" she asked in angst.

"Yes... perfectly fine," he answered.

Hands and legs never felt so nervous.
The way they are getting annoyed is hard to conclude.
Might they support the will of the mind ever.
This time they are expecting things from heart, becoming hard to exclude.

"I wanted to know one thing. What kind of motivational speech do you perform?," she asked.

"Ok... the kind for making life better for people in need," he replied with grace.

"Aah... like? I am not clear," she said.

"I guess, I won't be able to say all of that in this crowd," he replied.

"Umm... We can meet somewhere out," she said.

"Yes, that's what we can do," he replied, giving way to the passing passenger.

"So, let's plan this weekend," he suggested after a second before she spoke up.

"Sure, I'll check with my mother and confirm," she replied.

"Check what?" he asked.

"Checking if she has nothing planned with me for this weekend," she replied.

"Aah… it is important stuff. Let me know what it is," he said.

"So Miss, come I'll drop you out?" asked Mark.

"You are coming out?" she asked.

"Nah, just showing manners," he said and laughed with a matching smile.

"Oh… such a nice start of my day," she spoke in joy.

"And you already completed half of my day," said Mark, looking into her eyes.

"Yeah, I remember you said that," she said, with a smile before moving towards the exit.

Mark's sentiments weren't able to control themselves. Somehow a voice raised from inside him.

"Hey Superhero," said Mark.

She looked back while walking forward. But Mark shut his mouth and showed this voice to be from her imagination. And she walked ahead on her way.

That precious thing could be clenched tightly.

But a person gets frightened to lose that thing which visits their life hardly.

Do they have to blame themselves for loving things so badly.

Or it's just a matter of time, and they should let things happen accordingly.

Mark closed his eyes and said :

In a blink of your eye

He captured all those tones that you hide.

You can judge the level he gave to you.

The way he folded his hands over prayer, for just asking your smile.

Iceberg

Those love encounters which are planned by self.
Shouldn't be kept in books of mystery and become helpless.
If somehow your lips are blocked by your soul to reveal the truth.
Plan a way to not let your anxiety to break, so what if it asks for the hardest way you could.
Talking about those glaciers which meet each other in love.
Spreading iceberg over the sea like they settled several white doves.

"Where you are off to?" asked Mrs. Shivach.

"I told you last night Maa, Bangla Sahib Gurudwara," said Mark, trying hard to make his shoe fit in his foot.

"You told that to me but didn't say anything about the timing... so early?" asked Mrs. Shivach.

"Yes, I found it suitable," he replied, still trying hardtop make his shoe fit in.

"But skipping your workout isn't a good option," she said.

"Mark, be easy on your shoe. They've gone old, and can't accommodate your feet," Mrs. Shivach added.

"Well, your other long brown boots look dashing on you. Try them," she urged while going back towards the drawing room.

"Thank you, Maa," he said, before he ran to open the drawer and bring out his boots.

"So, you'll have breakfast or that is also planned with her?" said Mrs. Shivach.

"Her? I didn't tell you anything about her," he replied, carrying the shoes towards Mrs. Shivach.

"Things were understood to me by your gestures and that smile of yours which reveals a lot," she said.

"So now, as you know, won't you help me with it?" he asked, coming closer to his mother.

"What help?"

"Tell me what I should wear?"

"You already get dressed decently everyday," she said.

"Hmmm... I want to take your blessing," said Mark, picking up his sister's photo from the dressing table.

"You kept that out again," he said, holding the frame in his hand to show it.

"I know this pic is very close to you. But last night, I couldn't resist talking to it," said Mrs Shivach.

"Some things never die," said Mark, lost in thoughts while pointing at one corner of the wall.

"I am really sorry, Bacha," said Mrs. Shivach, with her dull voice.

"But why?" he asked.

"For letting you encounter this," she answered.

"She stays with me always. You don't have to," he said, placing the frame back on the wooden shelf and holding Mrs. Shivach's face with his palms.

"Now you don't get your mood low and waste time here," she said eagerly, wiping her tears.

"Wait, I'll make something for you," she said, again leaving Mark's hand, and going into the kitchen.

"Maa... don't hassle. I'll eat outside," said Mark, walking behind her.

"Ok, don't worry. I'll have the cake you baked last night before leaving," he said.

"Blessed to have a mother like you.
Things you never ask for but always do.
Your magnetic affection corrects all the false things that I do.
And I ever stay helpless, for fulfilling all your wishes back to you."

In an hour, Mark left his home and headed towards Gurudwara which was approx. 15 km away from his home. Questions took the lead in his soul, as he drove his car out of the courtyard. He began to speak to himself:

"I should pick her first."

"I don't know her address."

"So what, I will ask her. I'll ask her for the pickup location. I am sure, she'll let me know the address immediately."

"And what if she doesn't feel happy over all this?"

"I will get to know about her interest in first reply itself."

"And what if you judge it wrong?"

"If she really gets annoyed by me calling her now?"

"Ok, Ok... hang on, let me start. I am not calling her nor picking her up," said Mark as he put his key in the ignition.

"But Mark, this doesn't seem favourable. You must take her along," said Mark while driving.

This first meet of ours is of ample curiosity.
Like my cognizance covet to build it with dignity.
Your unsaid words keep on jumping over me.
Settle down this storm by conveying your emotions, no matter whatever they be.

"Aah, I reached, but now where will she be?" he said, with his eyes exploring the area around.

"I should wait for her at the main entrance.," he re-checked, while walking towards the entry door.

"Huh, where will I wait there? It's all spread with sunshine heat.

No shade."

"Now is it possible?" he asked hinself.

"Woah, that's the space where I can sit," he said, looking at a spot under the giant tree.

"I never make anyone to wait. Don't know why I have to wait for people," he said again, sitting down andwiping his face with a small towel he carried.

"A person should wait for special people in his life," a voice was heard from behind him.

"Yes, that's what I am..." said Mark, and became still after noticing who it was.

"Well, I also don't make anyone wait for me. Irrespective of how long I have waited for them before."

"I felt an immense shock with a smile which made me happy. A situation I have never felt before. That's because of you today, my super hero," he said.

"Well, I came before you and was waiting for you over there," she said, pointing her finger towards the opposite road, and laughing loudly.

"I can see this smile for hours, keep smiling," said Mark slowly, folding his one leg over the other.

"Stop. Come, let's get in before you make a scene here," said Tamanna, pulling his hand.

"I will never forget this pull throughout my life," Mark murmers with an excited face and joy in his eyes.

"Like this you will enter?" she said, holding his hand and staring at his feet.

"Yes, we kept our shoes already," he said, reacting innocently.

"And that's all we do?" asked Tamanna.

"Yeah," replied Mark.

"Cover your head, who will do that?" she said eagerly.

"Aah... how could I forget that!"

"Yes, how could you. Seems like you are at an alien place," she said.

"Though this place has been suggested by you," she said, stepping ahead into the water vessel placed below with her naked feet.

"Huhhhhh... I don't know how could I. I forget many things when I'm with you," said Mark, following her feet to wash his feet while tying his hankyon his head.

"Beware! Don't forget your name. Else I'll be calling you in the crowd and you won't realize it," she smiled, as she started climbing up the stairs.

"This won't happen," Mark shouted and followed her.

"Hey, easy, maintain silence," she said, keeping her finger on her lips.

"Not many people can I see here today," he said.

"Seems like you have booked a special appointment with God," she replied, facing Mark with a blunt look.

"This smile from the corner of your eyes seems dangerous," he said, while bending to kiss the floor.

Those quiet steps walking ahead of her on the floor.
My eyes want to see you, beyond every door.
Flawed to espy your swiftly moving feet more.
Trying to safeguard your impression above expression to get cure.
The life which never felt to breathe under someone else conquer.
Is now impaired to loose it's freedom, without any fear.
No one had asked this wind to flow with such a breeze.
But it supported those aspiring emotions, to stay away off any cease.

"Hey... let me come," he shouted and ran towards her.

"This air and all devotional walks have ever had love from me from my heart," she said, blushing from under her long scarf.

"Thought my heart got flat for you. For keeping all those things that I love to do."

"My all predictions are coming true," he crooned, walking beside her, keeping his actions away from her notice.

"You said something again?" she asked, before stepping inside.

"No, I didn't," he replied, making her look at what was in front of her topray.

"Yes, it's only you who gets lost in everything everytime," she said.

Walking parallel, they moved towards God, to touch it and grab that purity which they wanted to save. Eyes pointed towards the king who was full of peace and love. Their constant breaths started beginning to get a little louder. *They bended on their knees. Hands kept above to join and ask God about their needs.* Mark never asks anything for himself and he just wants everyone around him to be happy. *Tamanna, kept on taking a heavy breath with the same grin on her face like she's not afraid now of anything, whatever she'll encounter in this place. Mark was very happy to see her in such a mood.* It wass not easy for him to concentrate in his prayer after his eyes took a glimpse of her face in charm and peace. But he had to get back.

"The guy who can't make himself happy. Lend his prayer to be for everyone."

Mark heard a voice commencing above quote which was for him to open his eyes in shock.

"Why did these words touch me a lot?" Mark asked himself.

"Go round this place," an advisor of the place said whiletouching Mark's shoulder.

"Come," said Mark as he stood up.

They stood up and started to move around the pillars devoting worship and taking blessings from every corner of God's home. Sense of God's presence had already brought a smile on his face and it was only multiplying with Tamanna's presence and her every move. Her moves were making Mark feel exactly what he wanted to.

wonder

Those smooth movements with bowed head and joined hands.
Your prayers had once whispered, piling life with all smiling trend.
Whatever you grilled will come true.
As my prayers are also asking everything to flow in the way you want them to.
I don't know what is this and how it got built.
I just say what my mind says, to keep the jar of your smile always filled.

"Hey, what about 'Langar'?" Tamanna asked, stepping down from the stairs.

"**Langar**: *This is food facility provided in every Gurudwara round the clock all seven days a week. This is a priceless activity, treated as sacrament of intake here.*"

"Yes, why not… I never miss that," replied Mark, stepping down along her.

"Then we have to move and go there," she said, pulling his hand towards that way.

"Hey, why didn't you park your car here in the parking?" she asked pointing at the underground parking.

"I wanted to wait for you first. So that we both entered together," he answered.

"Is there any ritual for us to both enter together?" she asked before laughing.

"No, but I liked waiting for you," he replied in his thinning voice.

"Oh… Please don't sound low, I asked it just casually from you," said Tamanna, touching the chin of Mark to look into his eyes.

"I understand," said Tamanna, looking into his eyes for some seconds.

"Come let's have food, we wouldn't get an empty place or else," she said.

“When will you be making food for me to eat?” she asked Mark, after they both got settled and were about to get served in their empty plates.

“Soon, soon,” he replied with a cheer, taking a sip of water from the glass.

“You know, all males I know make classic food. My dad cooks amazingly,” she said.

“Yes… you told me once. That day when I spoke about ‘aaloo ke parathe,’” replied Mark.

Those desirous whisper converted their words into sentences,
Showing their’s intention towards each other.
Like someone or the other had hitherto decided to forge.
All those ways completely alluring and brimful of delight feather.

Squeezing Emotions

Calls from your heart are never loud that they can be easily heard.
But attempting to make it non-divulging, could produce something absurd.
Words are mastered by emotions and your will.
You have to convey it, apart from asking your heart ever still.

Two weeks passed and a difference was noticed in Mark's professional life. But he whirled around only one factor that none of his days went by without thinking about Tamanna. Everyday started with her memory and ended with thinking about her. It was the period when Mark was send onsite for a week for official meetings. He came back last friday and today was Monday–"Start of a new week". Some changes had been heeded by everyone over Mark's day-to-day operations. His smile seemed to be stolen and the way he was taking decision was without questioning the public. A fitness freak person who suddenly did not seem to be bothered about his workouts. Even after waking up early, he sits on his bed with his legs folded for an hour, lost in some unconditional wander. Mark isn't bothered about his time these days. Those bland reactions over several case meant Mrs. Shivach get edgy about Mark. The spark and cheer he brought in everyone's life through his elegant smile was now lost.

First day of office after a week :

"So champ, how's your onsite work? What about clients? How is it going?" asked Maunik as he punched his card to get into ODC.

"Seems you didn't hear me," said Maunik, entering the ODC behind Mark and walking upto him.

"Ah, you came back, brother," Mark said with a slight glow in his eyes.

"Yeah, I came back last tuesday and came to know that you too are on client visit to Germany," said Maunik.

Maunik works from the companies branches at Australia and stays ON and OFF to India.

"Oh! Good, you came," said Mark, hanging his blazer at the back of his chair.

"Have you lost something?" asked Maunik.

"What?"

"Yes, your stress relieving smile for others," said Maunik, opening the first button on Mark's shirt.

"From when did you start putting your first button on?" asked Maunik.

"It's winter now so…" he replied very decently.

"So what if it's winter? I have been with you since childhood, don't teach me," said Maunik.

"You never did it. And you were always agitated to put it on if anyone asked you to," Maunik added.

"Anything happened in Germany?" asked Maunik.

"Nothing happened, all went good there," he replied while bringing out the MacBook from his bag and switching it on to check mails.

"You can check those later as well, don't hide anything from me."

"Oh dear, not hiding anything. Why don't you understand?" he replied insistingly.

"I would have if I hadn't smelled that uncertainty."

A sound from the last cubical block of the ODC was heard by Mark, while Maunik was still lost finding the answers of his questionnaire.

"You are working under Mr. Pradeep these days?" asked Mark.

"This seems one question over the other which has been left

unanswered," replied Maunik.

"Answer to me, it's important which is why I am asking," added Mark.

"Yes, I am with him for some integration project," he replied, settling his emerging anger.

"You didn't hear, he just called you twice. You must go before he gets annoyed," said Mark.

"How come I didn't heard it?" Maunik asked.

"You were busy in untangling my emotions over every action of mine," Mark replied politely, placing his hand over Maunik's shoulder.

"You've been saved at present, but you will not be for long," said Maunik while stepping towards Mr. Pradeep.

"What happened to this guy, we've met after months and…" said Mark while checking his mailbox.

"I told him about your changed behaviour," said Uzeeta, who was sitting at the next desk unnoticed by any of them.

"Uzeeta, is it you?"asked Mark, standing straight to look over the cubical space ahead which was separated by a thin wooden shell.

"Welcome back, Mark! I won't ask you about your Germany trip because I know you won't tell me anything," said Uzeeta with her glasses onand her face directed towards her screen.

"Oh…I am really sorry for my last week's weird behaviour. Are you still thinking about it?" asked Mark.

"It's not about that thing anymore. But it's about the feeling you still have even after travelling to a different country," said Uzeeta.

"What?"

"It's your distressed face. The way you replied to Maunik," answered Uzeeta.

"Oh… Forget it, someone arrived early today," Mark changed the topic of the talk.

"I have been coming early since last week. I started coming early even before last week when you were here only," she replied.

"Oh… is it?" he asked.

"Yes and you noticed this today. See how you're living. Completely adrift," she said and left to go to the cafeteria, carrying her water bottle with her.

"Bring a black coffee for me please," said Mark, passing her a smile.

"I will, you just try to give us back our previous Mark," she said, before exiting ODC.

Your smile is very costly.
You don't know but it's been loved mostly.
You meant it to become universal.
You heart sprays a smile into other person's life, counting those as your personal.

The day passed by with Mark spending time on his seat the complete day. It's 05:00 pm now when he started putting his things into his bag.

"You're leaving?" asked Surbhi, she was a lady from Mark's team.

Surbhi was a girl with a charming personality and the way of living she had was the coolest. The best thing that Mark liked about her was that she lived in the present and didn't live in the future. Future will automatically get better she believes. Although Mark himself spread a variety of motivational messages, even he got inspired by her once.

"Yeah, I am feeling that I should go. I do not have much to do," replied Mark.

"It's the first time I am seeing you leave early," said Surbhi, passing him a bowl of grapes that she was carrying in her hand.

"So, what I heard is right?" she asked.

"Now what did you hear?" asked Mark, getting up from his seat.

"Your indifferent behaviour," she said, eating grapes continuously.

"Oh God… how do I tell you that everything is perfect. Nothing went wrong anywhere," said Mark.

"Now it's clearly revealed out of your agitation," she replied.

"No grapes today?" she asked a second later.

"Not wanting to eat," he replied.

"Not wanting to eat your favourite fruit. That's also weird."

"Ok, forget it all. I am not complaining to you about anything. You met Maunik today?" she asked again after giving a break.

"Yeah."

"When?"

"Early morning, the first person I met was him only."

"You know, in a day, how many times he talks about you!" she said.

"Even today at the lunch table," she added.

"I don't know why and what Uzeeta conveyed to him," he replied, developing stress marks on his forehead.

"She said exactly what everyone feels here. Why don't you understand the concern they all have for you," she said.

"What should I do?" asked Mark.

"Leave the past and walk into the present," Surbhi said her last words and walked away.

What they said, do they know about the insecurity going on in your mind.
Your changed reactions could be easily measured as they aren't blind.

Mark left his office and reached home at 8:30 pm that day. Wiping his sweat that developed over his forehead, he opened his home's electric door and stepped in.

"How was your day?" asked Mrs. Shivach.

"It went good," replied Mark.

"And what about your evening?" asked Mrs. Shivach from the drawing area.

"Evening? Why did you specifically ask that?" Mark asked, while climbing the stairs towards his room.

"I got a call a minute ago from our neighbour," said Mrs. Shivach, turning back to face Mark.

"And what did they say?" asked Mark, opening his room's door.

"Don't get into that Mark, answer me this first," she raised her voice.

"Answer what, Maa?" he asked, getting inside his room, throwing his bag over his bed, and settling down.

"What did you do at their home?" she answered.

"I only told them to not make that terrible noise the whole day at irregular timings," he replied.

"Can I ask why you became so arrogant now with your neighbours?" she asked.

"Maa, that's for you only. You know that, as I wasn't staying all day at home and you tolerate this noise that they create ever. It's you who does," he said.

"Who told you that I feel miserable with it?" she asked.

"You only told meabout it. And your tensed face while delivering wasn't accepted by my soul," said Mark while filling his empty glass with water from the mug.

"God knows how come you became so rude today. This is not what Mark is known for," she said, standing in front of his room.

"I just said that which needs to be in their awareness," he replied.

"So you have started making people aware by screeching at them?"

"That wasn't a quarrel, I kept my points justly. I don't want you to face any trouble."

"My child, they are our good neighbours. What happened to you?" she said, pointing her hand towards their house.

"What should I do then? Tell me?" he asked, with an agitated face.

"Oh God, what happened to him? Losing his senses as well," she said and left his room moving out towards the balcony that was attached with their neighbours.

"I will look into it now, don't think too much," said Mrs. Shivach loudly, facing his room.

Changing your overall reaction for a single change against your will.

And your functionality will make the environment intolerable, making everything still.

You are the only one to balance it out,

Need to forget something for the other to sprout.

Need to realise one thing foremost.

Life's struggle is a spice that works till the last flow of your smile almost.

I know they keep on saying, 'you can make everything with your effort.'

But love is something with whom your heart can't flirt.

Mrs. Shivach said and went outside. Mark thought about Mrs. Shivach words for a while. Soon, in sometime, his character emphasised him to make amends.

"Why am I unable to stay away of it?" said Mark and threw his glass on the floor.

Wider Sensation

Sometime its vital to persist some memories strongly inside.
Which wouldn't outshine showing any wreaks left beside.
As your weakness will make you more weaker.
You wouldn't even realise, that for these situations, once you are a good speaker.

Unintentional changes in Mark's life had left him stunned. Mark began thinking more than required on certain situations. His moves could be sensed to be dipped in grief. His many incoming phone calls stayed unanswered. He was talking less, making it weird for his surroundings and his teammates to accommodate him.

Next morning in office over the breakfast table :

"Something surely had impacted him," said Maunik, peering at Mark who was sitting across from them on the sixth floor cafeteria where Maunik was with Uzeeta, Surbhi and Divyansh.

"Maunik, don't be much concerned. Let him discuss with us himself if something is there," said Uzeeta, passing her bowl which was filled with sprouts to everyone.

"From when did you also start eating all this?" asked Maunik gazing into her eyes.

"Yeah, Mark made it my habit to eat these for breakfast," she replied.

"Yes, a good one he developed. Else nothing is helping her to reduce weight," said Surbhi, drawing a spoon of sprouts from the bowl.

"But Mark has a different lifestyle. It's really hard to opt his lifestyle," said Maunik, tasting a spoonful of the sprouts.

"Yes, but now this habit at least she will follow," said Surbhi, before laughing loudly.

"Why not, it's really helping me to reduce weight!" said Uzeeta.

"You keep acting like a kid only," said Maunik.

"Yes, I like it," replied Uzeeta, jumping twice.

Suddenly Mark passed them in the cafeteria to go to the washroom.

"He'll not have breakfast along with us?" asked Maunik, looking towards that side from where Mark had just passed.

"No, he does, but that too only as formality these days," said Surbhi.

"Means he's showing the colours of being a 'Team Lead' nowadays," said Maunik and laughed to make their dull faces smile again.

"Very funny. We all know he can't behave like this due to that reason," said Surbhi.

"Some vexing is there, he's not conveying it," said Uzeeta, lost in her thoughts.

"What the hell you are doing sitting like a dumb idiot here?," asked Maunik, turning his face towards Divyansh.

"Wait, I am on the final stage of my projection," said Divyansh, busy with a pen and a paper.

"Leave Maunik, he everytime does that. He and his star's astrological predictions," said Surbhi, showing attitude to Divyansh.

"But this is due to a girl," said Divyansh, looking up from the paper and spying everyone. He shut his mouth thereafter as he saw Mark standing at the doorstep of the cafeteria with his hands folded.

"What? What is it?" asked everyone at once as no one heard Mark coming yet.

"Nothing, I was saying, I have to leave for something urgent," said Divyansh.

"No, you said something, tell us. Come on, speak up," said Surbhi.

"Sorry guys. I'll catch you soon. Need to leave urgently," said Divyansh and left them. Mark sat in a hidden corner of the cafeteria with his ongoing secret thoughts.

"Why all these things so confusing?" said Maunik.

"Oh… Chill. Please don't get into it. If Mark hears of these concerns, he could feel bad as you all know," said Uzeeta.

"Let him take his own time to tell us," added Uzeeta.

Mark sat still in his place and kept trying to get rid of his thoughts. He stood up, now annoyed with himself, and went out to the corridor.

"Hey, good morning," said Mark, after dialling a number on his cell.

"Hi," replied Sayoni from the other end.

"So, how did your day start after coming back from onsite," she asked with her sweet tone.

"How can you make yourself so sweet after undergoing so many muddles everyday?" asked Mark with his low voice.

"Ummm," Sayoni murmers.

"Don't react like that. You know I am aware of the changes you are handling in life," he said.

"It get managed dear, if you try," she replied.

"And what if it's because of an emotion you can't cure?" asked Mark.

"Oh… I can feel that agony in your tone. Mark, please tell me first what is bothering you?" asked Sayoni.

"How do you realise my agony so easily?" he asked, sitting on a couch.

"I want to meet you," he said, after a few seconds break.

"Aah… something seriously not looking good now," she said.

"I am taking tomorrow off. Let's meet up?" she said again.

"Yeah, i'll also work over calls, have nothing to deliver as such," he said taking a breath of relief and moved towards his workplace.

"So let's meet at CP, 12 noon?" he asked, opening his ODC door.

"Yes, good enough," she said, before they both hung up the call.

"All good Mark?," asked Mr. Pradeep.

"Yes, everything going good," he replied.

"I didn't see you after you returned from Germany. Take care of yourself," Mr. Pradeep said and left the space and Mark settled down at his place.

New day, A new world of new words

Mark was wholly ready to meet Sayoni today. He went to workout after a long time. He was trying to be normal by keeping himself busy in other activities.

"What will be for breakfast today?" he asked Mrs. Shivach, after he just got out of the bathroom after a shower.

"It would be nut butter, banana and Chia seeds toast,"' she replied taking a sip from her cup of tea.

"After a long time you woke up to your routine," Mrs. Shivach said.

"Yeah, it happens," he said.

"Happens what?" Mrs. Shivach asked appalled.

"I'll be making breakfast today," said Mark, walking into the kitchen.

"It's been months now," she says.

"And it should be delicious too," he replied.

"Yea… it's one of your favourite things to do, so…" she said, watching him from his back preparing stuff in kitchen.

"Don't cut your finger today," she said, smiling.

"But the food taste should not get spoilt ever," he replied while slicing a banana with a knife.

"My child you are important, not food," she said, before walking away.

Everyone had Mark's made breakfast the day. The way Mark made home stuffs, was making his *Maa* to smile. He then began to clean his room and books got scattered all over. Afterwards he took an interest in watering the plants which were on his terrace.

"Everything won't get completed today only," said Mrs. Shivach, peering at Mark watering the plants.

"I know, there's immense of homework you do everyday," he smiled as he threw the water pipe, set off the tap, and went straight downstairs to get dressed and leave.

With his extra long loose shirt, biker jeans, and bluetooth hanging around his neck, he managed to reach the location he confirmed. Still trying to wear his newly gifted apple watch over his wrist. Noticing its features, though he did not have any intention of using them or not. Sitting under the sun light, he controlled many things which were silent inside his heart. His eyes were not examining the crowd and were focussed only on one blank space. Looking towards his phone had became his task every other minute. Staring at the blank screen after even though he was not looking for any call or message from anyone.

Something he felt deep first time in his life, is making him deaf.
Or it's his emotions, which like others he can't bluff.
Why his lips are getting dry.
If after taking enough amount of water, still he tries.
Should he be blamed for decorating his emotion in such a nice way.
Or that person who closed their eyess and did not want to see the output of his true pray.

"A guy is in love with the sun's heat," voice evoke from behind Mark.

"Yes," Mark said and turned to face the person.

"Oh, listen, wait… why are your eyes watery, Sky?" asked Sayoni, putting her hand with affection on his chin.

"See, there's so much of dust out here. So it could have been that," he said, pointing his finger around the local environment.

"Is it?" she queried, spying around to check on his words.

"If it is, then why are you sitting here?" she reiterated.

"I thought that you'll get out through this gate no. 07," he replied, wiping the tears from his eyes.

"Do you need water?" she asked, giving him her bottle.

"No… I don't, dear. You came, that is enough. Ok, I do not want so much shine, let's get under the shade," he said.

"But where do you want to go?" she asked.

"I have nothing in my mind. Seems my thoughts are getting blind." Mark smiled while walking with Sayoni, holding her hand.

"Mark, wait, Mark! Mark, I said wait," she said, being little agitated.

"Now tell me first, how are you holding up?" she asked.

"What? And nothing… why are you panicking?" he answered, halting himself without turning his face towards her.

"Such a guy in such a tone. It's not digestive, Sky," she replied being louder.

"I am spotting some heat over here, can we go in some shade please?" said Mark, closing his eyes and facing forward.

"Ok…Ok! I will reduce my questions. But at least say where you want to go?" she asked with her remorseful eyes.

"Nowhere, let's get into this bar, come," said Mark as he gave a look towards the right.

"This one, would it be worth it?" asked Sayoni.

"Come. It's you that's worth it for me," said Mark, holding her hand before getting into the bar.

He dragged one chair for himself and one for her.
Caring about all commodity around, that she wouldn't bother.
His eyes were staring at her, like a relief he found after so long.

That smile making his every coming second go strong.
Her care protected their pure nod of friendship.
Like she's praying for his health, in all her worship.

"What you'll take?" he asked, peering into the menu card served.

"I'll take your sorrow, your discomfort and plague that took away your smile," she said.

"So much you want… Ma'am, I don't have that much money to buy all this for you," he replied.

"Is it so costly, Sky?" she asked.

"Then just give your faith, i'll preserve it," she added.

Mark shut his lips and concealed the tears from his eyes.

Like she read something that had no price.

Getting anxious about her fondness after knowing this human emotion in which he guided many before but had now started feeling troubled himself now.

He filled her empty glass of drink. Served her plate with snacks.
But eyes still away to gaze at her and lips are shy, finding way for words go cracks.

"What happened, Mark?" she asked with distress.

"Ok, let me start. I saw that spark of desire in your eyes when we met last," she said.

"I was having this idea that it's due to your intense developed emotions of attachment," said Sayoni.

"Its not just attachment," he said.

"I found a perfect partner in her," he added with a heavy breath.

"So, my true assumption was right that it's due to Tamanna," she said.

"Aren't you both interacting with each other?"

"No, it's not the issue. We are interacting," he answered.

"You know well as tohow many guys I have helped to get them rid of such a feeling and stay free," he replied.

"Yes, I do. Though I am dismayed noticing this in you," she said.

"What's separating you?" she asked slowly while looking into his eyes, bringing her face closer towards him.

"Yes, tell me," she reiterated again in a second.

"Things aren't flowing in the right order," he told.

"And you are feeling insecure?" she asked.

"Not me, it's my reverence that is getting hampered," he replied.

"And you are scared of losing your belief over them?" she asked with a smile.

"I don't know what I am, and what should I do," he replied.

"Do you guys chat normally or there's any difference?" she asked.

"I don't know why I am directed towards her and want to give her my everything in this world," he said.

"You are pressurised, Sky. I can see it very clearer."

"By what?"

"By feeling the pain in such a nice heart you have," she spoke.

"You know my ways. I can't ask her to take the next step if I haven't conceived the same interest in other one," he told.

"But what's happening this time?" she asked.

"I can't control my thoughts abouther and my mind builds a home around them. It's not just once, but many times in a day," he spoke uninterruptedly.

"Please convey, where is your understanding lagging behind?" she asked.

"We talk over text once in two days and her reply comes after many hours about what she wants to convey," he said.

"Do her replies sound weird?" she asked.

"No, her replies are wrapped with proper sentiments and she answers everything well," he said.

"So what?"

“If I want to ask something immediately, she never picks up the call,” he said.

“After knowing about each other a lot now, I try to wait for her on my way, but her face seems to show that she doesn’t cares,” he addedintention.

“If you read her text, you’ll feel that how close these people are. But regardless of that, the glass remains filled partially only,” he continued to elaborate.

“Hope she is shy, as she got to know your intentions,” she said.

“Yes, I told her ‘By meeting you, my half of the day gets completed’,” he said.

“She would be knowing then as to how you feel.”

“Whatever, at least a clarity over these feelings is required, right.”

“I feel like I am dragging something along with me,” he said, exhaling.

“So don’t drag it,” she replied.

“What?” he asked.

“You won’t be able to do it,” she replied.

“I just want a relationship with her of knowledge and understanding which can only stand on clarity of thoughts,” he said.

“Everything doesn’t happen the way you want it to happen, Mark,” she said while filling up her fifth glass of drink.

“Why are you drinking so much, please don’t,” he said, whispering to the waiterto not to take her orders anymore.

“Yeah…. I wasn’t in mood to drink. But don’t know how come I’m wanting more of it,” she said.

“Ok, don’t take it anymore,” he said.

“Are you getting my point to think positive and not getting tortured by your unwanted thoughts?” she asked, pointing her finger at Mark under the influence of alcohol.

“I will,” he replied, relaxing his back on his seat.

"Yes, you should," she said.

"I was trying to show you that it's very easy to lose your control. But the game is about how you gain it back," she added.

"Listening to this I've realised the concern," he said, finishing his last pack.

Your tragedy is what is generated through your desire.
When you ask something and get something other than what you aspire.
Suggestion and words would be easily delivered to you.
Your work starts when you apply it in your life without asking how to do

"We are winding up," said Mark to the nearby waiter.

"Thats it?" asked Sayoni.

"Yes," he said, putting his card into the leather bag that had the bill.

"Come, I will be dropping you home," he said, pulling her up to stand with the help of his hand.

They passed their whole day on that spot. Time passed in a way it never went before. They wouldn't have realised it for sure. Dark evening time in winters. Those chilly winds took their place in outside air. They stepped outside slowly. Blessing each other to have a nice story ahed of them.

"Have you carried anything woollen?" asked Mark.

"No, but why?" she queried.

"Its cold outside," he replied.

"Wait, take my cardigan, I don't require this," he said, removing it from his shoulders.

"You are getting edgy worthlessly," she replied.

"See, the moon has taken its place in the sky," said Mark.

"I am responsible to take all care of yours," he said, spying her face while supporting her.

"This moon is partial," she said.

"Yes, as it's not a full moon day," he replied.

"Partial moon, like us," said Mark, getting lost in his wonderlooking up in the sky.

Look at the moon tonight :

The way it pretends to be complete but is incomplete like us.
The way it shows to be full, but most of the time its half like us.
Spreading delight through its shine,
It never reveals the loneliness like us.

Trauma Saga

The nights getting empowered by days.

What fault they meant, if wished you in their prays.

It's not a fight for wining anything.

They only tried to probe sterility of emotions, placing it bigger than everything.

"Hey, wake up," said Mayank, rubbing Mark's head with a towel.

"What happened?" asked Mark.

"If you are not at your home, you should wake up early," said Mayank.

"It's 08:00 am," added Mayank.

"I slept late," replied Mark, rising slowly, yawning while lying on his bed.

"What made a person like you to sacrifice his night?" Mayank asked while combing his hair in front of the mirror.

"Where's my tea?" asked Mark.

"Kept on your stool. It is getting cold while waiting for you to drink it," replied Mayank.

"Tell me one thing. Your home is just a couple of (km) away from mine. So didn'twhere did you go last night?" asked Mayank, as Mark took the first sip of his tea.

"I got late last night, so…" replied Mark, enjoying his tea.

"And what made you to be late? As per my knowledge, yesterday you hadn't gone to office either," said Mayank.

"And sorry cause I will again say that it's none of your business," said Mark before he let himself laugh for a minute.

"See again your special art of shedding things came into picture," said Mayank, giving him a bread toast.

"Thanks for this, as I'm already late, no time left to have anything," said Mark.

"Ok, I am ready. Have to leave, you carry on," said Mayank, buttoning his suit button while picking up his case to leave.

Mayank left leaving Mark in a hassle. Mark got out of bed, picked up his brush, and went inside the washroom

trying to get ready on time and finish up like his regular schedule. Missed half an hour and he would be getting late today. Mark realised this as he stood in his balcony gazing at the sun rays covering the space. He still wasn't clear why he was worrying about time. There's no time compulsion in his company. What his intentions were trying to achieve was still in dilemma. Somehow he reached the metro, where he began to panic to get in early. He ran to get into the metro that had just arrived. Even he doesn't savvy as for why his soul wants to unfreeze of this flow.

"Listen… Listen Mark… have you missed anything? Or is something running ahead of you?" Mark asked to his soul, somehow managed to get into the same metro instead of waiting for another 5 minutes.

"I don't know, but I am not wanting to delay as that same timing suits me," said Mark answering the query of his soul.

"What for heaven's sake is this hassle all about," crooned Mark.

Soon middle platform came where he changed to another metro. Mark tried to get down and take the next one from the platform that was up. Walking to the next platform, he saw someone whom he had been yearning to meet. A person standing on the escalator. His feet ceased to move with the advent of knowing if his illusion was correct. His heartbeat automatically took lead like finding something out of wonder. Mark was peering at the person who was standing on the parallel escalator. Lastly, he exhilarated and said :

"She's Tamanna, oh I was fool, she changed her way," he said, slapping his forehead with his opened palm.

Hundreds of thanks ejected from his heart for God. Praising him for making him get late today, making him encounter the one whom he adores. His blinking eyes severally sharpened their vision to not be in any dilemma like before. Steering his breath to avoid any other thought except the one flowing inside him through his mind's doors. He tried to usher out his optimistic nature like hell. Like someone rang his dancing bell.

Above the escalator, over the platform, he followed her steps, anticipating her to stop, for surprising her of his appearance. She hadn't stopped and walked straight. Mark's intellect got extremely excited of his presence on her. Though he walked behind and abruptly walked ahead to cross her way.

"Aah you, what's up?" said Tamanna with a very broad smile, bringing her hand ahead to shake. She pulled his hand, taking him to one side aligned couch.

"Huh, after so long, say how are you? And how's everything going?" asked Mark.

"All going superb… you say?" she replied.

"Cool, but where were you from that long time?" he asked.

"I started going into girls couch as it is safe. You know about my nail pull lastly nah? So for security, I preferred that," she answered swiftly.

"Woah… And I had wasted my time waiting sometimes for you over our previous platform space ...huh," he said, exhaling heavy breaths to stop his anxiety.

"I felt at times that you might be waiting at that place for me," she said with innocence, delivering a smile on her face.

"Yeah… I did," he said.

"Aww! ... say how is auntie's health?" she queried.

"She asked about you a day before itself," he said, before she gazed at him with those introspecting eyes.

"Yes, I told her about you. I told that to you nah that I do discuss every important person of my life with her. She knows everyone," he added with smiles sprouting out of both cheeks.

"Come, let's take a place in the back. It's crowded near the door," he said, as they both boarded the metro.

"So, what else is going on with your life?" she asked putting her brows up.

"I was shooting a comic video on guys demand, at my home studio," he delivered with craze.

"Wow... that's interesting. Again to say, so many things in you," she prompted.

"I just helped them in direction and provided space for them," he replied.

"How about your work?" asked Mark, breaking the silence of seconds as both stopped laughing.

"Work is somewhat tiring, it doesn't get completed these days," she answered.

"Umm... So that's why, your eyes seem spent," he intervened.

"Is it?" she said sliding her finger over her eyes curvature.

"Hahahaha... don't worry, you look pretty," he giggled on noticing her.

"See the name of this station got changed," she said, pointing outside from the glass towards the stations hoarding, again breaking the silence due to the lack of words.

"You know what my business partners say?"

"What? Please tell," her question arose with cheer.

"Noticing my craze and cheer of doing work to build our events start-up ," he said, looking out at the hoarding.

"Yes, now say," she said with her anxiousness.

"They say that our company name will be titled as a station name soon," he said. After listening to it, she crossed her finger.

Your ever tangled cross fingers on my every other wish.
Makes me more of you, the way you gave it such precious bliss.
You're projected to hit the right mark ever.

Though heart wants to be yours forever.

"Your destination came," said Mark, giving her way to go out towards the door. She smiled and stepped ahead, still engrossed in discussion.

Mark soul being disruptive. Mindless feet started following the spirit of his heart, getting out at the same metro station without any subjective. His eyes are numb to envisage more of her. But he couldn't realise what it was as he was stepping down the stairs, whether those desire wants him to do anything. Mark stopped her, after quickly walking to her. Those ceased feet of her gave a sign of bother at first.

Then her amazed face and that pretty smile, turning over a call facing aside.

Frozen those words of warmth, he carried on walking behind her, covering that small ride.

"Hey, are you getting late?" asked Mark.

"Hmm," she murmered.

"Huh... I missed to show you the video about which I said," said Mark with his dried innocent lips, with his right hand bringing out his phone.

"Oh... you know I didn't attend office yesterday, so I am in a bit of hurry to reach early and wind up the left work," she said with a decent knowing smile.

"Aah... I understand, let it be... I will ping you this one," he said.

"Yes, ping me. I'll check it," she said.

"Huh. I came as lacking to show you in front. But no worries you should move."

His unfinished words and desires wanted to jump higher.
It can't be his mistake for all that he desires.
Why those winds reacted being indifferent, being like others?
Not considering accustom undergone, before designing beautiful feathers.

The very next day:

Mark as ever was confined on timing, neither early nor late. In the perusal of intentions of seeing her today. But his characteristic wasn't confined to be like that anyway. Controlled and continued he moved over his way. But again those impressions weren't willing to stay away. He had an interaction over chat yesterday eve, he left it with asking her to meet today. But his true desires were knocking at the door. Saying him if that's so beautiful inside, then why do you store those feelings within yourself. Let them loose to flow out and live life. Before any trouble strikes and builds it tough to survive.

Yet after all such queries, his intellect asked him to traverse the same way. Mark as every day reached in the mid of his metro's way being directed to go straight. But something meant his feet to halt and stay. He stepped on the side of the platform where he stopped her yesterday. Stabilising his soul in alliance showing those true feelings for only one person. Waiting was becoming difficult, with every passing metro one after the other. His closed eyes, healing back to touch the wall. Inclined against, facing above towards the roof ball. Still closed eyes, questioning his desirous truth-worthiness. Before he listened a 'YES'.

A breeze blew to make him open his eyes. Face moved right to notice its price.

Those eyes, red hair and that glow over her cheeks. I don't know why heart has started beating those drums heavy beats.

Yes, he was gazing at Tamanna with her bag on her sleeves.

She didn't see him, due to standing off the track. Her attire floating inclined straight over the track. And Mark getting into consciousness followed her from her back and finally crossed from the front. To build a feeling, he showed her attending a call before he approached her.

"Hey yeah... this way," said Mark, with a gentle greet crossing her way.

She stopped slightly stunned followed by her pretty smile.

Striding back with him towards the next block behind the girl's couch, Mark directed.

Getting in the upcoming metro.

"Hmm... what's up? " she asked.

"All as you left yesterday," he replied with a smile.

"Let's get in," he said.

"No I'll be standing at the door only," she replied.

Stood futile discussion, standing right over the door. Like ever he tried so hard for her to not get bored. Stifly beating heart pursue to prolong its frequency. Like his every word showing its transparency.

"So at what time you reach metro every morning?" he asked.

"It's different everyday. Sometimes at 8:30 or 8:40 or 9:00 am."

"Oh... so it's hard to catch you," he said with laughter.

"Yes. It's just you who somehow gets to meet me."

"Hmm," he said and gazed over at the floor.

"Blessed me to get to meet you everyday!" said Mark carrying an intimate smile.

"It's all God's favour of giving a chance meeting you," after a second break spiting her reactions.

"Well. see you! My way came," said Tamanna. She began to start and again, Mark's sensation started to shoot.

He ever feels something he left as she leaves.

He started finding his happiness in her, that's what he believes.

"But something you wanted to convey," crooned Mark looking at her going out.

While moving out she turned a little.

Might be she heard those words he said when she stood still in the middle.

Due to immense rush, her sight didn't reach him.

She drifted, considering it as one part of a short film.

The last working day of the week: It's friday :==>

After meeting her for two regular days, Mark's hunch towards life got swanked which can't get built nor can be destroyed by any envy today.

Folks around had witnessed this change in his words. For Mark, happy professional life got attached with personal joining their gloves. Guys rejoiced on such a revival of Mark. The way he starts and ever sprays smile enlightening sparks. Those feet which never get tired of being spoonful to others got new feathers.

Mark's office time started getting multiple.

In his ultimate grin joining others for living practical.

There were dancing moves coming out of his body while he moved. He got something he asked from God, as they prove.

Amusing smile, capturing cheeks. The way everyone was wanting him to breathe. His clear answer over unclear questions meant realisation that he's back into his obsession. The way peaceful treats he's enjoying inside the same getting delivered outside. His ever first greet towards all, settling down its picture back.

Third regular day and his steps wanting to encounter her again.

It's Friday, his soul wished for that same aura to retain.

Mark left home very early today. Outstretched over the way, to start with jitter on his face. His anxious senses were giving him negative views. Getting tored due to his ever carried thought of Tamanna building queues. Mark saw a dream that she was getting hampered. The zeal of getting clarity by texting her which she never replied so instant. The text was still lying unread. Those ever scrolling eyes towards phone screen were getting queued. That gloomy face stayed in the hassle of spying her once. Though he negated time to play any role in building this relationship. He rushed a bit earlier, not to miss her glance today.

"I'll wait above only. Would be knowing when she'll be coming," crooned Mark standing out of the metro having not entered.

"I've never ceased in such a way. How am I into it now?" said

Mark after waiting intact for 10 minutes.

"It seems uncanny waiting here, I should leave," he said.

In envisage of her thoughts, he invaded scrolling his palm over side railing. Lost eyes in wonder.

Face giving the glimpse of worry.

He killed his all negative thought letting them get burry.

"I want to meet her today," he said, punching the iron railing.

"But how can you wait for someone every day over the way?" his soul queried.

"I don't know but the heart wanted to glide this way," replied Mark.

He stood inside the metro. Trying to vacay her flowing thoughts from head to toe. Mark's action stood numb. No queries, as he didn't want to go against his mind and hit the stump. But the empowering heart wants him to acknowledge those salient whispers. Shedding into what, his embellish started flowering.

Mark left the first metro to get into the other one.

But as he climbed, his treads were towing over the way where he stopped them from firing a rifle out of his gun.

Mark's eerie inside for doing something he never felt off.

But now the picture is such, he ever meant off.

Sudden sound and afresh disruption initiated within the crowd. Like one train left and people were ready for the other around. In such mess of a crowd, eyes looked for that beacon of light for whom his heart praised. Time for him to get healed. For whomever worthlessly his fright gets raised. Gazing the way she carried herself. The way he left her yesterday. Heart took its dense beats. Mind denied but he drifts ahead making her aware of presence even today. Mark didn't tapped her shoulder, regardless he came across her way with ample smiling cheeks.

"After following her four steps,

he came surprising in front in the zeal of making her impress.

"He envisaged to notice an excited reaction,

though doing such act, he showed his interest."

"Hey," he said waving at her, exhaling long breath with thriving eyes seeking her smile, decent face airing devotion.

She saw Mark bending his back a little. She kept a smile over her face. Lightening eyes like every day. Some difference Mark felt as he semi circulated in front noticing reactions of her body. She detached headphone from her ears and said :

"Aah... I don't like you chasing me every day," with a smile, stepping forward.

"But... But it's nothing like that," he stammered sustaining his muddled heart.

She stepped ahead and turned partial to face Mark and stopped him from saying anything by raising her hand.

"I understand, ok... I am going in the girls coach," she said with continued cherished face, pointing her finger forward in the direction of the girls coach.

Mark went completely in astray, standing over his place.

He's broken from beneath, like floor below feet he's unable to trace.

Gazing her left space, not able to see those away going feet.

As his eyes were filled with water, blocked flowing out through the corner of its street.

His presence wanted to take him away from this aura. His fingers raised above wiping his wet eyes, hiding those from present spread flora.

Mark hasn't expected this ever.

Something stood him so bad that he felt it never.

Questioning himself for the trust he did.

Why he ever tried something where no one cares leaving him in mid.

The whole day went worst for him.

Blaming himself of living a life that's not the way he film.

Struggling with thoughts, the day passed and night came.

He's unaware of an umpire, to give a result of this love game.

He kept himself for all blame.
As he doesn't have the capability to raise any question over her name.

Mark reached home with immense distress. Sat on the carpet, placing his back on the side of the bed kept next to the room. Crushed eyes wanting to get closed. He was noticing every notification light raised over his phone.

Peering constantly at his phone for a while.
He developed power, picked it up, and started typing in this mental style.

"Hey Tamanna, I wanted to ask you something. Can I?" asked Mark, texting from his phone.

There was no reply received for an hour. It wasn't even illustrating that she had read the message either. Like usual behaviour of her, observed many times. With stubbed and defeated face, he started getting back to his evening schedules. Mark didn't allow Mrs. Shivach to cook that day and took the lead. Mrs. Shivach till now was aware of his discomfort through his face and his actions. his request to cook made Mrs. Shivach's impression to build stronger towards his grief.

A couple of hours later, Mark was ready with his dishes. Aligning them to serve Mrs. Shivach, picking those as he kept his foot towards Mrs. Shivach's room when A notification bell sound and light over his phone lying nearby took his attention.

"Reply from Tamanna," said Mark, as he picked his phone. And he took a relief breath putting the dish plate on the table. It felt like some angel again came and kissed his cheeks.

"See, I don't want to be rude to you. Try to understand, I really don't want to interact with you. Hope you understand," was the text reply from Tamanna.

Mark stayed stunned for a minute. Thousands of thoughts all together started attacking him. Realising what she texted and what she pretended, actions became undigestible on the first glance. He was unable to walk as his feet got numb.

Nothing he's able to notice, nothing he's able to respond.
When his own colours are asking today to break the bond.

"Mark, I am hungry. Waiting for your recipe?" shouted Mrs. Shivach.

"I know Maa, I have to serve you first. But give me some minutes to check my emotions and to settle my panic. This is not for anyone but to my heart," crooned Mark inside.

"Coming Maa," said Mark, wiping those unwanted tears covering his face that were trying to drop on the ground.

Mark began to breathe heavily and kept his unstable fingers over his phone screen and wrote :

"Thanks you for conveying it all. You really don't know how much you helped me with it. As the uncertain way we interacted and slowly, steadily it became certain. That silence of your face and peace in your eyes, ever asked me to praise you. I was just trying to follow what my God guided. His words in my ears said you deserve immense love and smile and asked me to build it for you. It is perfectly fine if your emotions don't want to float towards me. Thanks for making it clear and away from what I should be. I remember every word you said and I felt close to each of it. There were no questions if you hadn't cared about those a bit. So what I tried to make it, I want to thank you for everything. Please maintain that ever, without allowing anyone to make it vary.

At last, I request you to not make fun of any of my words that I said to you. As all I said only what my heart wanted to say. Please don't convey to others those sacred peace of my life that I shared with you. I commit, that I will try to forget such a nice person like you.

Be happy

God bless you

Those last words I said to you.
The pressure they took to get delivered I can't tell you.
It might be very easy for you to walk ahead.
Which you could have taken to beautify life of both instead.
You felt wrong, but I walked with a desire of giving.
And you kept checking angels in your life, are they working?
Peaceful desire with pleasure that everyone admires, I tried to produce.
And you broke the silence and meant those smiles to reduce.
If that you felt right, then I also adore.
But it's really hard to forget, the way you shut the door.

True Angel
(Invades)

Those storms became difficult to handle.
One after the other he tried to light the candle.
Tried hard to maintain that gleam of smile.
He felt and realised, but his efforts aren't enough to make it fine.
Million of emotions, lakh of expression that couldn't be expressed.
Everything wrecked him from keeping his emotions to not get undressed.
Hilarious exertions started getting unwind.
The farthest his eyes could go, kept him from noticing anyone behind.

Mark wasn't aware as to how the very next day passed away. It was Sunday and he stayed away from everyone's eyes at home. Today is Monday and Mark did not seem to be in his unusual behavior that he carried. Answering every question asked very exclusively. But his unique smile and prosperous giggling is kept in some unexplored corner of his heart. Work floating like the way Mark's ever took the lead.

Things were sharply disclosed.
Whether they are a build up plan or something to cure.

Mark was delivering his speech without any break, any Halt.

But his eyes spoke louder, still asking him about his fault.

Suddenly there was water inside his eyes curvature.

Over the meeting, delivering his planned yearly research to every creature.

His speech stayed away to get fall.
Fingers willing his eyes stopping tears to cross its wall.

Though Mark was reliable with those last words of Tamanna. But somewhere those decent emotions got burned like hell. Winding up the seminar hosted by him, he carried his bag and snatched his blazer that was kept above a chair. Moved towards the basement and opened his car door to get in. The minute he kept key in ignition, his favourite music started which also was his dialler tone. Hitting the cltch with his left leg, he geared his car and hauled it generating brutal rush. Ceasing stereo to maintain silence that he wanted to feel.

Mark drove ruthlessly without any worries of any human, any being.

He started something in need of one thing.
He tried to create himself, not asking God to bring something.

"I followed the way you shown and the words you conveyed," said Mark with little aggression on his face.

"Then why I have to face all this?" asked Mark to God.

He passed loaded roads of traffic swiftly. Crossing one after the other vehicle sharply. Handling unknown pain, he passed those streets of silence. Mark wasn't aware of this change. How today instead of going home, he took some other lane being heedless of where the lane would lend.

Negligence of any thing isn't there in acts. Grief of not having even in bits, those emotions he wanted to make perfect.

Sudden a small child of around six in age came in front of his car, making it hard for him to save the child. Being in his accelerated speed, with ignorant feet and mind lost in those past deeds, his eyes broadened leaving him with a stunned face. Pressing break with his whole power, how hard it takes. Car concluded it's speed coming to halt, but no heed of saviour, spirits shouting in Mark's ear if he made any fault.

"Noooooo," shouted Mark, opening his door to move out. He rushed to check the safety of the child. Blaming himself, as to how he could be so blind. After a minute, child commenced crying with fear. With a girl curling around him on the road, she settled him over her knees. Her bent head scared of saviour, as she pulled the hand from the child's sleeves. Such hazardous situation meant her hit hard over person riding the car. She got crazy as to what happened. Sensed through her sweating scars and heavy breath.

With closed eyes, she was upholding child hard in her arms. Mark looking towards both, shuffling breathing heavily like he's praying God for their saviour against his all good norms. Mark's reaction implying that he was becoming conscious from unconscious one. Bending over his feet, he prayed for help, not wanting to run.

"What the hell you did here! Is it the way anyone drives?" the girl shouted still scared while holding onto the child, looking down the road.

"I was," stammered Mark.

"What? What haan? What you would have done just?" said Girl with high pitch voice, facing slowly up towards him.

"Oh Mark," said Sayoni with her dull face bending down.

"Huh... it's you Sayoni," said Mark with the same scare and his pressurising tone.

"What you would have done today," said Sayoni with her shattered emotions on her face.

"I can't express, what guilt I am into now," he replied in grief.

"This isn't dangerous for other's, it's for you as well. The way you drove," she screamed, holding the child in her arms.

"I am speechless, I should be punished," he countered in his dull defeated voice.

"It's not a matter of punishment. See once at yourself, you are already punishing yourself," she said leaving child's hand and giving him the way to go across the road with other playing fellow.

"You are with these kids?" asked Mark peering towards crowded children.

“Yes, you found it right. I brought my NGO people here so that we can make these orphan kids to celebrate a day”.

“You come often here?” he asked afresh.

“It’s not a matter of concern Mark. You are taking me away from what just happened,” she said.

“No... No dear, can’t you see I am already ashamed,” he replied.

“Yes, I come here twice or thrice a week. It’s the biggest pleasure I can give to my life,” she replied with grace.

“Not your pleasure. Pleasure of those who get the chance to accompany you. You are ever admirable,” he said.

“The way you think about everyone. It’s far from a common person realisation,” he added.

“And the way you crave for everyone’s happiness and in end leading yourself in grief isn’t good I feel?” she asked stepping close, pulling his muffler lying behind his neck.

“Come, let’s go there,” she took him towards the guest house built nearby.

“So you love to come over to this orphanage. Woah. I feel today that you are actually living, what I am just feeling from many months,” he said.

“Not specifically for this one only. I visit all across the state,” she said.

“Time with them goes the best I can imagine,” she said spying into Mark’s eyes while walking.

“I understand,” he said nodding his head.

“Ok, you relax here. I’ll finish up there and come,” she said.

“Well I wonder, you don’t have your office today?” she asked.

“I am coming from there only.”

“What about your work today,” he asked.

“Am on leave dear!,” she said smiling and went straight towards those children.

Such decent smile and devotion she maintain.
Ever scares of doing anything, which could hamper her beam,
that I want to retain.
If somehow any tear came into her eyes due to me.
Heart broke in a way, becoming hard for me to sustain.
Mark's trying twigging all lying obstacles across.
Yes, his eyes scrolled from one site to the other off-course.
Silent heart inert linger's away of all emotions.
Intensifying his eyes, those which were full of devotion.
He knows, that colour need to be changed.
He knows, he have to stop feeling himself blamed.
He strive to listen this belle of peace around.
But found himself heavily bound.
Mind struggled to open up closed door.
The much it does, heart throws it back over the floor.

"Aah. you haven't finished your glass of juice yet," said Sayoni getting back inside the room.

"Aww… what happened Mark, why are you so dull?" she added keeping her hand tenderly on him.

"Nothing… Nothing…! I was just," he said being startled.

"Why you're so worried, see your face once," she said wiping the sweat built on his face.

"See, is this why people love Mark?" she said staring at the mirror behind them.

"Nothing remains constant," he said, turning his face towards the left with a sharp twitch.

"Yes… But things get resolved with time," she intervened.

"I know," he replied.

"Then why has your ankle stopped tickling?" she said, filling her glass of juice.

"I am?" he asked.

"Now don't think too much," she said, raising Mark's juice glass towards his mouth.

"Am not willing to drink," he said, agitated, removing the glass from near his face.

"What happened Mark, what?" she asked matching her face with him, down over her knees.

"Nothing," he moved his head away.

"Mark say?" she shouted.

"We broke up," he said.

"Who? You and Tamanna?" she asked.

"How come you know this?" he asked.

"I wasn't aware," she said.

"I had read your heart Mark and you are not the person who gets low on every topic," she said, taking Mark's face in between her arms spying into his eyes.

He said her plainly.
Disclosing every factor his soul is playing making him lonely.
He split up everything with the flavour they impacted.
Covering every accruing intentions before, that he subjected.
That break of one twig after the other,
Didn't leave anything to breathe further.
He talked about his affection, informing how they developed.
Asking is it a crime he did, for which his every word she judged.
Falling on his one sensation and rising on other.
How hard he controlled his feelings to not get spilled further.

Mark told about all the rise and fall he went through last week. His continuing mental wreck and those confused tweak. His presently shattered eyes were unable to contact her. His bickering hand tried to put back the empty glass on nearby stool. His other palm was pressing harder Sayoni's hand.

"Wait, I'll put it," she said, carrying the glass from his hand.

"Don't go away now," he said, pulling her towards him.

"Oh Mark what? Am just coming," she said.

"No leave everything right here. Just be beside me," he pleaded.

Such thriving desires of belongingness. Changing colours over Mark's eyes. Desires provoking to sit close long being clubbed in her arms. Sayoni gave the best she could for him to get away of all hassles. The aspiring eagerness of Mark, giving every significance not required any elucidation. Her prolonged benevolence melted him to forge twig of what he actually contains.

"I have the best gift with me and was worried for," his lips whispered above her ears.

"I understand it very well Mark, what you're undergoing," she said trying to make space between them.

"Yes, I know and please don't make it go down," he said breathing heavily on the corner of her neck.

Those fingers and then those hands.
Everything is impairing to flow in present flowing trends.
Shades of past are getting covered with shine of today.
They touched every base, in need to finding some other way.
These delight are so unique, over which they want to breathe.
Slow starts and little body moves, they meant it in a way wanting to squeeze.
Hesitation and those fumbling voice came to an end.
When both wills are aligned, which they begun to understand.

"Mark, you are one of those few that I can really count on with my closed eyes," her lips pressed together, feeling the movement of his fingers on her neck.

"I ever feel good from your gestures," he said, lying her down on the bed.

"Check the door once at least," she said.

"It's locked," he said, as he raised his hand and touched the knob.

"It's me who had the failure of not understanding the beauty around me," he said as he took her again in his arms to let her lie down comfortably on her back.

"I haven't realised this before."

They were both getting engrossed in each other.
Like one is helping to heal pain of the other.
Sometimes words are not much to express desire.
That can only be felt by warmth of its fire.
What one said you know they aspire.
But it gets colour, when you praise the love you got, with admire.

"Easy Mark, don't hurt yourself," she said, beholding his impatience.

"I wouldn't," he said holding herin his arms.

"You have to deal with everything strongly," she said with her shut eyes astray in Mark's senselessness.

"You just stay together and I will deal everything well," said Mark.

"You know I am two packs down already," she smiled while saying.

"What you had," he asked smelling her hair.

"We started today with our inauguration party in the first half. So," she said moving him down to look at his face from upside.

"And you know, I only take Vodka. Nothing else," she said settling down her hair and moving her fingers over Mark's forehead.

"How are you feeling now?" she asked.

"I can't say anything," he said shutting her mouth placing his palm over her lips and pulling her closer.

"Mark, this is not good. You never reveal your internal storm," she said, kissing his cheek.

Whether its the bedsheet or bedside aligned lamps.
Nothing in will of maintaining posture, asking to make out more attempts.
Getting dipped in sizzling touch of one another.

Desires want to be more indecent while opening their feathers.
One wants to fill, what other one needs.
Making it their only present deed.
They arched their limits, by floating above sensation of each other.
And did what all their surroundings asked.
They expressed whole hearted feeling for one another.
Removing every unwanted sarcasm in their words that people mask.

Starting Again

Story crowned its cycle, still unaware of disclosing concern. Where Maunik with Mark knowing it's every bit, the way it ran. Maunik was not happy to hear how it began and the way it ended. Queries were still unanswered, like Mark left him unexplored of sheer film. Those exigency of resolving puzzle, could be sensed in Maunik's eyes when he was aware that this resolution can only pay the price. Mark was impressed after revealing all he just told. Maunik's face seemed to still know more.

Something they entitled, some others they govern.

Mystery needs to get solved, making things away of staying stubborn.

He sat to listen whole story, touching every depth.

Sometime he took and sometime need to hold his breath.

Story told dipped in absolute twist, but it wasn't the way he wished. Provoking confusion to stay alive in mind, doesn't matter how hard he kicked.

"What about Tamanna?" queried Maunik.

"Wait, I haven't ended yet," said Mark, he said rising from his place to have water.

"Could you tell me what happened ahead. We don't have time champ," said Maunik getting agitated with Mark's silence.

"What you just said? Why we don't have time?" asked Mark carrying a glass of water he filled for Maunik.

"No...Nothing! It went out unknowingly," he replied, settling his face in relief.

"Am about to disclose about that day between me and Tamanna. Don't panic! Relax, today I am in mood to convey everything," said Mark with cheer, handing the glass to him.

"You went back to Australia till the time. Bond between me and Sayoni forged sturdy in term of our cognizance. Sayoni asked me to loom Tamanna and convey my true heart spirit. Sayoni kept her hand of tender to help me out in such sorrowful times. Her attempts were ever performed to make me get out of myasylum," said Mark, leaving his smile wandering about Sayoni.

"She's a kind, devoted, good, human being who cares and spreads smiles in our aura," said Maunik, as Mark took a second break.

"Yes, like an angel in my life," said Mark.

"Yet again your words shun in silence, speak up what happened ahead?" anxious Maunik.

"It's last week, when you were about to come back to India (Delhi) and as you know, we both already had a plan to visit our home at Landowne. After you landed 'Indira Gandhi Airport'," said Mark swiftly.

"Yes what then, that we planned for yesterday?" Maunik said being desperate.

"I was sitting alone in market place across home already baffled with repeated thoughts of Tamanna and her departure from my life. Thought I would go out to make my eyes see something new. It was Sunday evening and I again got lost, after settling over bench somewhere in market area," said Mark with his stubby voice.

"Come on Mark, what happened then?" asked Maunik.

"Someone came and sat beside me. Time my eyes were astray spying queue meant by ant over lower part of wall stood next to me," told Mark with modest hoist in speech.

"Now what's the story of that person?" senile Maunik.

"She was Tamanna," replied Mark.

"Aah... is it?" Maunik was shocked.

"I was stunned, my body was set cold. I have nothing to say apart of staring at her with my pale face and opened eyes".

She took space next to Mark over bench. Facing him, whose eyes were struggling to hide from her to avoid interacting with her. Flickering fingers gone frozen with his feet not moving anymore. Concatenating still face and shut lips which contain an ocean of words to deliver. Not able to whisper, in spook of getting broken again. Collecting his left strength and stood up to step ahead.

"You left your things here," said Tamanna.

"Your wallet, your clothes," she said, bringing up the stuff in her hand as he turned and noticed.

"These are materialistic things which don't cost much, what you have already taken away."

"Sometimes things are contrary to what you feel," she replied staring at Mark going awayfeet.

"I feel, two close peopple should be compelled to unfold their beliefs for other one to understand," he said with static expressions.

"But what if the concern isn't clear to the person itself and they need time to think over it," she retaliated with her mushy hoisting voice.

"Everything... everything should be apprised... there is nothing which God will make you to understand. Human entail words to savvy the scene behind," he said turning towards her, bending on his knees while holding her hands.

"Don't develop such grief on your face. I can't see it," he said pointing towards her eyes.

"I was in alliance before with someone," she said.

"Yea say... am listening," he said settling down back.

"I haven't come out of its failure from a long time," she said.

"Yes... speak up all you want...I am listening," he said.

"Either after yearning your desires, I walked ahead with you. I know I supported you in your feeling. You are such a person who doesn't want to reap the fruit of your kindness. I know I sprouted things in you, to dig its dawn point. I lingered being confused for the whole journey that I had with you. At last, I know I did something with you that somehow I have already gone through," she said with her pleading eyes asking for sorry and body grilling relief.

"Is it good to anyone of us?" he posed, holding her fingers more tightly.

"I build it very purely, Tamanna. With everyone's awareness, as I already decided to walk my steps with you," he said.

"I can't say much Mark. I already find myself guilty," she said.

"Oh... please don't. Neither that time I can see your tears nor at present," he said keeping his arm behind her neck pulling it closer, staring into her eyes.

"Either I can't say much, as my storm had already flushed my emotions and barren my land once," he said spying forward.

"Let me find a way to heal everything," she said bending her neck, facing Mark with sober face.

"Yes, you can," he said inhaling comfort inside peering forward still.

What has been asked? What is in need of getting build?

Desires that had been crushed before, are in need of getting healed.

Those tracks which were spoiled before,

Heavenly breeze stood, setting them in cure.

Intentions evoking from aspiration to do,

All is for building love, which was asked before to flue.

"You hadn't realised, the way heart connected its nods with you," he said.

"I know... First your heart captivates words and then you deliver," she replied with a smile on her face.

"The care amplified from you to your family either," he said.

"I either erupted wavering, assuming my flaw in everything due to your behaviour. I blamed myself," he said.

"But it wasn't you, anyway," she said admitting.

"Things broke up the same way, for no reason," he said spinning face towards her.

"At least clarity of thoughts should be maintained," he said taking a step closer.

"Huh... what should I do," she murmered, bending her face towards the floor, tightening her hair back with her fingers, exhaling breath.

"Can't we build it again?" she asked, raising her bowed head and eyes stretching to raise a question towards Mark. Mark had gone shut after he disperses this last liner said by Tamanna.

"Speak... speak up Mark, now for what are you retaining stillness. Aren't you getting the curiosity of the person to hear from you," she spoke slugging.

***

"After that we got a hold of each other's hand and we walked for next couple of hours in the same park nearby," Mark said to Maunik and quaffed the partial filled water glass kept aside on thetable.

"How did you both plan to come down along?" asked Maunik.

"It's not just my hometown, but a place where her mother does stay," replied Mark.

"What? You know it," said a stunned Maunik.

"Yeah I know, our neighbour aunt, Mrs. Sinha, is her mother," he giggled.

"And I was feeling," Maunik intuited with impeding relaxation over his face.

"Hahahaha... I encountered in words much before," Mark laughed pointing a finger towards him.

"Ok... Ok! Would you not tell me, how you both planned to come together?"

"Things got conveyed and our journey was decided that night itself. That walk-in revealing secrets, forging beautiful plans," said Mark lost in wanders with his consistent smile capturing cheeks.

"Can you pass me a glass of warm water?," asked Mark.

"What happened? Hope you're fine or there's some difference in the body you felt. Tell me, buddy, I'll call upon a doctor," Maunik hassled noticing Mark moves.

"Nothing getting wrong dear. There's some force stopping me from conveying things. Like someone's hand over my neck," said Mark, coughing myriad times.

"Hey... hey... easy control. Wait, I am carrying warm water," Maunik ran towards electric cattle, pouring into the glass.

"Don't find yourself spared, tell me the complete story," said Maunik handling water.

"Everything was perfect, but mind got spoiled the very next morning when Divyansh met me," said Mark.

"Now how come he came into all this. It's been you and her only."

"Next morning, I sustained cosy mood that I ever prefer, relaxing inside our small cafeteria on our floor," Mark spoke with a dried going face.

"Now what he did?"

"He didn't do anything, but he spoke rubbish," Mark said while turning his face to another side.

"What?"

"I was into the last chapter of the story I was going through and he entered. Again with his books and predictions," said Mark.

"And what he predicted?," Maunik's broad open eyes staring at Mark.

"Nothing, you don't need to know it. I'll continue my story," said Mark getting up from his place.

"Is he aware of your and Tamanna?"

"Yes, he is... as such he's the first one whom I spelt it unwillingly"

"So, what he said?" Maunik asked in patience to hear.

"Why are you so curious to know?"

"Mark, you know well... he's into foremost proved predictors."

"So what .... see this time they proved to be wrong," said Mark.

"Wrong... what's wrong Mark?" he asked rigorously.

"He said that I shouldn't travel on the date, that's yesterday," Mark replied.

"And what he said would happen if you travelled?" he asked sliding his stool closer to Mark.

"Aah! he envisaged it could upshot for life loss of me or any close one. Though I condemn myself, as I stood conscious espying inadequacy around. But thing sets reliable as I saw and heard your words," said Mark spying outside greenery from wall glass pane, sipping from his mug.

Succeeding seconds of silence :

"Now where are you stuck, for what you maintained such asylum," Mark turned facing him.

Maunik being shut and shattered present.
Like something he listened and his senses gone vacan't.
He had already been waiting to hear the same.
But away of cognizance, how sour would be its pain.
Like some grief puffed by others.
Came in light, after someone opened his feather.

Maunik aggressively got up from his place and stood next to Mark. With burning eyes and in pain. Those non-resistive words, unblinking eyelids remained undimmed while staring at Mark.

"What happened? So abrupt," asked Mark with his eyes pointing up peering him, retaining a smile on his face.

"Why didn't you listen to his words? Why?" Maunik shouted, pulling his shirt collar towards him in extreme vexation on his face.

"What happened, Maunik? For what you're being so aggressive?"

"Aggressive? Do you have any realisation of what you did?" Maunik shouted plunging him.

"Easy man, I could get hurt," he said, hitting the wall.

"You might get hurt, but what about the life which is no more," said Maunik with tears in his eyes, over unbalance feet.

Mark gone strained, seems his disable going body had lost hope. Putting himself up supporting wall. He walked towards Maunik with sliding feet over the carpet. He spoke while keeping his hand over Maunik's shoulder back.

"What happened to whom? Tell me Maunik, what are you hiding?" asked with heavily going breathe.

"Not hiding anything, wasn't able to convey this cruelty of nature," he replied.

"Am exhausted now. Tell me before I'll lose my veins," Mark replied.

"I said lie to everyone, that accident did not go safe," he said pressing his wrist over the wall, facing opposite of Mark.

"Then what happened? please convey for god sake," Mark said pressing for an answer.

"Tamanna is no more Mark. She left us last night," Maunik screeched in vain, throwing his hands aside.

"What you said... haan? What? What is it? I didn't listen well, I feel,"

"I said what you listened, Mark. She is no more with us. Tamanna left this world due to yesterday's accident," he said, turning to face Mark, staring into his eyes while crying.

That vain had already touched the base of earth.
This light came to take away soul, as it was of death, not birth.
Magnets who had just found their perfect pole.
Nature developed in between a never filled hole.
Those eyes which wanted to spread out water over the floor.
Are still denying to accept, looking for the person to step in through the opened door.

Broken heart and those yellow going skin.
Shivering from pain, struggling with whom presently they live in.

Mark found his soul to be invisible in this aura. Trusting Maunik's word his sensation getting broken with all of his upcoming thoughts.

"How could it be possible, no I don't believe it. She can't go away," said Mark balancing his broken emotion twigs inside.

"For what you are producing such negation, can't you find truth in my speech of pain," said Maunik.

"We met after a year of separation. And leaving me like this ... it can't happen," said Mark lost with stretched eyes and opened mouth being abducted facing corner of the wall.

"Get into consciousness Mark. I need your help to handle all this," he insisted.

"Things been build so beautiful to 'start again' and ... how can this," said Mark holding steel railing aside.

"But we need to walk ahead in the present. I got saved when that natural disaster crashed our car last night. I came out, through window removing attached broken glass pieces. Everything became stony in front of my eyes. The time I realised to see no human presence to help us. I went straight to pull you both out from the front seat. I saw Tamanna's hand waving out of the window. I tried to pull her if I could. But when there's no space I found. I have to unlock the door somehow. I shouted and thumbed pressure over her lungs badly to feel her alive and breathing. My all attempts were going expressionless one after the other. I stood up with that grief and tears. Got extremely scared and ran to check you on the other side of it. You came out till that time and with a little consciousness but blood was running all over your body. I took you completely out of it. Called police and they took you and Tamanna to the nearest hospital where the doctor claimed Tamanna's death on the spot," said Maunik with his watery eyes trying to get over this tragic situation.

"Who took her? I want to meet her," Mark shouted and woke up with a sprint, running towards the house's exit.

"Wait... Wait Mark .... wait, where are you going?" Maunik clubbed him tight while he's exerting to run away.

Those pain of separation, torn him from beneath.
His terrible going hands and feet, want to run until they meet.
Those last words of her to him.
This unaware departure spread darkness in the aura, letting lights to go dim.
His cries and that crucifying fire inside.
Immense heat onto his emotions kept burning wide.

"You need to handle yourself, else nothing will be left," he said, continuing holding Mark's body from his base.

"Her father took her to Delhi," added Maunik.

"Why... why? You haven't told me this before? Why Maunik? Why?" Mark screeched.

"Who will give relief to my soul, how could I?" Mark tremendous creep in pain.

"You have to settle down," said Maunik dragging him towards one corner.

Maunik tried to settle his soul in peace. Constantly trying to make him drink water. Those creeps aren't getting stopped even for a second. Maunik stretched his leg forward, making him lie down with his back touching wall and base over the floor. Struggling to normalise his breath and then he asked :

"What was so important for you, that meant you to not take care even once about Divyansh prediction?" Maunik with anger over his sleeves.

"I was not."

"What you not ... Mark speak clearly."

"That morning I received a call from Sayoni's colleague 'Priyanka'". She revealed the tedious condition Sayoni was going through from last many days. Sayoni hadn't shared anything with me, even though I had word with her some days before. My mind which even can't notice her of being in pain and she was already bearing it. So, I went straight away to her home," said Mark.

"How is it related to what Divyansh said?" Maunik said in agitation.

"He said about night and the time is around 9. Though I had planned to leave early that day, to reach before sunset."

"And we exactly met with our accident at 9 yesterday," said Maunik.

"Aah so it happened yesterday 9," Mark thoughts stuck and opened mouth, wiping tears.

"Yes, and everything went deadpan everywhere. I don't know how I came out of it.," replied Maunik.

"I can't even imagine what I lost," said Mark again trying to get up, where Maunik just threw him.

"If someone is so important for you, then how come you didn't consider Divyansh words. I became thought proof, mesmerising such thing which could be cured," said Maunik dipped in vain.

"What was so important Mark, tell me?" asked Maunik in vexation.

"It was important Maunik. It's about Sayoni, she didn't say that she required my help."

"Was it more important than Tamanna's life to you?" asked Maunik staring Mark.

"Please... please get this off... I am not aware of anything," said Mark wrapping his face behind palm in extreme strain.

"Where you are trying to mould this now. It's something unaware that happened," replied Mark with anger on his face, spread with tears.

"Am not trying to mould it anywhere, just scrutinising your desires towards,"

"Desire towards? What you mean," Mark raising his pitch.

"Leave .... you know it," said Maunik getting into aside room.

"What are you saying? If you are talking about Sayoni. Then listen, yes she is prior to me and will stay ever," said Mark backing to peer his face.

Maunik shut the door ruthlessly over his face, when Mark was just half a foot away of him.

"Hey open it up, what you're trying to do," shouted Mark knocking door with his tight wist.

"Huh, how it happened? I haven't closed it," said Maunik running towards the door.

"Open up the knock. Damn," shouted Mark stubbing the door heavily.

"Mark understand, there is no knock. It's already open," said Maunik trying to open, hitting it with shoulder push.

"Then what's wrong with it," said Mark kicking the door.

Door tried to get opened from both the side and suddenly after attempts a push of Mark build the thrust, bearing which Maunik shagged far apart over the floor. They faced each other with a puffed face. And eyes trying to find what's away from their notice, that they can't notice.

"I am unearthing this uncertainty over the house since you have been lying on bed unconscious," said Maunik.

"You are uncovering, due to hiding those realities from me, which you shouldn't," said Mark turning to move towards the drawing room.

"Don't pull me. You can't vaporise it so quickly what you did," said Mark.

"I am not blocking your step. What happen Mark?," Maunik coming in Mark's upfront.

"I felt someone pulling me behind, holding my waist," said Mark with his discerning eyes.

"I didn't do anything," replied Maunik.

"Good," said Mark and walked away.

"You love Sayoni," voice stood inside the whole house, like coming out through its every wall.

Mark distorted faced like his roots got hammered and till the time he makes himself to realise. The voice repeated once more 'You love Sayoni?' His feet can't wait at his place and he ran back towards Maunik looking aside at every space.

"What? What happened Mark?" panicked Maunik.

"What happened? Can't you hear her voice?" asked Mark holding his shoulders with his palm with cherish smile over face.

"Whose voice you are talking about. I heard nothing?" said Maunik, settling his anxious reaction down by sliding his gentle palm over his head.

"Don't say that," said Mark, took a step back.

"You might hear something from outside. There's no voice inside Mark," replied Maunik in a slight shiver.

"Well, I haven't still told you anything about any such voice coming from inside," said Mark with his eyes trying to find the thing he wants from Maunik's face.

"What's the reason? Why are you shivering?" asked Mark.

"Nothing… Nothing, Why would I?"

"So, you haven't heard that voice? It came twice," asked Mark with those intrinsic eyes.

"I told you already, it's something someone said, from outside of the house. That you are concerned of," replied Maunik.

"Maunik, this house has no human living around it within 500 yards. Who can shout the way and that too calling Sayoni's name," said Mark.

"Am not getting what you are trying to say," replied Maunik, turning his back towards Mark, getting numb.

"You can't," Mark just said before pressured air came from his back and flown him to hit Maunik. And they both fell on the floor.

"What you did? Oh my back," said Maunik trying to wake up off the floor.

"Is Tamanna alive Maunik?" asked Mark.

"First I heard her and now that fragrance to my notice, the way she smells," said Mark trying to realise breeze entering house through opened windows.

"Tell me Maunik? Tell me, where is Tamanna?" asked Mark pulling Maunik back down over the floor to answer him first.

"Shall I tell you?" a big female voice of someone standing next to both asked.

It was a giant smoke sculpture which had builded, covering the whole space from the floor till the roof. In those shades of smoke, somewhere they both can visualise Tamanna wearing the same scarf she wore yesterday. Those dull eyes with water floating through them were containing many questions that need their answer. That shaggy hair getting flown wider into the surrounding seemed to show the anger with the desperation of achieving something.

"Look at her, oh Tamanna," said Mark looking above at her face. With those eyes setting in relief of not losing her. Slightly building cheer on his face delivering his heart in peace after encountering a look.

"This is what I wanted to know from you. You told me wrong info, Maunik. See, Tamanna is alive. See, she's in front of us," he said heading Maunik's face up.

Scared and silent Maunik turned his face to gaze at Tamanna and said :

"Tamanna died last night Mark, this is a spirit following me since morning," said Maunik in his extreme heart sinking and fearsome voice with his broadened eyes visualising such macabre look of Tamanna.

"What… It's Tamanna only," Mark shouted loudly.

"Yes, I am Tamanna, for whom you didn't care last night," a voice came from this giant fume and it started getting closer to both lying over the floor.

"Move… Move? Move Mark … what the hell you're staring at.

Tamanna isn't alive, she's dead Mark, she's no more with us," Maunik said being highly afraid.

That trundling body of Maunik over floor, repeatedly getting failed to carry Mark along. The way this smoke was coming closer to them had already shaken Maunik's heart beat.

"Mark move… move," he steers and somehow left control.

Whole house started howling with the sound of Tamanna. One wall delivered beautiful memories of the time Mark and Tamanna spent along. With other wall concluding Tamanna's grief of not getting the space in Mark's heart that she deserved. From other two walls, the sound of her laughter and wailing, shielded the whole internal aura. Chime of plunging flask from height, dropping photo frame the wall and those calibrated destruction of surrounding artefacts, with thrash of wind.

"This was the factor, you are wanting to know. So listen these haven't took lead just, am in gait of these since morning', Maunik shouted, the minute he intuit smoky spirit a feet distance off Mark.

"Yes Mark, its Tamanna's spirit," Maunik gigs louder, letting Mark off of noticing the face behind this white fumes.

Mark tries to make Maunik's hard words to stay unheard. Until he'll discover this face of spirit that bending towards him. Beats are still flowing in the same order, Mark's heart couldn't balance out his grief with those harsh border.

It *took seconds to come upfront of his face.*
That was the time Mark can hundred time recalculate.
Feel of fear isn't there on its place.
Like it had become his last desire to notice her face.
Encountering *same fragrance, as he discerns from her.*
When that spirt came closer, putting hands over his shoulder.

At present, both stood up in front of each other. One can see other one clearly. That face was still not clear. But he mesmerised that her dress was the same that she had worn. Face of the spirit is still shaded with white fumes, black hair. Mark eyes were widely open making every attempt to stare.

"You hadn't answered my question yet Mark. 'Do you love Sayoni?'," daunting face coming out with eerie effects. Black circled eyes and effects spread dread. Smiling and in front of Mark's face by an inch.

"Tamanna," said Mark, exhaling breath.

"Who will answer my question," a heavy shout evoked from the spirit and Mark dragged his body behind.

"She's Tamanna, Maunik …….. Yes, she's Tamanna……," said Mark facing once towards Maunik and then towards the spirit.

"Run Mark… come here," Maunik roared towards Mark.

The disruption erupted in an unexpected way.
The way they started finding place to stay.
Those build dreams came back showing its worst picture.
Letting eyes go scared to visualise, discerning what else came in its mixture.

"Come Mark … come here," Maunik ran to get hold of Mark's hand dragging him towards the out-yard room.

"Lock it up," said Mark as they got into the room.

"You know about all this from before?" asked Mark.

"I was dealing with these qualm since morning. The minute Mrs. Charles left the house and went to go to Delhi," said Maunik making Mark to settle down on the chair.

"Then I deceived her glimpse when I was washing the towel to clean your face. While washing it in the wash basin, the minute I carried it, the mirror turned to show its colour to be red. I'd thrown it over the floor to perceive the brief look over that voice. That came out as Tamanna in the same outfit she wore '**Yesterday 9**'. She came in front of me and roared badly with tears floating on her face. She went away in seconds, left me frighted. Wasn't easy for me to assimilate. I sat at my place, pointing out her actions since morning to correlate.," said Maunik, with goosebumps all over his sleeves.

"How could all this happen to her? What is bothering her? Does she reveal anything?" asked Mark.

"She hasn't said anything, nor she's answered my any question," replied Maunik getting closer towards door, placing his ear onto the door.

"See... she commenced again, fearsome sound and her terrible acts," said Maunik with his daunted face, harking those slight murmers that she already did many times before.

"What she wants?" asked Maunik crying, frustratedly pulling his hair with his hands.

"I don't know," said Mark.

"She asked you something? Tell me what's that," Maunik was crying and getting petrified.

"She asked anything... did she...," said Mark confused.

"Tell me ... Mark please settle this out," said Maunik in panic, suppressing ears with palms, afraid of noise.

"How can I? Let me see, which noise you are talking about," said Mark coming closer towards the door where Maunik stood.

"I can't hear anything," said Mark being hesitatingly afraid.

"But you can at least say, what she asked you?" asked Maunik getting rude.

"She asked me," said Mark and a deep silence on his face.

"I don't want you to sew your lips over my question. Please answer, so it can bring us any help," said Maunik.

Something isn't clear to his heart itself, but he has to disclose.
Questions raised in heart of others, which he's required to close.
Above everything, he's not able to settle himself.
Changes were not able to produce their clarity of arrival themselves.
Who is the culprit, why this disaster took place?
Do all his beliefs were false, that she conveyed through her face.

"So listen, she asked something that even I am asking my heart. She asked 'Do I love Sayoni?'" said Mark with his dried going lips.

"And what you answered?" asked Maunik.

"I didn't answer anything. But you already know what it is," said Mark facing up to Maunik face.

"What I know?" asked Maunik.

"You know that I don't have any word for my relation with Sayoni, but she is gigantically important for me," said Mark putting a hand over his shoulder.

"You haven't answered her question yet," said Maunik, holding his neck tightly between his hands.

"This is you who is asking me or Tamanna is persuading you to get its answer through me," asked Mark noticing uncanny behaviour of Maunik at present.

"Speak up Mark.... , bellow. She shouting in my ears," said Maunik.

"Where is she, why can't I notice?" Mark strongly yelled.

"Can't you just speak up," Maunik's eager to know had now adjuring him to confess the truth.

"Ok, I'll convey.... Yes, she has her position more than my love could be. So I preferred to check for her safety first before anything else Yesterday," said Mark eyes full of conviction.

The second Mark word took a halt. Maunik set in relief and a immediate strong storm found its accommodation inside their room. Spoiling every artefact one after the other and thereafter got collected over centre of the room. Maunik succeeded in opening the door he's trying too. Storm settling place got covered with evading belches smoke. Behind which Mark encountered the sketched arch or Tamanna standing. With her opened arms towards sky and face shaded through her hair. Heftily throughout air through her mouth in sky with anger. The minute Maunik saw her in such a position. He grabbed Mark's hand and plucked him out of the room towards courtyard.

They understood but his heart was still wanting to stay unaware.
He knows this is due to him, but he also knows he didn't do anything unfair.
He was still wanting to find that cheer on her face, he loves to stare.
But she's not alive and became a spirit now, that is away of anyone's care.
He hadn't felt that his love will end like that.
This is not the reason, the way they both met.

"Wait, I need to settle her down. She is crying," said Mark, getting his hand-drawn by Maunik.

"Get out of it Mark, now at-least. That's not more of your's Tamanna," said Maunik.

"What she is then?" asked Mark.

"That's just phantom, a shadow nothing else," replied Maunik stepping down through stairs with Mark.

They slept from its second step by un unknown thrust towing their foot. They went on bowling till they reach its base.

Ringing Phone

Everything decorated itself the way she wanted. By her black shadow and her footstep sound everywhere, meant this house haunted. Nothing is in its place. Her spirit hollers and crying wrapping everything around in her foil. Floating from one end to another and again crawling staring at these both mortal human lying beneath the stairs.

One after the other landline of Mark's home started ringing.
She hanged one and other meant itself to string.
Some message wanting to get delivered.
As something is trying hard to get revealed.

"Every phone is ringing Mark," yelled Maunik while they both are still struggling hard to get up after falling down through stairs.

"Yes, but she wasn't allowing to pick any," replied Mark in pain of his extreme backache.

"She had captured the whole house. She's hanging up phone repeatedly," said Maunik as he tried to stand on his feet.

"Whose bell is this?" asked Maunik.

"This is of my cell phone," replied Mark.

"Where is it?"

"It's lying above only. The room where we in before," replied Mark.

"Whose knowing every phone number of house," said Maunik.

"Yea... Is it Mom, at the calling end," said Mark while standing, putting his weight over the wooden railing.

"What Mrs. Shivach you mean?" asked Maunik.

"No, I am talking about Mrs. Charles. She only knows the number of every landlines at home," replied Mark stabilising himself breathing heavily stroking his chest.

"What happened?" asked Maunik.

"My chest stroked while falling and making me harder to breathe," answered Mark.

"Look up, II'll see".

"No, it isn't required. You focus on how to attend these incoming calls," said Mark.

"Her spirit had captured complete aura, her eyes staring us everywhere," replied Maunik with his eyes scrolling to notice this black shelter she had put on over.

"Have to do something early. I had noticed eagerness in her eyes," said Mark pressing his stomach.

"You have to talk with her, in between I'll pick up," said Maunik looking upstairs where he saw her spirit last.

"Yes, I also want to have word with her. Forgetting how hard it would be. I need to unwind the pain she's dealing with," replied Mark.

"Ok I'll be going backyard and will pick landline from there," said Maunik.

"Listen, I want to hear the call. Merge it with home speakers," said Mark.

"Ok, see its ringing, am leaving to pick it up. You call her now," said Maunik fearsome sipping out his swat developed over his face.

Maunik left with his scary feet. Gazing around every corner before keeping his next step. He gets trembled, the way she ever comes and asks his beats to run over the heart.

"Maunik, walk easy don't panic she won't hamper you," said Mark before air stream slapped Maunik face, forcing him to fall.

"Yea, she wouldn't do anything to me. I just saw an instance of it," said Maunik keeping his left palm over his cheek with his same scary scrolling eyebrows.

"Tamanna... Tamanna. Come and talk to me. You can't stay away and calibrate all this without any reason," Mark yelled louder gazing at every rooftop corner to its base.

"Who is far from you..... am close to you ever and will remain," slow steep sound whispered in Mark's ear and he turned in the hassle to see.

"Don't do that with me.... Stand next to me and talk," said Mark being agitated.

"And what about that you did with me," said Tamanna.

"What I did? Can you tell me, am despairing to know," asked Mark, turning back and he encountered Tamanna clearer. She was standing with the same conviction turning towards Mark.

"Huhhhhhh..... I can see that trust in your eyes," said Mark heading close to her one step.

"But you lost all that with my life. You didn't love me," she said haltering his neck with her hand and craned him up in the air.

"Tamanna... Tamanna. Leave .... Leave what are you doing?" said Mark as she took control over his body after slinging in air.

"You loved Sayoni, for whom you diminished you're heed for me. Letting me die last night," said Tamanna's hostile spirit.

"I wasn't aware of anything. As I don't believe in such things," said Mark with extreme tender getting hanged by his neck.

"Youuuuu.... Lier .....," said Tamanna's spirit while throwing him away to bump over the front wall badly. Mark slides over the wall and came down with his base highly bearing the pressure.

The time Mark is making himself to stand once again. That loud speaker spread the voice of Mrs. Charles crying talking over the phone with Maunik. Mark lost his least retainity to listen to those words said by her hastily.

"Why she's crying so much," Mark lost his power and fallen back after listening to those unstopped voice filled with the cry of his mother.

Maunik and Mrs. Charles over the phone :

"Yea... yeah... Aunty am listening please let me know what exactly happened," said Maunik pleasing Mrs. Chales.

"Mr. Charles .... Mr. Charles," she said controlling her repeated gasps.

"What happened to Mr. Charles? Please convey... he's fine nah?," asked Maunik furiously, Mark settled on his place with a stunned face noticing every word.

"Mr. Charles isn't responding... his body stopped functioning," she said with a larger haul and scream evoking beneath her voice.

"am getting helpless ..... He asked to meet Mark in her last voice," she said with gasps.

"We are coming to Aunty, don't worry about, please... ," he said and lost the connection. He shouted some more times Aunty .... Aunty ... and have to hang up the call.

Maunik ran straight down sneezing Mark's name before he encountered him lying over the floor.

"Come we have to leave," said Maunik picking Mark.

"I've listened to it all," said Mark sterling in pain.

"I've lost many things from my life from yesterday," said Mark threshed and defeated bending down over his knees.

"You can't go such Mrs. Charles need you, buck up," said Maunik putting him up again holding his arms.

Many things broke away very soon.
No one is able to hear those beautiful meant tune.
How could I stand and let it go the way it is.
Nothing happened even for a bit of the way, that I wish.
One after the other trunk, my tree lost its hands.
It's about that strong relation, tied to me like colourful bands.
That stray power of my feet, reels if I try to stand.
Have to stay alive and fight, before the power governing my life can understand.

Mark filled body with air, kicked its leg to jump forward. Maunik took those car keys lying next of the exit door. He ran towards parking to move his car out of the out-yard door. Maunik shouted asking Mark to join him in the car. Mark trying stepping faster but ultimately dragging his feet so far. Certain points over his leg started bleeding. Mark opened his electric door of the house, with the pain in the body he's carrying. His eyes turned to see the aura inside his house, he was leaving behind. Eyes couldn't capture her, as she was nowhere to be seen. He felt of her beautiful heart understanding his present condition, how hard it's been.

"I wish your soul to rest in peace," said Mark and look in front, over exit door.

He locked his house, carried his back over the shoulder and again started dragging himself. Maunik left the car, ran towards Mark getting known about his struggling pain. He took his bag and gave him his shoulder to lessen his strain. That face with lack of emotion and eyes lost finding place to sustain. Mark stood inside car next to driver seat, accumulating his power that he retain.

"You try to give your body relief. It will take time to heal reach Delhi," said Maunik, settling his seat belt across his chest.

"You saw her anywhere?" asked Maunik putting his head back with a relief breath.

"I wanted to ask you the same," said Mark.

"No, I didn't. Tried to notice her giving a look over whole house. Unable to encounter her," he replied Maunik.

"Even I didn't confront her. Was scared of getting interrupted by her, but came out safely," said Maunik.

"Let's move," said Mark handling Maunik the keys he had kept on the dashboard.

Confused mind not free from its past tragedy.
Have to accelerate life, to handle its left remedy.
Broken twigs need to be joined.
To fill the gap of all those uncertain developed void.

"What happened?" asked Mark.

"Don't know, it's not getting started," said Maunik before a whisper stroked their ears.

"Did you listen to something?" stunned Mark, asked facing Maunik hesitatingly.

"No, you?" asked Maunik as he turned to look towards the backseat.

"There's no one there, stop trembling," said Mark moving his rear mirror to see.

"Can't you hear that sneaking sound coming from below."

"It's nothing there, no sound, no spirit. You just gear up to drive," shouted Mark out of his black shield side glass.

"Hey! What was there, I saw something," said Maunik peering the mirror whose Mark's angry eyes are gaping at.

"Forget it and move, we are getting late," erupted Mark.

Mark spoke his last words to Maunik, before he opened his door ruthlessly and went out of it. Mark started shouting, as he was gone mad due to some rigidity. Jumping, throwing stones and picking up the rod lying near his feet was something he started to opt.

"Come! I dare you to come now... come make us get scared," said Mark, putting out his resentment, carrying that heavy metal rod.

"Maunik she's staring with horror through the mirror and she's only stopping us."

"Oh God! I felt her spirit had gone," said Maunik in dread.

"You don't come in my way... I want to save my left pieces of life," said Mark peering at his sides in a state of turmoil.

"Calm down, Mark, calm down ...," said Maunik leaving car running towards him.

"Settle down your soul... things will be fine," said Maunik before Mark's body spell down into his arms with tears of losing things from his fist.

"I am helpless and all this is tearing me apart. Give me life if you can," he said his last word before his eyes shun into darkness. Keeping his head on Maunik's bow.

"Mark... Mark...don't lose hope. Get up my brother, get up... things will get in control soon. You can't loose it like that," shouted Maunik stopping Mark's closing lids.

"Water ... he needs water.... where's water," Maunik said and ran to check car dashboard.

"This is the car you carried yesterday," a heavy sound with strong thrust came from behind the car and kept it half up from its back. It started shagging up and down badly making Maunik's head to stuck inside the dashboard.

"Get me out," shouted Maunik.

"I can't breathe... help me," Maunik insisted struggling hard to get out of it.

A hand kept hold of gear stump, with pressed acceleration setting it to first gear. Maunik got thrown out after the car crashed into pillar. Settling himself comfortable, getting up from the floor. He ran towards Mark, screaming his name. Slapped his cheeks in attempts of rejuvenating his consciousness before he ran for water. He took water pot, filled in garden for birds. Maunik finger sponged droplet over his face. Praying god over Mark's reliability. Lastly, his face started begging badly for help from God.

"Pleaseeeee.....let us leave," Maunik pleaded with his folded hands.

"Aaaahhhhhh...... why we are not going ....?," asked Mark promptly opening eyelids, hands attempting to stand.

"Wait, I'll be taking you. Hang on my shoulder," said Maunik bending over his hand on his shoulder.

Those timber of piano which Tamanna loves to play started sounding heavily in this aura. Mark intellect identified it in seconds of its play. He stopped Maunik to gaze once back towards the entrance door.

"This resonance Tamanna loves to play, I heard it many times," said Mark.

"What are you lost staring at, time already ran out," Maunik agitated.

"Yes, mom needs me," Mark turned holding Maunik's hand towards the car.

"You can't go, I won't let you," said Tamanna's spirit standing out in the frontal car, with blood running over her face and eyes in a desire to ruin.

"Why are you ominous of mean less concern, which has no consideration to reality," shouted Mark turning to point his finger over her face.

"Answer me, Mark ... answer me," she crept and slay down her left hand in anger.

Tamanna's dress started tearing of its place, enrolling anger over her face. Seems she evoked storm, from beneath. Which is getting heavier of flowing them away in the sky. Maunik kept hold of tree trunk next to him, with Mark keeping hold of water pipeline.

"Mark, why aren't you answering her," queried Maunik struggling this thrashing air.

"It's becoming miserable. I am losing my control," added Maunik in pain.

"What should I, she has gone off track," Mark's voice scuffling through the wind.

"I just know that now only you can control her," said Maunik and the pipe Mark's holding broke with sudden water-heavy shaft blowing him away.

"I ask what I did, tell me .... tell me, please. My heart isn't able to lug your loss and this poured pepper had already meant it lifeless," said Mark stepping towards space he felt her last glimpse.

"What you want from me? Aren't you seeing this birched, broken Mark," he said waving up and down finding her.

"None of my days had gone without thinking about you after your departure. I'd burned every day, the time you aren't there in my life. And you are reacting such to me. You've shoved wax drops over my heart," said Mark regaining the power to convey all to her spirit.

"Aren't you getting my question... answer me Markkkkk... Do you love Sayoni?" her spirit stood back of Mark, heading her face towards him to shout.

Mark even after hearing such a horror instance of Tamanna. Hadn't turned around, standing same he raised his voice to the peak.

" Yes... Yes ... yes I love Sayoni .... yes I love her," exhaust Mark said collective all his energy, crushing anger over the face.

"You listened ..."

"Say now... you listened to it?" he ended word before he thrashed hand looking against her for seconds. She was nowhere to be seen, as those abrupt storm stopped the same way it evoked. Leaving Mark in his thrashed face of anger asking question with those inspecting eyes. Maunik aspires again we evoked to move out, staring Mark and shocked with doubt.

"She is nowhere Mark... come .. come we can leave," said Maunik letting out his leg that's gone inside the small hole.

"Are you listening to Mark? What the hell you are lost in," Maunik shouted struggling to move out his leg. Mark still lost in finding him aside him.

"Let's go, before I'll get faint," said Mark scrolling his feet towards the car.

"Would it work, check once," said Maunik while walking closer to it.

"Wait, am doing," Maunik replied as he meant his foot out of the trap.

"Have to reach Delhi before the sun sets anyhow," said Maunik as he again attempted to get the car started, by squeezing key inside the ignition.

"And for me, every second is hammering," said Mark sitting straight looking ahead of the frontal glass pane.

Maunik with a deep breath kept screwing key in the ignition, with the hope of car to accelerate. His failure over repeated attempt had already faded his faith after some minutes and Mark said :

"Wait ... relax. It will get started, wait for half a minute and give your last attempt".

Maunik left his seat, moved out to open the bonnet. Slugged after not rectifying anything, he said Mark "things are in order" and he grabbed his seat, closed his eyes and with complete trust tried last.

"Huh, you said it right. It got," joy sprouted out of Maunik's desire.

"Yea, now just head it towards the hospital. My brain and body heretofore diminishing to respond. Need father meet soon," Mark gasping heavily, trying to stabilise his body.

No expectations, no desires are remaining.
Mind requesting storm, to settle down being a breeze for regaining
Those confusion sprouted inside the mind, still having opened question.
The soul is shouting to saving from dying, its left relation.
Eyes don't have that relief, to shatter their lids and sleep.
Every thought and impression wanted to think out very deep.

Letter from "Mr. Charles"

Travelling roughly for six hours, they outstretched over point they wanted to be. Maunik placed car over the hospital's backyard door. Headed out asking the way to enter from guard. Guard guided to park down car over parking and follow the way towards ICU ahead. Mark's eyes were slightly open with his feeble body and face staring Maunik. Maunik manifested Mark's condition to housing staff, asking to carry him towards an emergency. Handing Mark in the safe custody of those, he left towards Parking.

"Come soon," said Mark in rout voice with his body hanging in others arms.

"Yes, I will ... you please ask the doctor to confer him with proper treatment. Here is the doctor's prescription, he met accident yesterday," said Maunik, responding Mark and instructing staff member for ahead procedure.

"Don't wait please, hurry up !!!," said Maunik as he geared to move towards parking.

While parking Maunik got pointed out by policeman for car's miserable condition. It's sideboard got a giant dent, with its broken headlights. Front Number plate had also broke. Police personal was amazed at how they're spared for this throughout the way. After little word barter, he got informed that they travelled hundreds of kilometre before reaching Delhi. This man carrying two starts on his sleeves, being in charge of this area. Hearing all tragic situation Maunik is in, he let him go easily and either accorded him with his contact for any help he requires in future. This police's name was "Ravinder Singh".

Marking way towards ICU, after parking, he realised sense of peace over complete aura inside the hospital. He queried receptionist and got to know as it's national holiday "26th January". Sense visualising such hush continued as he entered waiting area of all ICU patients. Maunik, feeling pain onto his body but wasn't able to realise it due to storm of stress in his mind. He settled forging himself comfortable over the area. He produced his identity and patient information he came to visit. He asked about Mr. Charles health but they hadn't conveyed anything. Apart from their word "Sir, please take your seat, someone will assist you shortly". One more thing they gave him was the ICU ward number, he is in.

Mark wasn't interested to seek news telecasting on the big giant LED attached over the wall. That's was becoming the source of attraction for visitor sitting there. It's hospital self channel, specifically showcasing the hit news of hospital.

"What this reporter doing here?" Maunik crooned.

"Where did I see her?"said Maunik lost thinking.

"I saw her there just," said Mark with excitement pointing towards the LED.

Maunik gone stubbed as he gave his attention towards, listening out the current headline news. And he shouted putting his base above to stand in shock.

"When it happened, she said he's wanting to have words with Mark".

"Life can't teach such chapters. It can't be so cruel," he said and ran straight to enter the gallery that contains Private ICU rooms both sided. He hit three guards over his way, as well as running shouting "I am the son of Mr. Charles. Move away off my way".

"Where is room no: 303?" asked Maunik from one of attendant coming out of the room.

He gave way to Mark through his hand pointing towards the extreme left. Where he found the whole sort of crowded media people standing out of the room number: 303. All this had already meant Maunik's heard words into reality.

"No, my belief can't fall in such a way," said Maunik running towards the room. His tears had already started making his shirt to go wet. Reaching behind requesting everyone to give way he reached in front, where he found Mrs. Charles sitting staring at a point. She was completely lost and her broken desires were getting flattered like melting snow. Those sneezing sound of sorrow can be easily heard with her every breath. Maunik left hopes got crushed when the doctor said :

"You can take Mr. Charles body, we are done with everything," said Doctor to our Mr. Charles friend standing next to him.

"What you said him .... a body ... how can you say such to an honourable person," shouted Mark holding doctor's coat.

"I understand, a person of your family passed away. But you can't spoil the adequacy of hospital and behaviour to its personnel. The departure of Mr. Charles is already heart breaking not for his family only, but for the rest of the nation too," said the doctor.

"His research and achievements will ever be mesmerised as a beam of the incredible growth of the nation," said Mr. Singh closest friend of Mr. Charles.

"Yes why not, it will be and nation would be glad if you can share regarding the ongoing research Mr. Charles was in?" asked a reporter raising voice standing outside. Reporters from different groups avail behind the glass pane, listening activities happening inside in need to take interviewing Mr. Singh.

"We need to take Mr. Charles for burial," Mr. Singh said slowly pressing his finger over Maunik's shoulder.

"How could I say to Mrs. Charles, as am already not able to bring her son to meet Mr. Charles on time?" crooned Maunik.

"Can you please shut your questions, for now, I don't know anything regarding his present research," said Mr. Singh to an anxious reporter, as he went out from the space for a minute.

"You can understand the love everyone has for Mr. Charles," said Reporter.

"It doesn't mean that you will serve your task in between it. He left us, pray for his soul to rest in peace. That's it," said Mr. Singh coming back inside.

"These people will be taking Mr. Charles to a mortuary. Please ask your family to carry him from there," said Doctor to Mr. Singh and left.

"Maunik... please," said Mr. Singh looking towards Maunik.

"Aunty we need to go now," said Maunik with his heavy tone, settling down those tough sorrow of emotions being pragmatic.

Mrs. Charles got downright lost looking towards Mr. Charles lying over the bed. No tears, she was staring congruently without a blink of lids. Maunik bent over knees matching the height of Mrs Charles face and said.

"Things are happening very cruel in our lives. I don't know why this time is getting so tough" said Maunik looking towards Mr. Charles being stubbed.

"Where is Mark?" whispered Mrs. Charles, breaking her ongoing silence.

"Mark already struggling with injuries, gone unconscious, so I thought him to be in supervision first. I deceived mesmerisation of things being improper here," said Maunik gaping Mrs. Charles face.

"Whatever, he should be here," said Mrs. Charles with hush covered face staring unceasingly towards Mr. Charles body.

"Tell him, Mr. Charles kept his last wish to talk with him and when he came to know he couldn't. He wrote a letter before leaving all of us and asked me to not let anyone see it except Mark," said Mrs. Charles germinating words out of her dried throat after long stillness.

"Hold it, hand it over to him," said Mrs. Charles conferring the note written over the folded paper to Maunik.

"But we are going church along? He'll be reading it later," said Maunik.

"No, I'll be taking care of things ahead. You tell him to acknowledge Mr. Charles soul, wherever it would be, that he had the edification of what he wanted him to know.," she said stretching her feet to settle pending formalities.

"Go and provide him with this letter. Take care of him," said Mr.

Charles rubbing her hand over Maunik's forehead. Everyone left the place, as Mr. Charles got carried away by hospital staff. Mr. Singh and other folks commenced gripping out and it's just Maunik, left with an untold truth, that he carries in his hand.

"What could be so important in it? Why Mrs. Charles wants Mark to read it first? Before acknowledging father's dismissal," crooned Maunik and kept hold his head with all those tragic thoughts evoking in his mind in absence of getting settled.

Maunik ran towards the hospital's emergency cell leaving the room. With the assumption of Mark being treated there. He ran crossing the tracks. Going from one block to others and lastly, he reached the emergency cell over next building ground floor. Which is just next to the door from which they entered. Maunik buzzed the person sitting on the counter and resolving public queries.

"There's one person who entered here a couple of hours before, named Mark," asked Maunik bringing out his cell phone.

"Has he been admitted?" person over counter said.

"I have no idea, I am trying his phone," said Maunik dialling Mark.

"Give me a minute let me check," said counter personnel.

"What name you said, is it, Mark?" he asked.

"Yes, yes the same person," replied Maunik getting conscious from his distracted mind which was lost looking around. He peers at the computer screen from where that person just inspected.

"He left 10 minutes before after taking aid," said counter personnel.

"Where? I can't see anyone around. Did he tell anyone before leaving?" asked Maunik.

"No, you can check around outside. He's not able to walk properly either. Would be somewhere nearby only."

"Tell me please? I am worried," asked Maunik before his face is about to break down in tears.

"Today it's very less crowded, you'll find him. Please look once outside," he replied.

Maunik ran out throwing that glass door densely, with his sluggish voice calling Mark going heavier. Those spying eyes struggling for getting his one look anywhere. Legs wanted to cover a bigger distance with their every step to cover-up more area.

From entry checkpoint to the exit gate,
Maunik ran looking everything lying in his sideways.
His eyes were unable to notice the presence of Mark.
Making his belief for him to become darker.
Spots are dull that needs clarity of vision.
Without Mark, the words will stay like, kept behind the prison.

Maunik beard temple bells. Which is meant in its premises. Someone rung bells louder, whose evoked sound remained for a while before vanishing. Under such influence Maunik ran towards the temple, answering his raised questioned of Mark's presence. He stood inside the temple without giving a second thought and gone straight to the priest inside and asked :

"Is there anyone who came, who rang the bells louder in such an order?" asked Maunik.

"I haven't seen that person, he came to bendin front of God and left after ringing the bells," replied Priest.

"Oh," said Maunik and ran down towards the temple.

Maunik saw Mark strolling with his walk. Mark with his folded hands swirling around the temple. He came closer and noticed his closed eyes

"Mark, is everything ok?" said Maunik bending his head down to stare face.

"Yeah, what happened?" Mark replied.

"Why aren't you picking the phone? I wouldn't have found you if those bells you didn't ring," said Maunik.

"Leave it... tell me how's father? I was getting extremely scared, so I came here to platen my emotions," said Mark carrying Sacrament.

"Don't make me get low now.... Would you speak up?" said Mark after staring at his face for half a minute.

“Mr. Charles wanted to have a word with you and he wrote it all here,” said Maunik raising that knit paper.

“What are you saying. I can either hear this from him,” said Mark ruthlessly snatching it off Maunik’s hand, stepping towards the hospital.

“Mark, why don’t you understand, please read it. Mrs. Charles insisted,” added Maunik above his pressurized tone.

“Come fast, that’s what I want. I’ll be hearing it from him only,” said Mark boring his leg ahead over the way.

“No, Mark it can’t be,” impeded Maunik with his dull voice.

“But why?” asked Mark.

“He’s not with us now. Mr. Charles left the world,” he screened answering Mark, turning opposite to Mark.

“What? What you said? No,” Mark’s tearing voice coming in front of Maunik’s face.

“It can’t be Maunik. I can’t lose everyone from my life like this,” he roars with his stretched brows, compressed face staring at stacked bowed head of Maunik.

“How can I handle this?” mauled Mark sat over the floor after fall.

“How is mom?” asked Mark resolving his upcoming tears, moping his face.

“She’s a strong lady, said you to read this letter of Mr. Charles and not to care about anything. She said she’ll manage,” he replied.

“I want to see father once,” Mark yearns.

“Readout the letter first, she said so, very strongly,” said Maunik holding Mark’s shoulder to make him get up.

“That could be done. I want to see him once,” requested Mark looking into Maunik’s eyes.

“I hadn’t denied Mrs. Charles words ever. But seeing Mrs.Charles before he gets buried is much important,” replied Maunik.

“Thanks, my dear,” said Mark sliding his right hand over his cheeks.

“Which church they carried him to?” asked Maunik in dilemma.

“I think I am aware of it, let’s go,” said Mark and pulling Maunik’s hand towards the exit.

They travelled their way to reach Church,
Desires had already broken with the inspiration of life not left too much.
One is soothing another one, noticing the tears of each other.
Both lost hope such, as building themselves up is very hard further.

Maunik atlas reached the location for Church instructed by mark. Instantly came out opening Mark’s gate, helping him to move out.

“Are you sure, we’ll find them here?” asked Maunik taking equity of Mark’s arms, gaping around.

“Yes, it’s behind this building,” replied Mark.

“I’ll be able to walk, you don’t worry. A broken person inside can’t get broke outside,” said Mark removing the hand of Maunik off his shoulder.

“No need to walk slowly either. We don’t have time,” Mark noticing Maunik’s steps.

“Mark, I don’t want to lose you. you understand?” said Maunik covering Mark’s way.

“Yes, I do it very well. But I think God’s unable to balance happiness and pain in my life,” replied Mark, putting his hand over Maunik’s shoulder casing difficult smile.

“See it’s there, we came,” said Mark, heading towards the Church speedily.

“Mark, I don’t know why Mrs. Charles said this. But you please have a look of Mr. Charles from distance,” said Maunik noticing his speedily going steps.

“You don’t worry. I’ll take a look from a distance. I know what’s mom uptight off," said Mark and kept hold of Maunik's hand to walk behind the wall.

"You said it's there, then why are we walking behind this wall," asked Maunik.

"Church is there, but burial happens that side. To sojourn spared of other eyes we are walking behind this," said Mark bending his and Maunik's back, hiding themselves to eavesdrop people around.

"People are in extreme vain, due to Mr. Charles departure. But I don't know why those aloof people obsessed gossiping over his present research?" said Maunik while walking, listening around.

"They are his teammates with whom he's engaged," replied Mark.

"They imply utterly unaware of his work."

"Leave that... just try to treasure Mom in these," said Mark being slower.

"See, there is she sitting next to Mr. Charles grave," said Maunik, evincing finger, moving Mark face to acknowledge.

"Oh, Dad," said Mark with a gloomy face of depression.

"Hope you are able to espy both of them?" asked Maunik.

No reply out of Mark's throat, apart from that green grass assimilating wet through his dropping tear. Seems his shattered face, lost all aplomb through which he balanced his state of mind, quite a time before. Imbalanced feet, depicting the extent of pieces his heart distributed into. Peering one another life of his loved one getting crashed had already left aught inside Mark. Hoisting rare belief in his eyes, he tried to stand. Body beating raised wrecks. Eyes stopped dropping tears. Adorning Mr. Charles was enormous. The curvature of eyes filled with water and a desire of caress Mr. Charles evolved inside Mark.

"Mark, is everything ok?" asked Maunik couple of minutes later when Mark didn't move his head.

"Aah... yeah... I am," he replied wiping his eyes with a slight head shake.

"Do you need anything?" asked Maunik.

“No, nothing,” he replied and stood up over the place he bent himself.

“Are you ok, Mark?” asked Maunik.

“Yes, yes I am. Let’s leave this place,” he answered.

“Have water,” said Maunik passing him a water bottle, he carried.

“Yes… it’s required, anyway much of water had already come out of the body through tears,” said Mark with slight giggling with a tear still floating in his eyes while carrying a bottle from Maunik.

“Everything will fall in place Mark… believe in positive acts too,” said Maunik.

“There is nothing left to fall in place,” he replied before stepping towards the car.

“I want to read that note, come fast,” said Mark looking back towards stifled Maunik.

“Yes, even I am eager to know it,” said Maunik stepping out of Church premises.

“We can sit here and read ‘The letter from Mr. Charles,’” said Maunik as they get into an open space with spread benches.

“Yes it can,” said Mark, settling down over the rearmost bench.

“Take your space. Let me open it up and see,” Mark said Maunik.

“Am reading it out,” he said.

My child Mark,

We haven’t met since many years. I know that I had given more priority to my work than my family. We don’t have a colossal family, but still I have not been able to give time to you and your mother. Even if I tried to get away from my work somehow, my essence pulls me back. Today I wanted to share with you my work. This could be heartening for you to listen to something from me, that I should have shared over the period of my livelihood. But I believe that you can settle down your feeling calmly. Discussing my work and especially what I designed is something hard for you to relapse. I wanted to

present this to you only after its successful achievement, which I had committed to my heart much earlier. But unfortunately, I didn't get time to test it after its completion. And my health went worse with every coming day. I got anticipation of my time period getting over. Then I clinched to let you know everything about my work and research of the past many years, that's in everyone's agony to know. Those with whom I work, even they don't know about it. So you might encounter gossips about my work. People in the greed of its knowledge. I barred myself to divulge. As I was in the study, a make up hut which isn't only governed by science. But embroils diverse effects to set it true and functional. So my child, let me reveal to you that I was working on "Time travel". Over my scrutinization, I'd gone through every round clause finding out the buildup of time, as of how it gets built and how it gets destructed. How time retains its state and how can we cover those layoffs again that cruised our way. I was not able to achieve100 per cent accuracy yet, but I assume my work satisfactory. Yes, I worked on Time Machine, which we can travel time. Time travel I am able to achieve was not of much span, but it will work perfectly for 24 hours past and 24 hour future from the present stance. The biggest innovation of my life, which had only pictured by many but not testament practically. I wanted to share this with you first, what I committed to myself. My research and practice that I hadn't revealed to my supporter either. If this invention gets handover to the wrong hands, it could lead to major destruction. So I wanted to safely hand it over to the government after its completion. And this didn't happen as I had just tested it once practically but not got satisfied by results. Making satisfactory changes, I wanted to travel time once again probing its perfection. Then this disease and my health's worst condition impacted me in such a ruthless way. It made me realize of my passing on soon. I wanted you to come along with your mother when I asked hospital people to call my family. But noticing her coming alone, I queried for you at first. She would have called you, but unfortunately, I couldn't wait much. So I felt to write all this to you. So that you can complete my last task and take my all previous year's efforts to

their completion.

I want you to take the final test of my meant machine. Where you required to travel time and check it's efficiency. My work has no flaws but still I wanted it to get checked once before leaving this world.

I know you'll receive my note after My dismissal. But mind it, don't use this for my saviour anyhow. My death is not instant, as it's due to a prolonged disease and heart issues. I want it to stay innate with my specified time period.

I believe you will test it over every ground and make my research of many years to grasp its triumph mark.

I have mentioned every detail about my lab and making it clear to you to encounter everything to perform what I said. I designed it to be somehow helpful to the nation for taking its help in securing positive issues.

Check the next page for all awareness. I want you to get completely comfortable first to use it thoroughly, both mentally and physically.

Thank you
Your Father
Mr. Charles

"Why you've gone quiet? Is it done?" asked Maunik over Mark's silence, folding note.

"What life wants me to do?" he said.

"What the hell you started thinking now?" asked Maunik bending in front, gaping his astray gone face.

"I can use this within 24 hours… Think it what I said… its 24 hours," said Mark picking his eyelids up to peer Maunik.

"So what if it's 24 hours? What you're into Mark?" asked Maunik with heavier going pitch.

"I have many questions, which will get cleared from Tamanna," said Mark.

"What's going on in your mind Mark?" Maunik shook Mark, acute his shoulders.

"I will secure what occurred "Yesterday 9"," he said smirking towards Maunik.

"What mess you are creating out Mark? Nothing seems easy," said Maunik.

"You aren't there with me last night, so you don't know. I'll make it happen. I'll make her stay alive. Yes….. I will do that …. I will," said Mark and stood on his feet with directed eyes of dedication.

"How could it be done? Mark don't panic such, you are stepping against nature's will," said Maunik, stood abruptly holding Mark's face.

"Nature either can't go such cruel to my life. If nature can, even I could," said Mark inhaling rooted gasp.

"I will handle that, you don't have to get distraught," said Mark putting his hand over Maunik peering those blown shaded balls.

"Ok fine…. Leave what all I feel here only. I am coming with you," he replied.

A desire sprouted like small water droplets.
Dropping down off sky, crafting those emotions with a golden bracelet.
They hadn't asked for this favour from God.
But their massive sacrifice, aren't even got handled by Lord.
Such beautiful designed thought and way to achieve is in front of them.
Though they started climbing a tree, taking the help of its strong stem.
A bright light started building that crushed emotion into bricks.
They just have to build the house again, through their tricks.
Asking, telling anyone about it is worthless.
Before reaping its fruit, as this help and attempt of God is priceless.

Way with "Time Machine"

Started way towards location mentioned by Mr. Charles for his lab. Maunik drove in the hassle of reparatory time, of sooner embracing place. Still unable feet of Mark to walk, with shimmering courage in his eyes.

"You wanna have water?" Mark asked Maunik whose driving.

"No, I don't," he replied.

"But I need it. Could you see, if we can get it somewhere over the way?" asked Mark.

"Ohhh sure. But can encounter a bottle kept aside. If you can have it," replied Maunik picking the bottle in the back seat.

"Do I have to drink such water now?" asked Mark.

"Yes, what's wrong?" replied Maunik.

"This water has been kept for car rinsing," said Mark.

"Oh… is it?" said Maunik passing smile.

"Would you please look ahead else slow down its speed," said Mark.

"No, we don't have time," said Maunik gaping Mark.

"A person like you, dictums me such. Time changes briskly," said Mark.

"Yes and you are going to stop it," said Maunik giggling.

"There's nothing to laugh," said Mark, taunting voice.

"Oh... see... see Maunik someone's there," shouted Mark as a person came in front of their car.

Maunik gets hold of breaks heavily, the second he espy Marks face in holler. Maunik gazing Mark couldn't able to realise what and who came in front of the track. Tumbling down the road after getting stuck in their car. Mark opened the door in a hassle and ran towards the font.

"Hey... ya... are you ok?" screamed Mark stepping with pain to check out if they endangered someone's life.

"Hello ... hello can you hear me," Mark yelled over a person lying facing the ground in front of their bonnet.

"Ohhh.... It seems to be a lady. God, nothing would have happened to her," said Maunik reaching the car's frontal space.

"No, don't worry the breaks were on time. She'd fallen after you met it," said Mark.

"Please get up. Let us know If you need help," Mark solicited.

"Could you please pick her up through shoulder? Might be she's unable to," Mark asked Maunik.

He gave her his hand of favour to let them stand,
Sometimes people require that support you have to understand.

"Hey... Sayoni... it's you," said Mark as Maunik raised her.

"What the hell have you done with yourself? What is this?" asked Mark got stunned the minute he sees her crummy condition.

After seconds of try, she meant to settle her breath winded by some blow. Maunik said:

"Wait, Mark, let's take her in.....let her recline. Nothing seems good".

"See.... We don't have water, how could we serve. I can see anything around," said Mark as he adjusted Sayoni over the back seat and gazed over aside aura.

"I have... check," said Sayoni passing her bag to Maunik.

"Hey calm down... We got, you won't get anything out there," screamed Maunik pouring water from a bottle to glass to be carried to the back board.

"See... she helped her herself again," said Mark.

"Would you both get quiet for a minute," Sayoni in a slight displeasing manner.

"Hey wait... she's getting annoyed," said Maunik.

"Sorry dear, now please let us know what happened with you?" asked Mark graving towards the concern, taking space next to her inside car.

"She is following me," Sayoni replied with fluttering lips, being intense petrified.

"What happened? Who followed you? Let me know, don't be so frightened... calm down," insisted Mark.

"Can you please tell me, where is Tamanna?" Sayoni asked Maunik.

"What happened with her… why so instant?" asked Mark with his fumbling voice.

"Her spirit's following me. She wants to take the hell out of me, without any reason," said Sayoni sprouting out her fear

"Though I was in wonderwonder as to why she's quiet," said Maunik exhaling breath gaping forth back towards the frontal way.

"And I felt she understood and favoured my difficult situation," said Mark.

"But she started a new chapter," replied Maunik with aggression.

"Don't create a mess. Could anyone convey me what's the incident and console my anxiety," said Sayoni getting frustrated, pulling hair through her palms.

"Hey… heya… please don't panic and let your eyes go wet. I can't see your tears".

"What would I do. Her spirits following me. I am either not aware whether her eyes confronting me at present," startled Sayoni with evolved strain on her face.

"Defray yourself, I'll give you clarity of everything"

"It started due to 'Yesterday 9'," said Mark kept holding of Sayoni's back peering upfront. Mark took him into the same ambience, for giving the best interpretation.

"What "Yesterday 9" you left with her for Lansdowne yesterday only?" she asked.

"Yes I left with her yesterday night and," Mark commenced developing gloomy sensation before his pandemics words spell out, instance he traversed.

He conveyed a factor faced that's hidden from her eyes.
Anywhere she queried, he told twice.
He wants nothing to endure in a bucket, which she's unaware of.
Relief mesmerised over his face for conveying what his heart stood off.
He asserts every desire, phrasing so plainly to her.
That whenever he stops his stanza, she has nothing to ask further.
Need for dispersing knowledge for settling things down, he wished.
He tried apprising everything before any word gets missed.

"Can get it, with what you are going through," she said perception, rubbing his face blackened due to dust with her hand.

"Was worried as to how would you react over it," replied Mark.

"You both were those being, with whom my life got blessed. How could your words be ever disabled of expressing themselves," she replied.

"But why did you summoned her spirit, as you love me? I am wholly happy staying aware of the relation between you and Tamanna," conveyed Sayoni facing Mark with querying eyes of urgency to get answered.

"After her repeated question, my realisation stood to be straight. My heart loves you foremost and I said," Mark controlling breaths delivering what is in his soul gestures.

"Mark," abruptly she replied, with her opened mouth and sober eyes, shedding with every covered second.

"Please don't mind it the way I asserted. But when I scrolled myself and found this conation took place over the period of time, where you tackled my every exhaustive emotion so calmly. Time Tamanna wasn't even tending of my presence in this time world. Then how could a person attempt to come back by their will? Asking for the place they lost long before. It wasn't aware of my such inclination towards you, till the time her spirit repeated questioned my desire pulling out the truth," said Mark unstopped, not letting his feeling to break.

Sayoni quietly listened to Mark's every word. His stressed lines and confused forehead. Delivering every piece was making her realise his adherence to what he's saying.

Her deficient eyes to provide him with healing. Face taking up a smile to let him know things will be resolved soon with what he's dealing.

"Don't be afraid Mark, for anything," she said pouring her hand of kindness.

"I don't know, what's life wanting next," he said folding his sorrow under his exhaled air through the mouth.

"Guys, Nothing will work if we passed more time here only," said Maunik gearing up the car.

"You get started. She'll be coming with us," said Mark with a serious face.

"Me as well?" asked Sayoni.

"Yes, I won't be able to leave you a minute away from me now," said Mark as Maunik accelerated car towards the way.

Those untold developing desires had revealed their emotions.
Whatever he said from heart, not require any promotion.
That covered wet shed over those aspiring devotion.
Scared of hassle in relief, after such biggest confession.
Hopes again took their lead to sprout seeds over barren land.
He was building trust over life again, giving it a try to stand.
Having faith over the last spark, shown twinkling far apart.
He kept hold of her hand to move ahead, over a new start.

"We are heading accurate, I feel?" asked Maunik rushing the car across tracks.

"Yes, we'll be on spot after this right turn," replied Mark.

"Do you feel that I should come along you?" asked Sayoni hesitatingly.

"I won't let you sacrifice any emotion from now onwards. These present words negate your desire to come along. Again for someone," said Mark as he tried to find out that last letter he wrote to himself.

"Is everything alright Mark?" she asked.

"It's missing at present, else I would have shown you what I really feel for you. I understand what Tamanna has undergone is nature's cruel approach. One day she has to go away from me anyhow. I am not her love, I meant to be her need. Is what her spirit conveyed," said Mark eyes convoluting in the surrounding, atlas holding her both hands peering into her eyes to deliver.

"Guys, we reached the said spot. But I can't see any lab over the jungle," conveyed Maunik scrutinising the place as he stepped over.

"Sometimes things require some effort to erect," said Mark moving out of car.

This place seems to be no man's land. No person could be mesmerised through its farthest location. Due to the setting sun and darker going aura, initiatively becoming horrible. Mark shouted, checking if anyone responds to his voice. But nobody came to embark, except echo's which returned back to their ear.

"See it's right there," Mark pointing towards small cage meant nearby. That's covered with green plants over its roof.

"You're sure it would be?" asked Maunik.

"You can check, I heard of some research centre of Mr. Charles at such place," said Mark.

"At least you can say him your father now," said Maunik.

"I say it... he is my father yes..." said Mark.

"If I convey you something, Please don't judge me after that," said Mark.

"I don't want you to come along in examination of invention," whispered Mark.

"But why, Mark? What happened?" Maunik tone carrying a furious face.

"I want you to look after Mother, whom we left alone," replied Mark.

"So instantly," said Maunik you changed your statement.

"I haven't committed to taking you ahead on this path," said Mark and opened the gate of Mr. Charles hidden lab.

"You are aware of its passcode?" asked Sayoni being stunned staring at it getting open.

"I don't. But I remember the generic code Mr. Charles uses," replied Mark.

"My words are the same for both of you. Please try to understand. I just realised how risky it could be," said Mark stepping towards its centre.

"You can't do it like that Mark. Please stop this," said Maunik.

"What wrong am I saying, If my soul can't carry to lose more. Please ... please try to understand it's not easy for me," said Mark facing Maunik.

"Go and take care of Mother. She'll need you," said Mark.

Maunik left in response to Mark's call. He thrashed door ruthlessly, throwing his feet hard outside.

"Wait, take her along," screeched Mark gaping Maunik diminishing off his vision.

"How can you say that. Once you said that you won't let me stay away for a while and now you're dropping me the middle way ," replied Sayoni, standing backside of Mark.

"Understand that my words are not pointless," Mark said before his feet got scribbled as he heard runaway voice of excelled car wheels.

"Hey, he's gone alone. How could he?" said Mark running towards the door.

Maunik left the space with heavy thrust where Mark running hooves could only see one slight glimpse of the car, before it vanishes away. Mark shouted twice hanging over the cage's door, balancing his unstable body unable to stand either.

"See Mark, look over your body once. You would have fallen down just," said Sayoni after she ran and kept hold of Mark shoulder above his disabled feet.

"Am perfectly alright and will manage everything to come on its place," said Mark.

"Don't even think of keeping me away from you now, I won't leave you even for a second," said Sayoni where Mark dragged his body to go closer towards central yard.

"So things start from here," said Mark as he opened central legroom door.

"What you found?" asked an astonished Sayoni, as she reached towards a room's corner. Trimming Mark seated over the central stool surrounded by many operational machineries with red, green and blue emulating lights.

"What's this? Can you hear it?" Sayoni spoke, as she entered.

"It's metallic sound. This place is shouting about the work he did from years effort. I read everything he told me and this was exactly the place he said.

"Who's he here? I am confused Mark," asked Sayoni with her intrinsic look towards every artefacts she's encountering around.

"My father," said Mark.

"This seems to be the time clock and here's the handle to rotate it," said Mark with astonished dispersal and sparkling face, touching a round shaped wooden steering.

"I am seriously not getting, what exactly you want to do," said Sayoni.

"No time left for me, Sayoni. Many things I have to secure, you stay away from it and please help me by not coming along with me anymore. This could be dangerous," said Mark before his words ended, with those sharp creeping shout of a lady crying badly for relief took lead.

Sayoni, scared enough. With her closed eyes and shivering body, she squeezed herself over a corner, sticking her back over the wall. Mark being stubbed and stunned tried to get up from his place, scrolling his left leg behind right towards Sayoni.

"Calm down... nothing happened. What's bothering you to be such?" asked Mark reaching next to her, whose shagged in fear.

"These were the same sound, with whom she tore me up," she replied carrying dread on her face.

"Who is she? Sayoni," he screamed placing his hands around her over the wall.

"Tamanna," she said exhaling air after all heavy breaths that she took.

"No... No she can't come again to tarnish me further," yelled Mark rigidly punching the wall.

"But I did Mark," a hauling sound stood his ears.

Shagged hooves moved right, finding such point of ejection. Gazing out, Mark perceived complete divergent aura, nothing left outside expect room they are in. It implies there's no existence apart of the room they are in, over the place. Forested surrounds started a foot distance off settled place.

"Don't panic, I'll resolve everything," said Mark as he spins bumped pleasing face towards Sayoni, holding her face in between his hands to stare those fearsome eyes.

"You can't do anything Mark. As you have already cruised me," a voice stood up from the ground underneath Mark's feet.

"I haven't done anything... can you listen? I haven't done anything," he yelled towards the floor.

"Can you see her?" Mark asked Sayoni with those heavy breaths.

"No I can't," she replied with her feared fumbling words.

"I saw her before, but now I couldn't," said Mark boring feet towards the machine.

"Hey, it contains days setting as well, with its 24 hours day setting," said Mark with a sprout of smile on his face.

"What happened to you? We are not out of one thing and your mind is trying to get into other," asked Sayoni, letting her voice out of sheer strain.

"I asked you, not to think about her spirit. I will go for it anyhow, for what I came here," replied Mark whose hands are struggling to understand functioning happening behind the machine glass board.

Spider scrolled from corners of the wall and started covering Sayoni's body parts to get them over to the wall. Disturbed and bewildered Sayoni not aware of those changes, rubbed her face through palm removing her hair nods from the face. Every second her one or the other organ is going in control of those tales. Mark engulfed in solving technical difficulties he encountering to get the "Time Machine" started. His eyebrow raised to notice silence stood inside.

"Get away from there, come out," shouted Mark towards Sayoni whose started getting dissolved into the wall.

As Mark's voice spread over the room and stroke unconscious Sayoni's ear. She was stubbled in anxiety. Her confused face and agitation produced in her body to move started. She gave her repeated attempts to break down a mesh of fine tough scleroprotein threads build by a spider from its secreted liquid. Till the time her hands, legs and waist were already caught in spiders web rolling over her body from both sides. All her attempt getting wasted as if these spiders thread are getting more thick and tighter. Helpless Mark unable to stand from his place. Seems like Mark lost all the power left inside his body.

"What is there above me, why can't I raise my waist," shouted Mark creeping badly as he kept all his power to save Sayoni.

With every passing second, Sayoni's body is getting in Invincible state, making eyes to get away of her visibility. She started shouting for help, founding her efforts getting ruined one after the other.

That request in need, like her eyes staring at Mark, whose not even standing to give his hand of saviour towards her. She's smashed inside, after suspecting Mark still sitting on the same place and defined towards his task resolving "Time Machine". She left the hope of getting saved from this tragic mystery and lost all hopes of getting out of it.

"You wouldn't be saved today, I can't see you in Mark's life," a passing wave whispered into Sayoni's ear. She shouted Mark hearing this voice.

"Why you aren't trying to get out of it? Please get it off," shouted Mark.

"I can't do anything present," she said.

Every obstacle started wobbling off its place. Keen shifts over land curvature below. Those bottle's, interments, books kept over shelf attached to wall evoked falling down. So far, Sayoni went partly immersed inside the wall. Looking at her in such mundane, Mark's eyes started crying due to his helplessness.

"Sayoni, I can't let you go," shouted Mark while applying his whole energy against the thrust that was blocking him.

That dread on her face with building hush had already settled Mark veins to stop pumping. She gave away in such a manner, meant Mark to pull her out anyhow hoarding all left vitality in his organs. Mark kept hold of his zest. With extreme roar produced through his mouth, he tried enabling his body to move. Looking towards wall submerging Sayoni, with her diminishing presence. His body had already torn down, telling his mind to save her or die himself. Mark's all whoop aren't getting outstretched to her ears any more, as her unresponsive frame about to get dissolved completely inside the wall.

Deadly tittering of female sound commenced out of every wall. Mark started pleading for Sayoni's saviour, as his ears rectified it to be Tamanna's act.

"I beg you, not let her go away of my life," tears sprouting out of Mark's eyes, were now in need of a favour.

"Take my life instead but don't let her go," begged Mark peering abandoning Sayoni getting way immersed.

"You can't die. You have to live for me," howled Tamanna's spirit impending in existence, standing upfront of Mark. After all her horror expression came visible over her such an eerie face, which till now stayed back of her appalling voice.

"You are taking the life of a true soul, what worth would it make of your bloody spirit," said Mark.

"Whatever... I have to do, what I want to do," dark shaded spirit of Tamanna said wiping out blood off her chin, dropping over the floor below those thirsty lips.

Her savagery was transmitting its desire through her smile overtaking life.

She went blunt shedding her hair round in air to generate complete hurricane inside.

"Look over her forming shadow over the wall," Tamanna's wild gone spirit yelled louder, giggling, pointing her finger towards the wall. Where Sayoni was about to get complete pierce brick-walled alive.

"See I am begging you... I beg you, let her go... leave her life," screaming Mark with those silenced gone cry, lost turning Sayoni's meant lifeless sketch above the wall. Her lost presence and those last memories of her into Mark's eyes were making him impeded insane. Silenced pushing Mark is away of thinking about those present destruction in his aura at present. Those falls with distortion of every artefact around him is deff unable to make any change in his posture of peering sketch build over the wall. Cipher isn't able to change his dispassionate, stony tone face with those opened abduct eyes. Seems his life lamp has been shaded inside the wall and he became blind bearing the left darkness. Those not blinking opened eyes, dismissing defeated of getting shut due to air thrashes.

His working breath, taking the time to get rid of their maintained flow.

As now Nothing could make her back to life,

apart from the body moves that her lifeless portrait meant over wall show.

Those smile and her generous words are still sounding louder.

Then shaft of those wild killing him, for being a love founder.
Dried saliva inside the mouth, air wanting to stop passing inside out.
Something needs to get watered inside, for those seeds to sprout.
Life steady flow became unsteady.
Shouting internal soul to scrub feet and get ready.
How could a body that lost all living aspiration can stand,
For what sake life took the person off and asking him to understand.

"Haven't you heard me?" yelled Tamanna's spirit with her frightening anger.

Those awaken eyes blunt badly, not blinking before they get to heal.
As calamities had already broken, all ways that's helping his life to deal.
Her anger burned fire around,
She meant her spirit so cruel, raising pitch the way she sounds.
She took off all colours lastly left alive with him,
Burning the last twig with the fellow he was an appetite to stand with.
This crude air she spelt around,
Making tough to breathe for him, the way it surrounds.
The pain of losing the one last hope, he was left to live.
Meant all those newly grown flower to get stiff.

The weary puffs which took their place covering every space of the room. Their flow upside down making everything to rupture down. Those terrible creeping of Tamanna's spirit inside has slashed everything to be in her control.

Tamanna's spirit recast shouts and call towards Mark, stopped getting into Mark's ear. Mark became a statue staring at the wall, like a lifeless worm. Passions of her spirit were broken exhibiting dopiness of Mark, as she lastly threw her power to thrash his body.

His unreceptive frame bends lying down over his back. With hand's gripping a shaft. This is the ultimate start of "Time Machine" after all setting he previously meant.

Being unconscious, his hand plunge on a shaft to set it on,
A new phase of life was waiting for him to cure, what all he left on.
Something would be asked before the rest can be told.
Life rewinded itself, to set alive a couple of chapter's that were untold.

U-Turn

The day started arranging discomforts to help comfort step ahead. Everything evoking with a beautiful morning and those twittering birds over the window. Something which Mark dreamt as a perfect mixture of nature delight to start a day. White veils shaded over opened window pane stretched their arms to cover those pink painted walls moderately. Those recasting devotional song raising from the ground, giving a glance of a cultural setup. A sweet celebration through small collective people wearing orange and red. Clock ticked 8 in the morning and the alarm kept inside Mark's room rang loudly.

"Wake up Mark, I won't say it again," voice of Mrs.Shivach was heard coming out of the speaker lying next to Mark's bed.

Mrs.Shivach, after getting irritated of Mark habitually ignoring his alarm, planted a speaker in his room. As soon she heard the ringing bell of his alarm, she utters in the microphone inside the kitchen to set Mark's excuse false of not hearing his alarm every day.

"What happened to this boy! He was an early bird before and see the change he's into now," said Mrs. Shivach after she didn't get a reply from Mark.

"Could it be little slower?" he said, removing the blanket off his face.

Some abrupt moves he sensed in his body. His hands rubbed his eyes. His eyes got stunned as they set to light, throwing their heaviness aside. Garnishing surrounding like a pendulum with every passing second. He held a jar filled with water in his one hand and jumped to grab glass in his other hand.

"Is that a dream?" Mark queried himself, blowing air out of his mouth.

"No... it can't be...my life is dupe, nothing I've lost," said Mark, taking a relaxed breath while putting his feet down on the floor.

"How cruel it was. Life shouldn't show such bad colours to anyone," he said, taking sips of water from the glass he just filled.

"No.., no, life doesn't have authority to take my loved one life such, the way it did," He shouted, making the glass to spelt down into pieces, throwing it ruthlessly over to the floor.

"What had happened? Is everything Ok, Mark?" asked Mrs. Shivach peering up through the stairs.

"Yea... yea... Maa .. everything's alright, nothing to panic," said Mark.

"But I heard the voice of penniless," she asked in anxiety.

"Why she cares a lot of me. Who actually don't deserve," crooned Mark.

"Nothing happened, it's these people downstairs, who again started clamouring their holistic activities," he hissed stepping towards window pane gaping down and his face towards those devotees dancing below.

"What language is it, Mark? They are doing a thing that you should also do. Praying God isn't a crime, it's in our deeds. I understand being an atheist, you don't believe in all these. But you shouldn't say like that," she said to instruct.

"But doing it every day like this isn't required I feel," he replied closing opened window.

"Who does this everyday? It's once in a year Mark," she replied.

"What date is it?" he asked with stretched brows.

"It's 17 January," she replied with a loud voice, going back to the kitchen.

"17 January... how it could be?" Mark crooned, with his face struck with dilemma.

"I couldn't believe this," he said collecting ample amount of strain over his face.

“What you couldn’t? Don’t forget you’re only one day far from helping your friend Ritesh. Tomorrow you have to leave for Lansdowne,” Mrs. Shivach said and giggled.

“This boy never takes things seriously,” she said slower with a slight smile.

Listening Maa’s last reveal. Mark’s legs became inert. He fell down over the floor itself losing all his balance. Fingers touching rug, realising of his being. Eyes glancing around everywhere perceiving his presence.

“Has it happened? Did that machine worked and thrown me over past phase?,” Mark vexed finding the answer of his question off himself, sliding over rug madly.

“How it could be if that “Time Machine” just works for 24-hour clock and the time I am in now is double,” Mark started pulling his hair fiercely, rubbing his head sharpening his belief. Exhaust, stubborn Mark have nothing to generalise.

“It can’t happen… Nothing has happened, it was just a dream Mark, just a dream,” said Mark existing in front of the mirror. Mark hastily went inside bathroom opened the shower nob; keeping his face below to get squashed. Stood to abduct underneath encored with the same dilemma, till his phone bell rings.

“Want to inform you that Sayoni is calling, please pick up,” Mark’s phone bell tone.

Gripping out of the bathroom carrying a towel in hand, he fastened steps towards phone lying over the floor. Rubbing hair, wiping mouth. His hand succeeded in picking it up before it gets hanged.

“Huh… by God grace you picked your cell. Else my mind had realised hearing your ever-constant busy speech, next second my cell dies,” said Sayoni as Mark held it onto his ear.

“It’s not for you dear, you know it well,” said Mark.

“Yes, I know,” she replied.

“And you cling to your habit of calling back again, once call gets missed," said Mark.

"I can, but get into the realisation of your being busy. So," she said.

"Some people allowed to make me interrupted anytime and you are at top of it," replied Mark, throwing the towel over the couch.

"Forget all that, tell me you are going for the show today?" she asked.

"Which one?" asked Mark.

"The one for Ritesh. Aaaahhhh how could you forget, you are performing to raise fund for those cancer deficient children's. You only said a couple of days before?" she asked.

"Either Maa statements this, but the date was before and the much I know, it already got cancelled," said Mark putting his left palm over the speaker.

"Mark... Mark... can you hear me. You are at home and I know theirs no network issue. So dare you said that," said Sayoni with her louder pitch.

"Hey... hey... yea am listening. Phone got dropped from my hand," he said.

"I don't understand your immediate lost vibes over mid of calls, when the real important thing is going on," agitated Sayoni.

"Aah... its Ritesh calling me. Wait for a while, I'll get back," he said before keeping her on hold to answer Ritesh.

"Mark! Congrats my brother. I got the approval of our show today. Nothing to get worried now," said Ritesh with an extreme buzz in his voice, the second he received.

"But you said it got cancelled?" asked Mark.

"When I did? It got cancelled as was on the verge to happen. But lastly, we were saved with sponsors and approvals which flowed the way we wanted. Else my NGO and all those kids would have suffered a lot," Ritesh spoke in cheer.

"Are you able to hear me?" asked Ritesh, noticing silence at Mark's end.

"Yea... am able to... listening to you only," he replied.

"So, how it's planned?" asked Mark.

"You get prepared with your dance troop for performing today's eve. Will start at 05:00 pm," said Ritesh with pent up motivation.

"What? 05:00? Isn't it too early?" asked Mark.

"It needs to be protracted, as many big corporate invites we have which were coming over different slots," replied Ritesh.

"So, whose their for anchoring?" asked Mark wearing his aside lying trouser at the corner of bed.

"Aah sorry Mark... it would be you only," replied Ritesh with his slower going tone questioning Mark.

"What? You hadn't appointed anyone to control crowd?" Mark was getting flushed, dumping his base over the couch with his stunned face.

"We have Mark, but he'll be able to do nothing in accordance with your grace. So ultimately it's only you, who can manage it out," replied Ritesh.

"Ok, you shut the phone for now. I'll be at a location with my guys at 03:00," said Mark tucking up his shirts button, picking up his black coffee, just served by Mrs. Shivach.

"Seems you got conscious after having word with Ritesh," said Mrs. Shivach stepping down the stairs with a slight smile on her cheeks.

"And you heard it all, what I said?" asked Mark, putting his cup down and questioning eyes.

"Talk to Sayoni first, whom you kept on hold," replied Mrs. Shivach.

"Maa... not that," said Mark with his stretched tone of irritation.

"Ohhhh sorry Sayoni, I kept on hold our fight," said Mark putting his phone back over to ear.

"Hahaha... oh, is it, rockstar?" giggled Sayoni.

"You leave it. Just stay reminded to meet me over the venue at or before 03:00 pm".

"So everything got settled down so early," she said.

"Yes, he managed somehow. It's left with me now," he said.

"I know you'll rock the show," she replied before they dropped words and got busy wrapping up all things.

Steering his songs to perform today. Mark was getting a glimpse of the date same as Tamanna's organised fashion show. His repeated peering over the calendar with a mind stuck finding an answer. Making Mark head to get exalt, mesmerising all that's becoming hard for him to devise. Wanting someone to settle down all those questions arose in his soul. Aligning his bag while taking last left sips from his coffee mug. Mark realised of repeated activities with words performed. His disbelieve rehashing back to make him realise of its actuality.

"This couldn't be the truth, it's not a repetition. Things seem similar, but aren't in existence," said Mark, while rudely finding cloth in his cupboard and throwing other out needlessly.

"But how can two things come again and that too on the same date. Tamanna's show and this charity event," said Mark, dumping clothes into his baggage.

"Had you felt to drain that dress you brought yesterday," asked Mrs. Shivach from her microphone off kitchen.

"Yesterday... yesterday what I did?" asked Mark rejoicing his memory with his Maa raised words.

"What is it? Why I can't correlate," said Mark before his eyes stood over his just silenced vibrating phone, displaying the name of Tamanna.

"Aah, Yea ... I was with Tamanna yesterday night. How can I forget her crazy asserts over dresses while shopping," he said picking up the phone.

"Hmm," he said.

"Leave it, we don't have time for this now. Tell me, Mark, at what time you're leaving to reach my show," asked Tamanna with her words in a hurry.

"Aah for today's eve... ah hmm," Mark in his baffled voice.

"Yea... I told you yesterday nah," she queried sipping her tea, chewing snacks.

"Yes .... you did but," he said folding a sheet of paper in between his lips.

"But what Mark, you couldn't say that," said with her annoyed voice.

"Our show is fixed, that one for raising a fund of cancer children's".

"But I told you to leave that, I can't spoil my mood with it Mark," she said with every word clearer and going dipped in agitation.

"That was important dear. It's about those children livelihood," he replied.

"What about me, Mark? I insisted you yesterday and you committed," she spoke with her sharp pointing tone.

"Now how could I explain that to you," he said with his deff tone.

"What you would say... you just keep shut," she said and hanged call barbarously.

"You can realise it if..." Mark tried to spoke as she ended, but call gone cancelled before that.

"What is this now?" Mark hashed his phone over the bed in such a way that it showed vexation.

He left everything he started to align, over the bed itself and sat with his palm balancing the weight of his head with fingers getting into hair.

"What should I do of such understanding," he said, as he beat his right leg over the floor.

"I can't do anything, it's their problem," said Mark stepping to pick his Bluetooth lying over a stool.

"Why am getting this glimpse, that I had attended her show after other one's cancellation," he said putting his dancer's prop in baggage.

"My eyes have a clearer memory of her walking on the ramp with her models," said Mark with eyes lost in wonder.

"I can observe it clearly. This happened!" said Mark, throwing his baggage being messed in his perturbation.

"Again... again these conferring such relegation, all that I have seen is true," said Mark giving flicks to his right hand in pressure.

"How could it be... that was hell... and my life couldn't get thrashed so callously".

"No my game would be such," said Mark stepping downstairs, hanging bag over the shoulder.

"You hadn't taken bath either," said Mrs. Shivach noticing Mark.

"You tell me first, did you had word with mom recently?" he asked settling down over breakfast table.

"You know it evidently, as we both talk every day," said Mrs. Shivach place toast over Mark's disc plate lying in his front.

"I tried but her phone isn't reachable, so couldn't check her comfort," he said.

"Oh... my child seems worried for the first time for his mom," said Mrs. Shivach with that nostalgic smile over her face while putting butter over his toast.

"I care, but you know, I am weak in revealing. Tell nah?" said Mark.

"Oho... she is perfectly fine, enjoying her NGO work. And listen, she got worried-less of you after laying you in your second mother's custody," said Mrs. Shivach gazing Mark's face and carrying glass jar filled with milk.

"Yes, as I love this custody the most," Mark catches smile taking his first bite.

Something sounding to get settled with perfection.
Like others wanting my help in implementing correction.
Breaths worried of what's done and what will come in return.
Like everything is coming back into life, taking a U-turn.

"Will you be going today for checkup's, doctor prescribed?" Mark asked Mrs. Shivach, signing to pass jam.

"What? Mark, you are talking about something that happened a week before," she said, handling jam.

"Oh I see," he replied.

"What do you see?" she asked.

"I felt like other things it would also happen again," he crooned slowly taking a sip of his milk glass, with his stretched eyebrows.

"What? What you just said? Speak louder," she asked with anxiety.

"Don't you feel you are in some other world today," she asked pulling a chair of the dining table to sit, gazing at Mark.

"What would I sense, everything is repetitive in this world," Mark vanishing his breakfast with the last pick on apple from the vessel kept on the table.

"Repetitive? Means?" she asked walking distant.

"Nothing Maa... you don't get stressed. Believe your child, I'll be managing everything," Mark said picking his car keys reaching next to outdoor steps.

"Why you leaving right now, I feel you have to go in eve," she asked.

"You heard that as well," he said raising fingers moving in the air while gaping Maa. His toning cheeks and smiley eyes letting her know the catch.

"Ok, I tell you. I require mental peace for a while, that you know I find in books. So going library at present and leave for evening show from their itself,'" he said exiting the door.

"I will be out for some work at noon, will hit back late eve today," said Mrs. Shivach taking those untidy utensils back to the kitchen.

"Don't wait for me tonight, either I'll be late while coming back. Might not be coming back as well. Will inform you," he said and crossed the door.

The heart isn't deficient to trust what is seen.
Wanting ever to forget everything, feeling it a dream.
But it wants to make everything clear, that's unrevealed.

Every other word of such impression is hitting and weakening those beam.

Situations decorated to make themselves critical,
Being normal before time and stayed a lot feasible.
My struggling emotions getting vaporised.
Wanting me to judge the truth behind those thoughts, I repeatedly mesmerised.

Satisfaction Above Desire

Mind flowing in others instructed way. Mark reached the site, struggling heavy bound traffic over its way. Mark lost in that silence spread over library space, forgetting to depart on specified timing. Toiling to strike short cut way through "Purani Delhi". Cornered in traffic, Mark got at first stuck behind a vegetable seller lugging.

"Could you please carry your things away in one go," said Mark honking his car stuck in an alleyway next to the market place.

"Can't you see how they are spread out," said vegetable seller named Ashish.

"I can see it, but if you want to carry them along then why you can't carry them in more quantity and dump into your trolly? Why only single one at a time," asked Mark waving out half body of the side glass pane.

"You people never understand, see it's time for us to settle our stalls. It's evening time," said carefree Ashish, in his free mode.

"So, how could I care of it. Can't you see you cease traffic, till the time you vacate my way," Mark said in irritation.

"I don't know why you people took this path for passing through," said Ashish, inspecting his tomatoes quality before dumping each onto his trolly.

"What? It's governmental recognised path to pass through. Are you showing your bullying," asked Mark getting out of his car closing its door.

"Why do you panic '*bhai*' help me let's move it together," replied Ashish.

"Why should I?" asked Mark getting extreme ruffled.

"Then see you have to wait. Can you seek anyone here except you from last 15 minutes?"

"No," Mark replied with dazed face giving a look towards the way.

"Yes, No one comes on this way. You are a fool, so wait till the time I'll complete this all," said Ashish.

"Why am arguing with you?" said Mark.

"You would be knowing it. How could I?"

"You are right. I am a fool that's why am doing this," replied Mark opening car frontal door.

"What happened Ashish?" a person standing next to Ashish asked.

"See this guy is affecting my mind to get disturbed. My mind is already disturbed of tonight IPL final," said Ashish.

"You again speculated your money over it?" the person asked.

"That to a bigger amount over "Chennai" win," replied Ashish.

"Change your decision as today 'Mumbai Indians' will be winning by 48 runs," said Mark right after he turned towards after encountering their words.

"How could you know? Even with so exact number," amazed Ashish.

"Yes true, how could I?" Mark slowly murmered.

"Ok. Ok it's your wish, I said what I felt," said Mark before he used the key in the ignition, tuned car to went off. Leaving a stunned face Ashish.

"What happened?" the person standing next to Ashish asked.

"Don't know, why heart wants to get concede is words," said Ashish as Mark receded.

Mark moved to take another alley which also directs towards the way he wanted to. Mark felt smooth to start over, but questions raised inside him aren't settling down over the match result.

"Why that guy was staring at me, had I said scores of any other match," Mark crooned.

"I know I don't watch a cricket match, but I stay updated with the result being a good observer," said Mark, gearing his car, in due of time running heavily.

"What should I'd spoken? I said it right, as its final score. I remember correctly," he said, slight happy recognising finest way over the track he took.

"This glimpse of time travel, will make me mad," said Mark before he trusted breaks heavily to control his accelerated car getting stuck with tempo.

"What happened now?"

"Now why you blocked way?" asked Mark avoiding out his car.

"It's not me, see this hollering person. He made me to stop," said the tempo traveller.

"What you said? Why don't you say, what you did to my bike," said Rahul, the biker whose bike's back indicator was broken with rashes over metal creating after thumping of Tempo over the back of his bike.

"Can't you see, condition you meant of Bike?" asked Mark.

"I got impotent, as he's trying to overtake," said tempo driver.

"And what about those honks and signals I am giving before. Hadn't you gone already aware before of my acceleration?" asked Mark.

"You don't know this is my area, our transportation happens every day by the way," said Tempo driver.

"What you are trying to say by 'This is your area', you can't take the privilege of driving such," screamed Rahul getting enthusiastic with his extreme vexation.

"And what will you do if I did?" said Tempo driver, bonded stepping towards Rahul.

"Let me show you what a person from "Agra" can do," said Rahul as he draws out his punching gloves off his bike sideways attached leather bag.

"Ohh… you both please keep a distance. Let me sort it out," said Mark as he held both avoid physical harm.

"Please, you both sturdy guys, nothing will get out of it," said Mark in the equity of both, keeping his hands over both chests, deterring them come closer.

"Pull him out of my way… right now," said Tempo traveller.

"I know you are an overbearing guy, and why wouldn't I will know such, as had worked with you once in TCS," said Mark with sparkling smile peering Rahul.

"Oh. It's you Mark… Amazing… how could I miss realising you," said Rahul graciously opening his arms to hug Mark.

"How could you have. While being dipped in anger, same like before. Myself either noticed you, by the way, you took the name of your place 'Agra' and punching gloves that you still keep in your bike bagging," said Mark while helping him to pick up his bike.

"'*Arey,*' I wanted to spray substantial lesson to this guy," said Rahul.

"If you both have strengthened you memories of belongingness, then can you clear my way," said Tempo driver in arrogance.

"Let me clear this for you now," said Rahul treading towards him picking a brick in anger of road.

"No Rahul , no fight I want … nothing, calm down," screamed Mark keeping hold of his waist with both arms.

"You please vacate this space. Path gone cleared," Mark said Tempo traveller.

"Forget about him, acquitting your mind of such annoyance," said Mark making tempo traveller to pass away.

"I want to witness my jolly 'Rahul Saxena', who sprouts seed of splendid grin in life's around," spoke Mark carrying him along to his car.

"Huh, this bloody exhausted me! I was in a hurry to take mother to the railway station and how this goofy guy hooked me," said Rahul settling down breaths of anger.

"Slacken yourself and have water. My first project's enhancing UX designer," said Mark smirking passing him a water bottle.

"So where you have to drop Aunty?" asked Mark.

"I need to drop her at Railway station, she has to head for 'Allahabad'" , he told.

"Allahabad.... aren't you aware of the news of it?"

"What news? No, I haven't?" replied Rahul.

"Don't let Aunty go today. Haven't you heard the news of communal dispute over 'Allahabad' railway station?" queried Mark.

"No such news came still, Mark. Things that weren't normal had settled down".

"Nay, Nothing settled in peace there. It's visible to me clearly," said Mark with those adrift eyes peering a space steadily.

"Ok, but how can you be so sure? Now don't say that you can see the future as well," asked Rahul with those cheek in a grin.

"I don't know... Really I don't know... How could am getting such beliefs since morning... I am trying to analyse, what is happening with me. But for now you please scrap her travel of today," said Mark looking pleasant towards Rahul.

"That I will. But I wonder, how it arose in you?" asked Rahul.

"I couldn't grasp, as of why such pictures are coming alive to me? Why nothing getting crisp, making me aware?" spoke Mark.

Mental ability becomes unable to solve a cube.

Meant by such questions, whose answers you know but still waiting for a clue.

The time becomes more critical for you when they ask,

How it came and what will you do to prove your task.

Knowing the reason behind what happened, never helps.

You should silent down your tone in present aura to acknowledge, what it tells.

Understanding can be provoked and relation can be built.

But they retain flavour when you sacrifice something over its every field.

You shouldn't imagine anything if you aren't realising the exact thought.

As your versatile imagination will miss abandoning the perfect slot.

You can't walk by just relying on some dreams.

Because life is a lot more than what it seems.

"Let me drop you somewhere?" asked Mark.

"No... I have a bike, it's working fine. Guess some fixes need to be done over it," replied Rahul scrutinising bike functioning by accelerating it, above the stand.

Two things meant Mark to get late over the spot. Where everything bustling quieter with time succeeding to commence. Omament were properly meant till the time Mark reached the stadium. The venue at "Jawahar Lal Nehru stadium," Mark got little confused as which gate he need to park his car. Mark can't even inquire, as people will recognise him and his time will get spared. So with his closed blacked window glass, he struggled to unearth insider way. Somehow those shaded eyes behind black glasses stocked Ritesh passing through.

"Can you tell me, where's 'Mark' performing today?" asked Mark scrolling down his window pane.

"Ohhhhh.... Yea why not. It's our show only, you need to take first right and," said Ritesh before he ceased in between encountering Mark.

"You? Have you seen your phone even once?" screeched Ritesh, with his terrific face of annoyance.

"Oh Man ... It got lost somewhere over the way," replied Mark.

"You hadn't either realist, the pressure am carrying today," said Ritesh.

"Hey come, get seated inside.. let's talk," said Mark.

"You aren't generalising complexity of today's show," said Ritesh, pulled car door.

“Forget everything, just let me know how’s you babies health at present?” asked Mark.

“We admitted him yesterday itself, but I hadn’t told you yet,” replied Ritesh.

“His fever isn’t getting seized off his body and the age he’s into is a point of concern. Doctor asked to take him under observation,” added Ritesh, eyes shun in grief overflown words. Mark faintly listened to all.

“Maa conveyed me about it in the morning, that too when I pinched my questions over her raised concern for you in every word. You said her not to reveal me Why?” Mark.

“Your revere concern is the reason behind. Not wanting to smash your rhythm for our show today,” replied Ritesh putting his palm over his shoulder.

“And you enhancing work for a charity of cancer children’s leaving your child struggling,” said Mark gaping frontal way, breezing words in his respect.

“No…!!!! No you needless worrying ‘*Veena*’ is there with him to take care”.

“She came back from her Dubai campaign?” asked Mark wiping his wet gone eyes, hiding them behind while putting on black eyeglasses.

“Yes… She came a day before.”

“Work you and Veena’s NGO are doing for humanities is unbeatable by any other devotion a person can generate for this society,” said Mark before heading onto Ritesh dictated way.

“Eyes wanting to seek your baby ‘*Farhan*’ getting in good health soon,” said Mark.

“Wish your words come out to be true.”

“He’ll be fine before the day ends, you’ll encounter it. As I can see him happily playing in my lap,” said Mark parking the car.

“Sayoni needs to direct your dance troop in your absence. She’s the one who managed everything till now,” said Ritesh, moving out of the car.

"She's a superhero for me ever. She hits the place like a miracle, where my heart requires her," replied Mark, locking the car.

"Now you're guiding me the way?" asked Ritesh, whose hand is carried by Mark walking ahead.

"You know I remember everything, it just I need support at the start. Man, I had performed in this stage many times before as well. You know it," replied Mark, spinning facing Ritesh while walking.

"Great! Take the ownership as it's you only, who have to set up the show," giggled Ritesh.

"Am aware, my brother. Just don't burn the fire of time underneath my feet," said Mark heading soared confident face.

They broke their way: Mark went on connecting with today's performing team. Ritesh got inclined probing fitment of all at the administration level. Mark already pulled out Ritesh's stress of his brain. That craze in the environment seems anew sprout bump into Mark's presence over indoor practice auditorium.

"Are we performing indoor?" queried Mark, pulling auditorium balcony gate.

Mark's troupe practising inside got appalled for a second the way that voice had resonated inside whole surrounding. Mark carcass came out in light becoming visible to everyone staring up towards the balcony.

"Hey keep on practising, we don't have time," said Mark as he descends stairs.

"Good to see you have a concern for time," said Sayoni perceiving up towards Mark.

"Is this booked of us only?" he asked, checking something in his bag.

"It's a practising place given by Stadium authority. We are here since 12:00 noon and you came at what time you just check," Sayoni with her worn-out voice after practising from hours.

"You had already saved me, I know," said Mark trying to come down straight from balcony to ground hall.

"There is no way to come, you have to go back to pick outer stairs for entering this floor," said Sayoni, signing everyone to not distract and keep on practising.

"I don't think I have to go back for reaching where I want," said Mark before he jumped from his heighten place railing towards the base wooden floor of the auditorium.

"See, how easy it is," said Mark to all frightened faces astonished gazing what Mark just did.

Everyone's weary opened mouth and stretched eyes hadn't realised yet of what he actually did. He jumped off the balcony, at a height of 30 feet.

"This shows your tenacity, what you are actually perturbed for today's show," said Sayoni coming closer Mark, pointing her finger over chest turning into his eyes.

"What? What? What happened," asked Mark with fumbling tone. Getting pushed back step through her pressured point.

"You are asking what happened, do you really understand how much everyone here cares for you. And you dismissed someone without even informing one," she asked slowly carrying annoyance in her voice and scrubbing teeth of anger.

"Sorry... really sorry, can't you see in my eyes," Mark pleased.

"What is this that you did just? Anything could have happened," she asked before a voice from backside came, fitful's their eyes interaction.

"Ma'am do we have to carry these," a girl from Mark troupe asked Sayoni speaking louder lugging buckeye of flower in her hand.

"See, you meant my people yours already," said Mark with a smile, bending back ahead peering Sayoni's eyes.

"Yes, this would be for our third song," said Sayoni coming towards the team.

"What would be for our first song? please tell that Ma'am," asked Mark taking the sprint from his place and coming upfront Sayoni, ferrying such cherish face spelt with fun and smile.

"Mark move, we don't have time for these," said Sayoni pushing

Mark bit right.

"Hey… Hey …listen dear, see how much you got drawn. You need to rest now," he said.

"So you will take care of it?" she asked.

"Yes I came now, don't worry I'll take care of it," he said putting his hand across her face with a feeling of affection in his eyes.

"But you have to perform today with me," he said Sayoni, whose picking her towel and bag to step towards restroom.

"What? No, Mark, I was here to make your team groomed. It's only in your absence to help you," she said with a staggered face.

"Please don't deny. I really need you. You'll add spark to my show," he requested.

"I have no words for such weird expression you make," she said confronting the insipid gone face of Mark.

"Your performance will sway like ever. What are you worried off?"

"Wanted you to perform with me, Everything doesn't enclose reasoning," he said.

"Ok…could you please be silent for some seconds," she said putting her bag down.

"Will perform with you," she said embracing grin on her cheeks, as she picks her bag again.

Sayoni spoke and moved towards the restroom. Mark interacted with his members and performed over some songs of the day. Mark ordered the whole show. He met with other well known musician and singers who were invited to perform in mid of their performances. He couldn't let this event fall at random. Whatever awareness and contribution they want from it. He meant it to come out with the same receipt. Mark spent precise but quality time with all performers of today's show. Accomplishing more comfortable feel for everybody at the place, before the show took it to lead. Being at mid of his interplay, a voice stood from the back, took off his heed.

"Plum you reciprocated with all. It's vital as well," said Ritesh nearing Mark from auditorium backside door.

"Aah… you here, how's everything conducting below?" asked Mark.

"All established and else you came, so things will work out towards there excellence surely," said Ritesh, smirking shaking hand with all invitees artist sitting around Mark.

"You have to initiate event Mark, with your '*hello*' to the crowd that ever blaze flicker," said Ritesh as he darts behind moving Mark.

"What? You never conveyed it?" asked Mark.

"I told you nah, that though we have '*anchor*' you have to take care of it," insisted Ritesh.

"I never discern, how you make such things. When I just wanted to centralise on my performance," said Mark picking up his water bottle from the floor.

They said nothing after to each other. Ritesh sat across the wooden stairs of auditorium coping Mark, keeping his hand curling around his shoulder. He sipped water from his bottle very intensely. Feeling how his words could start this show with a boom. Mark peering in front with those musing eyes. Ritesh saw his watch twice.

"Come, let's move," said Mark, abruptly raising of his place, giving his hand for Ritesh to stand.

"What happen?" asked mulled Ritesh.

"Nothing, Don't you have to start the show," replied Mark calling his dance troupe nearer with his hands.

"So?" asked Ritesh.

"Hey, don't hassle I will be joining you over our first performance, as soon I generate spirit in the crowd and broken ice by starting the show," said Mark to his troupe people.

"Yes, it's either required. As many people had come here to see you," a guy from his Team spoken passing smile.

"See, I also said to you," added Ritesh.

They moved out towards the outdoor stage, where people started entering padding the empty ground. Everyone getting engrossed over discrete food stalls available from every state, settled across corners of the whole ground. Some took place over a bench, some found meandering to be the best option. Spread savour over faces, while looking decoration meant at every specific place of ground can be witnessed fair. Relish produced over the arrangement was amazing. Swings settled for children's after every small defined space. Making aura to revere through their squeals.

Everyone's building enthusiasm whether it's a couple, family, friends or any organisation people came to visit. Light rolling music had added rosiness into the aura. Mark and Ritesh climbed at the backstage for letting show get institute any minute. A sound stood out of working staff :

"What an arrangement they had. Am really glad over its organiser's," a person said.

"See, it's all your efforts that's held out of every mouth," said Mark, putting Ritesh shirt collar up.

"Oh… please, just check mike voice level. Is it good for you?"

Eventual silence in the crowd reported, right before the second Mark placed his finger over the mike. Mark scrubbed his finger and stroking mike twice spoke to test the voice level over it. Everyone attention was directed towards the stage.

"See, you haven't yet started and craze sprouted with your even small whistle," said Ritesh and Mark took his entry over the stage with his same giant word of greet.

"*Halo…. Everyone out there!*"

"Hope you wouldn't have waited for long and we started on time…." shouted Mark.

"Yes," a big joyous sound reported from the crowd.

"I would like to produce my honour, to every single person present over here. As we all had gathered for a helping concern. I love to see these colourful humanities of all good-hearted people came today," said Mark in heavy pitch.

"I wouldn't count the number of devotees for the cause today.

As this alignment of all politicians and celebrities, will make you realise that what it means to Indians when it comes to charity," yelled Mark, picking a glass of water.

"Hope you can see this water filled glass in my hand. You can get any colour decorated in its inside out, but only till the time this is in collective mode. Once I spell this to the ground and its every single drop moves on its desired way. Nothing gets left after that. Same like the way we are like garden and can do everything till the time we are together. Once we got distributed, the achievement, grace, charm which we meant, broke into pieces," said Mark, emptying the glass over ground.

"Love everyone provides me, is something for me that I am unable to interpret. It ever ignites my spirit to give away my best performance ever to you," said Mark asking Ritesh from the corner of his eyes to call someone, whom he could hand over.

Running time with running words of Mark. He was trying hard for not letting such treasures spread a smile over faces to break down. Whatever he transmits touches people excited mood well. Mark constantly peering helpless Ritesh face, whose trying to find today's anchor. Mark gave a look to his watch and enlightened the crowd towards the time of first performance. Lastly when no one came. He implicated crowd and left stage settling mike ahead of the piano person.

Ritesh settled lights over the stage to go dim for seconds. Till the performers capture stage. From the time Mark left the stage and till dancer didn't come, Ritesh's breath remained blocked.

"I hope everything goes the way it should. I wish Mark succeed proving his perfection, today either," crooned Ritesh in dread.

Show evoked already, as after all background dancers Sayoni have to lead again in Mark's absence. She entered to join the group as lyrics started. Their moves, coordination and steps, all clutching crowd love. But everyone eyes seems to be waiting for Mark.

"Where is Mark in this song, so he's not performing," a person from the crowd said to others. After hearing this gossip in the crowd standing next to them, Ritesh either started getting goosebumps of something wrong to happen. He straight away went to backyard standing vanity van.

"Where is he? his presence is required," crooned Sayoni with her face in vexation while performing.

"Why he's not coming," murmered Sayoni with a stressed face peering repeated back over stage entrance.

"Don't worry Ma'am, we will manage somehow," girls said while dancing at the back of her.

"Nothing will be managed. Can't he see people want him," said Sayoni earning impatience.

"He's not even here, where is he?" said Ritesh getting depressed, viewing his empty vanity van.

"Why he does like that? Things will spoil if he didn't came," said Sayoni staring through the corner of his eyes with hope towards entry space over back.

"What would happen now," said Ritesh as he came into crowd peering over the stage.

Soon light flashed from the back stage with a giant explode in heed of all. Everyone stuck noticing a being shoot out of it, landing over the stage. Everyone's feet stopped over letting only music on. Everyone left whatever they are having in the third hand. And they stood up on feet turning to notice the person just landed.

"What's this now?" said Ritesh.

"My show hitherto on its verge to get spoiled. And now this," screamed Ritesh hiding his face with his both palm.

With the other beat and afresh start of the song title track. That person raised of his place, stepping ahead with his crossed feet, snapping fingers. Giant howl over the crowd evoked. Forging Ritesh to let off his hand from the face with slowly dispersing grin.

"Woah," crowd hollered pushing their hands up in the sky.

"He'll never change," said Sayoni with that beam of happiness evoking over her twinkling cheeks.

"Last start," said Mark propelling Sayoni, passing her beckon.

"Thanks Mark," said Ritesh blowing air in between of his joined hand touching lips.

"Come up guys let's show our natural colour," said Mark holding the hand of Sayoni with his one hand and others asking troupe to join them with beats.

All performance ahead happened in their specific order. Mark managed everything very pleasantly tacking good care of everyone's interest, whoever came as a guest today.

Ecstatic flowing music and all sophisticated arrangement around the courtyard, thrilled invitees desire. The move away of corporate leaders, with a relish on their face. Generating big contribution towards the NGO's funding had already settled down the aim of event occurrence. Mark phenomenal performance and unparalleled anchoring had flue of everyone shoo. Those reconciling breeze with their gratification, enlighten eyes of Ritesh with good hopes. Mark settled the show and announced the last performance of the day. The performance of Sufi singer "*Harshdeep Kaur*". The time she started that outflowing love of people took its lead and everyone flew over its rhythm. Mark rapped his work over the stage, rushing to his vanity van. Ritesh sitting inside, encountering the show with his eyes filled with tears.

"What happened, dear? Is something I missed in the show?" asked Mark wiping out his eyes.

"No my dear… please don't say that. You already accomplished my and many others dream from today's show," said Mark, putting his hand over his shoulder.

"Ok forget that, first pick up your phone it's ringing inside your pocket," said Mark.

"Yeah let me," said Ritesh wiping his left tears before picking.

"Hello… Ritesh," said Veena (His wife) from another side of the call.

"Yes Veena, what happened? Is everything Ok?" asked Ritesh being frightened and afraid.

"Yes, everything's alright. I felt I should tell you that our baby is fine now. The doctor even allowed to take him home," said Veena.

"Aah… I can't disperse my pleasure," said Ritesh.

"I understand. And you don't hustle to come here now. Am taking him along to home, you came there directly after winding your show," said Veena, her last words before she hanged.

"You worked as an angel to my life today. Everything… everything had settled down Mark… Everything," said Ritesh folding hand with tears in eyes upfront Mark.

"Hey please… Please don't do like this to me… I did nothing," said Mark and a voice stood Mark ear, someone's calling him.

"And if you want to know more about what I did. You can ask from Sayoni standing outside," said Mark spreading grin while opening vanity van's door, stepping on the ground.

"Why you want my blood pressure to go higher every time, Mark," said Sayoni.

"So that I could notice those twinkling cheeks over you," giggling Mark.

"We did it Mark and that too successfully. You should have seen their face while moving out. What an impression you kept on everyone," said Sayoni rubbing black streak over his forehead with her scarf.

"Huh… what happened?" asked Mark.

"Just Wait… something is there, yes it's gone now," she replied.

"What was it?" he asked.

"You might have not wondered and you painted your head," she replied looking precisely over his head and ended giggling.

"See your fingers, it came from those," she said looking down towards his hands.

"From where it came? Shit... I spoiled my jeans as well," he said gazing for water around.

"Nothing you'll find here. Use this scarf to wipe it from your hands at least," she said removing scarf off her shoulder, handing over to him.

"I painted this on you when you hadn't given concern to me crossing from my front," a voice came from right-sided alley.

"Tamanna... she is here only... Tamanna... are you there?" he asked being furious, acknowledging her voice.

"Yes... I was there, it's just you hadn't seen me, being messed in your work," said Tamanna.

"I am really not even wondered that you'll be coming here," he said handing scarf back Sayoni, stepping closer to her.

"So what, if you aren't able to come for my show... I can come to yours," she said checking her phone.

"Where is your phone?" asked Tamanna.

"I lost it," he replied.

"Like always," she added.

"Hey forget it, tell me how was your fashion show went through?" asked Mark.

"Passed well, I rapped it early to reach here," she said retaining spark encountered by Mark in her eyes.

"Was calling you as I reached here, But wasn't reachable," she said.

"Hey, you guys get settle inside vanity and talk, I just make sure that theirs no hassle for artists," said Sayoni.

"Either I need to go for it, wait," said Mark picking up his jacket kept on the first seat of the van.

"You don't have to panic now, I'll look into it," said Sayoni.

"Are you sure?" asked Mark.

"Perfectly Sure," replied Sayoni with her bowed head and closed eyes.

"Come Tamanna, let's get in," said Mark as Sayoni left the space.

"Am not coming anywhere Mark, you need to come with me now," she replied bearing anger in her eyes, with a brief smile on her face.

"What's gone wrong, can you tell me? Nothing seems to be good with you from the time you came," asked Mark spelling out his every word with breaks, clearer and slowly exhibiting his concern.

"I want you to be with me tonight, that's it," said Tamanna like she crushed all cheering emotion together off her face.

"That's not what am asking you. My concern is the way you're pretending".

"Am pretending? pretending what Mark?" she screamed.

"Ok wait, you want us to go together nah .. we'll go .. would that suffice you?" he asked holding her arms with his those stretched eyebrows.

"But tonight the team asked my presence for a while with them over the party. At least, I must inform Sayoni about it," crooned Mark checking his pocket.

"Looking something you'd already lost," she said putting her hand carrying phone ahead towards Mark.

"How can I use your phone," Mark murmered.

"What? You said anything," asked Tamanna with her heavier going voice gazing Mark's confused face.

"Why are you reacting such today?," asked Mark peering towards her unpredictable face in queer.

"Don't you feel, that you should be punished for all you did today," said Tamanna.

"You really feel bad still?" asked Mark packing bag.

"You didn't come to my show Mark," she said in anger.

"Opss, what happened to you dear, you don't seem to be good," said Mark coming closer toeing her hair nod back with his one hand and other sliding finger over her cheeks.

"See your body is burning ... is it fever, let me see," said Mark holding her shoulder tighter enough and pulling her closer over his chest.

"You just come with me. It's what I want," she whispered with her lips closer to his ears.

"Aah... will go together.. don't you worry," said Mark putting her face clubbed in between his palms and his every staring into her colour changing eyes.

"You are looking so beautiful today that your eyes reflection adverting in various forms to me," said Mark kissing her forehead.

"Come where you wanna take me," said Mark holding her hand, giving her inclination to follow.

"I wanted to walk over the sky with you," she said and carried him along towards parking.

"Why she's reacting such today, discovering someone else in her," he crooned rubbing the head with fingers.

"I'll carry my one," said Mark poignant towards his car.

"Leave it here itself, let me drive for you," she said grabbing his right wrist, staring at his feet walking away.

"Well Miss, as you wish," he said pretending placid reaction.

"No need to tie seat belt, you'll fly safe tonight," said Tamanna with intrinsic reaction sitting on the driver seat.

"I never felt before, that I'll see you such ....," Mark voice stopped as he gazed in the rear mirror.

"Carry on Mark, for what you stopped speaking? say about my beauty," she said laughing pulling car in high acceleration.

"What's that over the mirror, she's the one I saw in my dream," crooned Mark with those pent up breaths.

"No ... no .. have I lost you ... is it true? no, how it could be," said Mark within, with those discomfort tears, covered eye curvature.

"Say that quote of yours once," she said smiling giving a look facing towards him.

"Which... which one?" said Mark, pelting up his depressed fumbling tone.

Tamanna said "That one you once said as :

The first wish wouldn't be you.
Last wish wouldn't be you.
Life will be lived in between of this passage.
Where you say something and I keep on listening to you.

"What are you scared of?" she asked hastening car wheels over the road, beating every vehicle they encountered.

"The way it's running, you never liked this sort of driving?" he asked being baffled.

"This you could have asked another way as well. Why are you sweating? Should I lower down the temperature?" she said continuing her uninterrupted smile.

"No, it's completely fine," he replied.

"What she wants to do," crooned Mark, staring out of side glass pane.

"See we landed at our home. I said you of having smooth flight tonight," she said pressing brake heavily.

"How come? We were just over the bridge, 20 km away from here," said Mark stunned looking outside towards her peacefully settled home, with fine lamps glowing green grass of the garden. Enlightening the track that's moving towards the entrance door.

"Sometimes things happen in this world without one's knowledge," said Tamanna abruptly moved out and stepped semi circling car from the front towards Mark's door.

"Do all that I had seen last night actually happened?" Mark whispered with humming sound sitting inside car noticing her moves.

"Come my honourable, house is in wait of you," she said as she open Mark's door.

"Why everything is weird?" Mark murmered, getting out.

"You said something?" she asked.

"No I didn't," he replied.

"Don't get bewildered, Nothing is creepy," she said as she turned towards her home to walk.

"Everything is happening in accordance with nature's need ," she said.

"And what actually nature wants?" asked Mark, senile face and hypnotised feet following her way.

"It wants just me and you," she said turning abruptly with intense craving on her face, holding his collar and pulling his face to touch her lips.

"Hey wait... your parents could see us," he said with those shivering hands.

"No one is there.. the house is abandon of any human except you," she said and turned to pull him over her back though entangling finger in his pocket.

"Human except me... what it means?" crooned Mark while getting back dragged.

"Lay down ... let me take shower," she said trusting to Mark over big giant couch lying in the living room.

"What was that such a force," he said making himself stable after bearing such push.

"Aaaahhhhh my hair, they get ever entwine," said Tammana while opening her hair nod in front of giant mirror tryout.

"Mark come, help me with it?" she asked.

"Why water tap of your bathroom left opened. Even if the tub is filled What is that?" said Mark as he gazed aside opened bathroom door, where water flowing out of tub containing red colour while the tap is passing bleached water to it.

"Forget it, the concern of my hair, that needs the touch of your prosperous fingers to get untangled," she said before heaved Mark with an unseen impetus towards to come and club her body tighter.

"The smell I get when your breaths are such close to mine makes me unhinged," she said taking up intense breath, whirling her neck in its sensation.

"But ....but what's this Tamanna, how you did it. Am dragged towards you from my place," he said menacing with her stunning face and left opened mouth.

"Why you're winning flexed about unfounded things? Come put your cheek over my shoulder," she said being maudlin in her sensational desires, with his closed eyes face pushing head over her shoulder.

Those emotions she's willing to react were all beyond Mark's imaginary.

Getting completely dipped in her unknown covet of tragedy.

She developed an unknown stir of her desires.

He was confused to reply to her back, who previously admires.

Her willingness coming alive, as she's aware of her last day.

Why she isn't worried about such thing without whom before she can't stay.

Might with my reactions, she noticed things getting revealed, she tried to preserve.

Though she provoked her magic building over me to get something, that she meant herself to deserve.

Wearing saree 'black in colour', handling its flap every other second has already shown a flavour to Mark. A Desire she to wear it, being with him once. Her high heel welly over her feet, were other thing making him realise of her provocative wish.

"She can't wear these today. As she said to wear it on our coming special day," crooned Mark muddled with his beliefs.

"Why she hadn't asked me for it and saree in black with her black lipstick? Why am unable to answer my questions?" Mark got baffled, as he took off his chin lying above her shoulder and turned behind.

"What happened to you? Can't you smell this enviro flavour shouting to get us aligned," she said piercing her face into mirror slithering her fingernail overbuild wrinkles below her eyes.

"Am not feeling good. I feel we should meet tomorrow," he replied.

"Or you don't like me?" she asked yet gazing her face in the mirror.

"What are you saying?" he said swelling his last word in his lower tone of shivering lips in dismay, as he turned to face Tamanna.

"She's not her, am talking to a spirit. I felt it right," crooned Mark, as he adorns her actual glimpse over the mirror. Slowed down his breath. Tiding his fallen hair over the face to settle above with hand, while his face gazing towards with stunned eyes. He Wiped sweat of scare developed above his upper lip.

“Can I know the reason behind your silence, over my question?” her spirit in beam tone.

“Aren't you getting me, Mark?” she shouted in a couple of seconds ogling his eyes.

“I am ... I am, was wondering how could you even feel to raise such questions,” he replied getting destitute, removing the lid of glass filled with water kept over stool aside.

“Yea.. have water at first. You jumped a lot on stage today,” she said stepping toward kitchen turning her face against with smirk.

“You doesn't pretend to be happy, about my today's show?” asked Mark swiftly delivering his every word with break bending little heeding her away going steps.

“Where're her feet? only her heels are discernible,” he murmered above his hassled body feeling uneasy to spare even a second here.

“Let me lock the door, else it would come out,” she said bolting the door of her kitchen next to the bathroom.

“What's there inside? Why such sound of birds chirping is coming out from it?” he asked placing water glass back over the stool.

“Why you're so concerned about it, you should be concerned of answering me only,” her spirit replied in cruel reaction coming closer ogling Mark.

“Are you scared?” she asked sliding her finger over his cheeks, pulling his belt nod tighter, making his body get attached to her.

“What's happening to me, even after knowing it as her essence,” crooned Mark with his hand responding by holding her tight off back.

“Get into me the way you want. My body wants to feel every touch of yours,” she muttered next to his ear, removing strap of saree covering her shoulder.

“Am not in my control, my body seems spellbound ,” said Mark, as he gazed down, hypnotised by the swirling tide.

"I want to be inside you, cuddle me tighter," she said sliding her hand from his back towards his hips.

"Your fragrance getting mixed in my soul," he said pulling her hair back tightly to stare her face.

"I wanted to make this night with you," she said.

"So do you wore the one that you said once to do?" Mark asked with his intense eyes turning on before his lips slide over her neck to reach her ear and she whispers.

"My desires can't get crushed by anyone," her spirit said holding his hand carrying him towards the bedroom.

Settling him over place corner of the bed, like a toy in her control. Mark eyes couldn't realise anything beyond craving evoked inside him of lust. Her sensual desire of erotism, dropping off her moves. Such sexual agony and those intermitted moves, displaying Tamanna's spirit desire to write an unwritten chapter. Her spelt over mood and that climatic affection she builds across, already started vocalising her voice. Conceding her to achieve what she wants. Accrediting her to keep dots wherever she wants. Her leg moves and the way of setting lights to leave the room. Forging her passionate face to come out with a hidden desire behind intoxicant eyes. Studying Mark, walking towards him dismantling her cloths. Mark's spilt eyes with those desperation blue. Mark's tollway working reaction. One saying to get blended in her arms and other in the aphorism of staying away.

She kept on her favourite song of light music, that's spreading sensuality.

Desiring to bring output, that's compatible with her desire in equality.

She doesn't want to shout, prefer whispering in the ear.

But this time she wants to wear her wills, making all in fear.

Both souls had inclined their desire, dipping inside one another.

Wanting to check colour they left, which they wanted to be on their feathers.

Those siding fingers, over a hand of others.

Wanting it to get hold of it, to start flowing out their's intention further.

Those emotions aren't governed through one-sided wave.
They both crossed boundaries, becoming single body one cage.

"Which one will you take," said Tamanna opening drawer flooded of flavoured wines.

"One you'll be having," said Mark staring at her carrying void face.

"Don't flow such in my mind, let me stream you" she said drenching both glasses equally.

"Can you make me drink this," she said handing her glass to Mark, putting her body to bend back with face peering roof.

"Your hair are wanting my hand to titillate them," said Mark as he dropped sip by sip wine to get into mouth crossing her lips.

"Press them harder, they want to get pulled," she said, unfastening the glass, pulling him closer towing his collar.

"Bring down your shirt," she said in a cleft of the studs of his shirt one after the other.

Laying him down and getting above. Those hands away of chagrin, taking all they dreamed. Words had stopped like short breaths pandemics their place. Body needs are wanting to picture the aura as beautiful, being specific what they taste.

Those rapid moves of body siding over one another. Increased temperature disbursed through their body into the surrounding of each other. That glimpse of Tamanna and again the remembrance of her being spirit, getting raised and settled in his soul. Like something isn't allowing his mind to open its door.

"Hug me tighter, Mark," she said above him, smelling deep through his neck.

He clubbed her tighter, through the waist.

Her hands had got settled to hold his base.

Pressing each other harder, to tear down the complete wall in between.

That intense reaction had meant their moves over each other body, to go lean.

Removing clothes from each other body, wrapped like feathers.

Their arms getting open to explore inside the sky of one another.

It's meant to become smoother, as time helped their motion to become dense.

Which is hard to breakdown, that spirit they enlighten in between to go immense.

The flow of one's breath into others, in dim light, generated love in many form.

Like their taste of each other lips, became uniform.

"**It feels so right when you hug me so tight**," she said lying with Mark on the bed, covered with sleek blanket above.

"Hug me until I smell like you," he said dipping same in her sensual sensation.

"I know… I'll never have enough of you .. never," she said putting his face in front of her for a second.

"Cover me with you. I want the line between us to flue," he said pain in her last line.

That chemistry they created, build jumping limits reaching across.

They left loose inside each other arms, making a cross.

Their body hanged over others, to let other control.

The way they shredded from bed to floor.

Mark said one last liner before he got dozed off :

"I love you yesterday, I love you still. I always have and always will."

"Yesterday 9"

"I would have killed you if you haven't said that," said Tamanna getting into her eerie spirit look. Reacting ghastly and shouted loudly beating her breast with a tight formed fist.

The house had all groomed into an appalling look. With her louder screams, after Mark went unconscious. Those haze coming inside, following her tone.

It went darker, as the moon is also imperceptible today to spray light from the opened window of this dark room.

Devotion

"Without Heart's Awareness"

New day arose with its brief yawn before stepping into the room. Messed room with scattered cloths over to floor with broken veils of their places. Some veils hanging partly over a rod and others detached completely, whose formerly covering the wall. Those tidy white pillows are now away from their cushions. Their scraps of cotton inside came out, spelt over the entire room. Inspiring with air drift, closed glass pane whose window got broken yesterday. The third person couldn't conjecture except both, of what stumbled inside the bedroom last night. That bird which came every day and sat outside the window grill next to her bed. That fowl had today and sat after encountering Tamanna's incessant sleep. The fowl gazed inside with fierce, wondering another person she found with her inside the first time after a whole year. Fowl hit her beak repeatedly over a glass in a mean to make her aware of its appearance. But today it was not Tamanna who woke up, it's Mark keeping his body up over his base. He wakes rubbing his eyes, starred this bird, poring him from outside.

"What was that?" said Mark, as he stood up off his place, knocking window the same way like that little bird.

He's amazed to see with a smirk upon his face noticing the same count of repeated knocks that birds doing after every attempt to Mark. Mark stood still right in front of the glass not letting bird see Tamanna. This cute fowl stepped right faster with her tinny feats to wake Tamanna, letting her aware of her presence.

"What if, I don't allow you to let her awake?" asked Mark keeping grin over cheeks

Creeps of bird started towards Mark, letting her do what she wants. Mark doesn't know why he's denying Tamanna's sleep get disturbed. Enacting to silence bird, with his pleasing face keeping a finger on his lips.

"Please allow me to talk once with her," Mark heard, noticing bird flapping lips.

"You can speak like us?" he asked being perplexed, putting noise, touching the glass in front of the bird.

"Yes, I do. Now you please let me see her," the bird said.

"Why are you panicking such? if you see her every day"

"She was captured by some spirit yesterday and today's her last day over this earth," the bird said bowing her neck up and down.

"Huh… who are you? How you know it all?" he asked with a stunned face.

"Are you God's send angel?" Mark added to ask.

"Don't waste my time, she's rid of black spirit present, I want to meet her," the bird said.

"But who are you actually, please convey," asked Mark.

"You already went against nature's law. Breaking what had written already," the bird said and flue away into the sky getting disappear inside those white clouds.

Time Mark achieves realisation joining one fact to others. Mark got informed about a factor of clarity, that got cancelled before and how he boarded Time Machine to get back into his past. Mark eyes drenched with water, as he felt of Sayoni. Not able to conclude his vain. Glimpsing those picture of her getting submerged inside wall kept alive in front of his eyes. He broke from the centre and astray even the last drop of energy to stand. Dumped over the floor, with crossed legs, both elbow on knees and face kept above both hands forming a fist. Shouting out of tears scrolling over his cheeks.

"Everything ruthless happened and my memory and vision left with broken terms," said Mark.

"How could I save everything from her evil spirit? How could I?"

Mark added.

"The bird said that she's away of her spirit now," he said gaping her innocent sleepy face holding pillow underneath the face.

"I don't know why such happened but will secure your life to stay along," said Mark after he came and sat next to her head and scrolled his hand gently over her hair.

"I can't go broken, I'll firm everything for which I started," said Mark wiping tears.

He starred her virtuous face.
Sewing all those happy moments they spared over a certain place.
His eyes lighten to get her wake and hug him tighter.
Letting her know that if she's away of his life, nothing would stay lighter.
Trying to strengthen his belief of getting back in control everything.
He knows he needs to fight with time to bring back many-things.
He wants to portrait the strength of his walls.
Those through which he'll handle all disaster without getting fall.

The time Mark's eyes were lost in sliding his fingers over Tamanna's face with his again gone wet eyes. Tamanna's phone ranged.

"Aah… It's Tamanna's phone bell, where she kept?" he said, scrolling his eyes round finding cell.

"Yea… that drawer," he said pointing, walking towards the drawer.

Mark ragged himself faster and as he opened the drawer and picked the phone. He heard

"Mark….. Mark … is Mark there? Are you listening?" said Priyanka "Colleague and friend of Sayoni" the other side.

"Yes I am," said Mark raising his eyes towards clock showing 08:00 AM.

"Priyanka here," she said.

"Your phone isn't reachable, so tried calling Tamanna to know about," she said.

"Yea….. listening speak up, you aren't sounding prosperous"

"Yea… yeah, Priyanka says… why you aren't speaking?" Mark repeated.

"Are you fine? Mark," she asked.

"Yes … yes I am, please let me know, is everything fine with Sayoni?" asked Mark in annoyance.

"Nothing seems adequate, the way you sound. Any trouble?" she asked with pent up voice.

"Tell me how come you realised the concern would be of Sayoni? You react so different Mark, I don't know you realise it or not," she said, the time Mark settled himself calm, having a glass of water abruptly.

"Ok… Ok .. I was in mid of something, though you noticed inconvenience in my voice," he said being tepid over his words.

"She stood panic, as she called me. Due to some moneylender had called her and tortured repaying away money that her father took many years before for his business," she told with agitated voice.

"What? And she never conveyed such to me," said Mark frightened.

"Yes, either I got its awareness today itself when she called and conveyed. Never seen her such anxious before. This money lender is one biggest gangster and he harassed intimidate for sexually exploiting her and small sister," she said all that in one breath and halted noticing Marks silence for a couple of seconds.

"How could he speak such to her," said Mark carrying heavy vexation.

"They said to come to her house and will be coming anytime," she replied.

"Nothing will happen to her. I know what I have to do," said Mark before call hanged with rising resentment on his face.

"I have to save this from happening, before any other I want to."

"I know what and how I have to deal with it," said Mark wearing shoes settling himself over a corner of the bed.

Left in seconds, carrying his wallet. With jacket lying over his shoulder. Picking up Tamanna's car key he looked towards her face once and said.

"Nothing will happen I will secure everything either if I have to place my life on a stake,"

said before he ran towards the exit. Getting off from bedroom, reaching living room and then to the exit gate, slipping over the silky carpet lying across the door. He meant him safe by holding the ankle of the door before his eyes affirm the bird again. Crossing his face kept out of the door while the body was still in. Eyes gently noticing bird passing across, turning towards him like apprise her said words.

Mark felt a very strong impression of her again due to flashes of her last word "You are going against the law of this nature. You can't break what had written already". Mark stood abruptly, in favour of breaking questionnaire iceberg building inside. Bird flue passing through promoting her impression in his eyes once.

"Wait, wait.... You can't go away like that," shouted Mark.

"Yes am not doing anything wrong, I don't have to scared off," said Mark buffing his jeans after stabilising himself to stand over his feet.

Nothing got cleared yet,

What those intentions trying to do? What actually they meant.

Efforts are floating bidirectional, wanting to secure its both end.

One should be settled, before the other empower making you to bend.

Boasted with power, sparkling his energy.

He wants to secure lives of both the poles that were source of this energy.

With complete hope of not giving up, tracking above bigger going life cracks.

He meant his car to paddle faster over every tracks.
What those burning heat of sun could have told him, that he told himself.
Without caring about what he lost, he asked every breath to strengthen themselves.
He doesn't want to leave any question unanswered asked by his soul.
Finding whose answer he even silenced his desire, before opening a new door.
Every facet he faced over the way, meant him to realise what bad can happen.
And he spared himself sharply from those, those tried making him fallen.

"Noooo... I can't stop by this," said Mark hitting hard his hand over staring. The time he got stuck in a traffic jam over the road.

"I can't handle it anyway, it seems longer," he said opening car door, stood over it to gaze the reason of this uncertain blockage.

Mark left his car there itself, instituting running over foot tracks. Carrying anxiety to reach early, he crossed multiple streets running altogether. Touching tracks directed towards her home, body revealing desire. The crowd he crossed stood still being amazed of the way he's running. With jacket sailing out in the air like wings, below his conscious desperate face. He reached her colony, striding over alley which ends over her home's door. Mark took a heavy breath before he started to shoot left alleyway of around a hundred metres. He ran without nurturing of blood coming out of his knees, that he stroke over a pole in mid of way while running stupefied. Blood covered his half jeans of the right leg, shaded with red in colour. His eyes were just speculating to spot Sayoni. Asking her the reason for not letting him know about all this. Mark gazed big sized hooligans sitting outside her house. These monster glimpse people encountering Mark coming towards. Their eyes kept staring Mark, he avoided them raised a hand to knock the door.

"Mark you ... how come?," queried Sayoni opening the door

before Mark knocks it up.

“I saw you running towards, through an upstair window and I ran below to acknowledge what happened,” said Sayoni pulling him inside locking door over his back.

“What’s this? asking me of what happened, without telling me the truth,” said Mark with tensed liners over his forehead.

“Thanks Mark you came, I was feeling highly solitude and fearsome,” said Sayoni holding Mark tight in her arms.

“They are still noticing you, though I reacted such,” she said cuddling him tighter, keeping her face above right shoulder.

“Who are these? How can they stand outside house such,” asked Mark.

“I don’t know, I wasn’t having an idea that they will jump to my home with such stubbornness”.

“What? Means you are enduring it in past and never conveyed me?,” he asked, keeping her face upfront to stare in between his hands.

“Life isn’t that simple Mark,” she said snatching, turning opposite.

“You could have at least talked to me over it,” he said stepping behind Sayoni pulled her shoulder to give her turn.

“I would have, but you’re already dealing your sorrow and I don’t wanted to burden you,” facing towards him she said.

“You know I can’t bear, those tears in your eyes,” said Mark offended.

“Where? I am not Mark,” she replied wiping his eyes and face along.

“You will do such I can’t even realise. Is such a frail nod attaching you and me?” he said plucking her palm she kept on him, facing aside of her.

“It isn’t like that Mark”.

“I hope it could be such as you say. Don’t you feel I should be known of such throbbing over your life? Atleast,” he said.

“Father took business loan 3 years before. After that he passed away from our life, nothing he could utilise. Everything got crashed and business came to halt," she said swiftly looking into Mark's eyes.

"And this is the money for which they are here?," asked Mark.

"Yes Mark"

"But why this way? they can't do that. You should have given control of this to me much before," said Mark.

"You have all authorities in my life, Mark," she said with eyes enclosing flavour dispersing intimacy towards Mark.

"Mark, things aren't such quite as you felt. You have to understand," she said before door gets knocked badly with thumbing sound.

"Heyyy... hello ... if you all had polished your 'Drama' talks, then give away our money, else you know," heavy weighted colossal person carrying bold moustache with his fierce voice approached over door.

"Why don't you understand, I don't have anything to give away you. Why don't you all go from here," replied frightened Sayoni screaming while crying and fastening her hoof towards the door.

In her immense agitation, she opened the locked catch of door. Gazing with extreme animosity, towards who knocked. Her face set of pique. the person laughed allegedly for certain seconds and kept hold of Sayoni's hair exceedingly tight from behind. And pulled them twice to generate pain, before he earned a heavy punch over his right cheek.

Shagged, losing his control this person fallen aside over door-side lying crappers. With his bleeding nose and shuffled hair. The second his 'co-gangster' encountered such, they attacked Mark carrying all weapon artefacts they bear along. Mark blazing with extreme vexation on his face. Breath was already gone heavier, heeding such an attempt over Sayoni. Mark pulled his socks to have a ruthless fight afterwards. Firstly he picked a two-wheeler small cart kept empty aside of a vegetable vendor. Which he threw over these gangsters, centralising his energy. Getting thrashed bearing such a heavy weighted cart thrown over. These hooligans left unable to sustain its pressure throwing them across. Either after getting injured, these hoodlum people meant themselves stable to ran with eager behind Mark.

"I'll just look after these," said Mark gaping Sayoni being confident, keeping his watch over door-side shelf.

"Please be safe," she screamed over Mark outstretched steps.

"You want me to be in the picture. Then see ..," said Mark and gave a bullish punch on the face of the much howling guy, standing in front.

Being forlorn, they jumped over Mark, get him beaten. Mark presented his extreme strength and vigour through his smartest acts. He proved to be the superior in their every act, those they tried to make him fallen. Mark placed himself in such a way by his body moves so he could handle these 8 bandits separately. He pulled one person at a time inside the house, beaten him badly before throwing out. Then other and next one. Throwing one and grabbing others to pull inside. Efforts of these goons to grab him outside gets crushed ever, due to Mark's smartness which carries one along. They kept on knocking the door and atlas attempting to break it, till the time Mark beat one of their person inside. Their shocked face gaping Mark face while he throws out the body of their person after broking his twigs. Decors a funny stance the way they stare each other, once he swipes another one inside and locks the door.

"Wait, you took him inside before as well," a bandit from those all said looking Mark holding the collar of repeated person, whom he took inside at first.

"Ohhhh... you all look alike," replied Mark throwing the person, picking the one who said.

"Hey stop him," a bandit shouted thumping his hand over door, the second Mark closed.

"What the hell, you all even can't break this door," one bandit hauled picking a wooden beam in his hand and pressing repeated over door, letting it go open.

Soon other bandits joined, holding the beam tighter tangled between their arms. Instituted thumping door with it. Repeated thumping with their left strength, after getting ruthlessly beaten by Mark. At their copied 6th pressure, getting ahead to stroke door. Mark opened the door so instant, dumping all over insider floor. Earning fallen along with the wooden brick, due extreme coercion they kept on.

"So you came to drop down on my feet," said Mark laughing loudly guffaw.

Their anxiety of slamming Mark gone faded, go vanished till now. The fright of Mark could be easily generalised over their face. A person scrolled inside staying unnoticed of every eye. As Mark astray relishing that cute smirk evoking of Sayoni's face. Implying she'd relegated of her not being alone and fear. Her thrilled breaths were now committed to prove that strength in her whispers, which Mark aspire to hear.

Bustling benefit Mark's ignorance. That person elects up side-lying metal rod 'a broken piece metallic cupboard'. Picking it he raised being buried over Mark's staying unnoticed. He pulled Mark abruptly a smacking it hard over his neck, making him hard resisting pain. Mark screamed extreme pitiful in the desire of indeed help.

"Mark... save yourself," shouted Sayoni running towards carrying steer stress.

Mark plunged down over floor, after his shaggy legs unable to balance his body above feet. Things implied reverse changing whole tantrum, getting in control of those culprits. Getting back in power, these bandits pushed Sayoni heavy back taking her in control. The time she handled sinful Mark head in her bow, making him active, opening his eyes slowly.

"Help, help... Mark wake up.... wake up Mark!," being forlorn she raised her voice, being dragged by those miserable gone bandits.

"Sayoni !! … Sayoni," Mark either shouted charging hand ahead, intense face inquisitive stopping it to happen. Helplessly lying over the floor due to his broken strength, blurred vision.

One person from those merciless muggers carried Sayoni above his right shoulder. Took her along upstairs. Other followed him carrying dread smile and face of lust. With their every step, Mark's panic heightened producing imitated whinge off his mouth. Mark tried scripture with his elbow and knee contra towards these muggers climbing stairs. Sayoni moved her hands after shuffled legs being carried, getting wriggled. Yelling beating the person back with her fist. The environment of creeps and shout capped home. Such steer stress and pain over Mark's body, not avowing to stand. Pain in Mark's back meant him to go thrashed, though broken. Mark desire to get them stopped taking Sayoni away off his eyes. The clasp of getting beaten now sensed off his face. They were a step away crossing stairs, carrying her into the room before a person aghast louder over entrance door.

"Who the hell.... did this to my cart?" vegetable seller shouted.

"What happened? You go away don't disturb us. Else it wouldn't be good for you," said mugger one of those carrying her into the room.

"You tell me first. Else I'll don't make you left doing anything," said Vegetable seller pulling up his sleeves with his lower lip getting bitten by his teeth.

"Hey 'Fahim' who is he, teach him a lesson," muggers ruler spoke.

"You just wait over there, let me see you, said Fahim, stepping downstairs.

"Fahim look after him, he shouldn't reach me," he added.

"I will reach you and to your father also," said Vegetable vendor coming onward.

"Huh... It's Ashish. The guy I met today over my way," crooned Mark lying over the floor.

Ferrying hockey stick, walking in anger fronting the person approaching him. Ashish carried an artefact in his left-hand fist enclosed tightly. Battering the person badly who uttered to see him coming closer. Hammering such strong over the shoulder. That the bandit becomes complete unconscious after bearing his single hit. Whirling around over his own space, Fahim shattered over the floor within seconds. Ashish climbed stairs to tackle others. His potential amazed all, like the way he strokes these people. Settling a sensation of fear inside them.

“It’s the same person who wrangled with me today’s morning,” murmered Ashish as he noticed Mark lying over the floor.

Ashish stressed-out brain trying to a considerate story happened inside. While walking slower above stairs towards left out muggers. Ashish confined to keep Mark over his positive affection. Till the time Ashish saw girl carried and teased by them. And atlas, reading a foot distance off these bloody ruthless people. He opened his hand carrying paper containing red chilly powder, instant dumped over every face.

“So, have it,” said Ashish, dumping red chilly powder.

Disordering screams started getting of throat these bandits. Before they again started getting beaten up badly with Ashish’s hockey stick. He pressed it hard and harder over them. He splined down rolling their body over stairs, from top to bottom. They’ve been rubbing their eyes and Ashish didn’t stop pressing it hard over the body, even for seconds. Scream hauling inside out their mouth, bearing those strokes meant by Ashish. The much harsh he could, he treated them. Till the time even Mark is able to get rid of his pain and took stand onto his feet. Mark raised every person above holding their collar and started punching their face. Mark kept his peace of stroke over them then. Handling them one after the other, Mark dropped them off stairs rolling above its steps. Mark centralised his energy and meant them to exhausted. Till the time Ashish brought their last left ruler below badly.

“Rise if you got left with the courage to attack,” said Mark standing aside Ashish aside staring fallen muggers.

“I respect mankind. Got aware you saw me and what you did after had filled my heart,” said Mark facing right towards Ashish.

“Don’t worry, I won’t let them harm you,” said Ashish, stepping ahead throwing them out of the house.

“Am really sorry, forgetting you wrong at first stance,” Mark murmered.

“Let me show you now, as to how well it can be played. You wanted to take benefit of a girl .. haan,” said Ashish, jaunting his hockey stick tight inside his palm, staring at bandits in extreme gall.

"Wait once! Let me talk," said Mark stepping contra holding Sayoni's hand.

"For what? let them get treated well," said Ashish carrying extreme pique over the face.

"I don't want this issue to be screwed later. Let me talk to them," said Mark.

"So, can anyone from you tell me what amount of money, you came to draw against lender?" asked Mark, stabilising his discomfort body finding comfort to deliver.

"Could you speak out now…?" strongly screamed Mark.

"What are you doing Mark? What is this question for? It isn't required," spoke Sayoni.

"It's required. As I don't want this to be carried for any day ahead," said Mark removing Sayoni's hand kept over his shoulder.

The other second, doorbell got pressed. Everyone shocked wondering need of pressing it either if the door is opened. Mark step that was heading closer to these gangsters before, now crossed them to gaze behind the door, encountering person behind.

"Can't you see the door is already open. Still, it's required to ring the bell to generate hassle," said Ashish through directing every single eye towards the door.

"Oh… It's you Mayank," said Mark as he kept his face out to gaze.

"I was waiting for you only. Come inside," said Mark.

The person came inside with his document pulled inside plastic file and briefcase carried in both hands. Stepping inside, Mark asked him to sit over the nearby couch.

"What's your manager doing here, Mark?" asked Sayoni.

"I asked him to reach, the time I started to come here," he replied.

"But for what?" she invited again.

"Wait ... I said that already," he said picking up a file he Carried.

"Answer me, now what you started finding in this?" she asked.

"Yes these were the paper of property you asked," Mayank said.

"So let's close this with it," Mark said Mayank pointing that file towards.

"See... You bloody people, after this day never ever even try to look after this house," Mark said stepping towards them carrying a file with eyes full of vexation.

"And if it's done after this day. I will make your life miserable," said Mark while opening the file and his pen's cap handed him by Mayank.

"What the hell is going Mark. Why aren't you revealing us?" asked Sayoni.

"Hey, you don't take even a bit of stress. Seems I Know how to tackle these such people," said Ashish coming closer to Mark.

"No Sayoni and my brother, it's not for today only. I wanted to get this thing to end forever," said Mark signing paper kept inside.

"See you, predators, this would be much more than the money of loan you are looking for. For what you had already hell life of someone. Carry It along away and show out to your lender and never ever visit this place," said Mark while handing over that file to their leader.

"What you did Mark? What you gave them? Let me know," asked Sayoni meddling in between.

"I'd checked, this property would get sold in a month and from it, their money could be floated," said Mayank raising from his place stepping towards Mark.

"You are giving away your property, Mark?" asked Sayoni with her intrinsic look.

"You please don't think about it. I request," said to Mark giving his body a partial turn to let him get face towards her.

"You didn't even ask?" she said swiftly looking Mark with her those confused eyes.

Time their leader was checking out the validity of those papers, handed over by Mark. Mark smile concludes something for what he raised. The way they turned out pages evokes their cherish spirit. Which could be easily sensed by the gratitude they attained while peering those. Other bandits copied their leader, putting up their facial glow of smile fulfilling their aspiration.

“Don’t be such happy. It’s due to my will you got this. Else you won’t be able to take this from anyone if my heart hadn’t said me though,” said Mark getting irritated with their creepy smile.

A bird stood that place, Floating faster flapping her feather.
Singing loudly, as no one heard of such beauty in voice ever.
Capturing the whole area inside, bustling from one end to other.
It’s the same fowl Mark encountered in the morning, making him bother.
That same species with duplicate colour, like he saw those same feathers. Trying believing her presence, the way it again developed such ecstatic weather.
This bird becoming the only point of concern for everyone.
Lost looking her moves, letting her do what’s left undone.
Mark tried following her, listen out any clue that she could give.
As he doesn’t want to make his life more ravage, making hard to live.

“What is it? this isn’t a normal bird,” said Ashish, interrogative towards the active bird.

“Even I feel so,” said Sayoni noticing her whole input.

“What you all feel? Please don’t judge something so soon,” said Mark diverting their attention.

“Hey, you !!….. hope you’d checked these paper. All were proper. Now get lostfrom our house and show it to your lender. Just go away,” said Mark, atlas screaming over muggers.

“Yes... Yes… who wants to stay. We are going only,” said muggers leader.

"And listen, remember this very clearly, that you got these due my wills. Else you aren't able to take it away from me" said Mark, rubbing his head that's aching.

"What happened Mark? Is it paining again?" asked Sayoni placing her hand over his shoulder, coming closer to him with her concerned face.

"Oh Ohh… stop her… what are you looking at me? Stop her," said the leader of muggers when that bird getting spared from their eyes. As bird flue away plucking those paper in her beak, that Mark just handed over after signing.

"What the hell is this?," shouted Mark raising head above to gaze.

"Now what she's trying to do through this," Mark murmered discerning towards the bird.

"Hey…It's going outside stop her," a mugger said running behind.

"She's not a normal bird, I told you," said Ashish staring at his blank face towards.

"Now at least you don't say that, please. Nothing will happen, let me see," said Mark, making his feet to fasten up following bird's way.

"Where she went… Look that side," voice stood out of these muggers as they stepped out l behind her.

"Look nah… you look left and you look right," said the leader of those slapping back of their head.

"What happened now… is it missing?" said Mark moving with difficulty to gaze outside.

Everyone came out, trying to get only one glimpse of her to track. Sayoni and Ashish eyes also started capturing sky to look after for bird.

"This is ridiculous. Now tell me Mayank, how can I have an additional copy of those papers," asked Mark with a grudge.

"Those were original copies, not easy to have immediately," Mayank in sedated voice.

"Oh… What's this, means that bird needs to be tracked anyhow," said Mark as he sat over the doorstep stairs, holding his head with his finger inside the hair.

“Have you heard that sound of the bird, something came from that side,” said Ashish while pointing his finger towards the left-sided track.

Hooligans ran behind Ashish over the way he directed and found her situated accord over a string. Ferrying papers in her beak, dotting them in a mean of a tease. Theirs pent up the spirit to hook and ran behind her. She didn’t yflew high, but some meters above land. Hooligans ran around the buildings aside jumping from balconies in a mean to catch her. But nothing seems attainable, from all the effort they kept and build strain. They covered miles to catch her. Showing their obligation towards.

A couple of hours, from the time they started catching the bird. Still, they all are following her like a mad and Mark was lost in his suspicious muddling. Sitting in his same constant ideal way over his place, Mark speculating about his journey overstory “Yesterday 9”. His failure to save everything occurred over the way. As he got in consciousness and moved his hand up to perceive his watch strap. He encountered hefty voice floating across him.

“Hey Mark, what are you up to? Why don’t you stop all this? Nothing will go anywhere, things will get resolved,” said Sayoni settling down next to him over door-sided step stairs, cosseting him.

“Aah... it’s you,” he said with his stunned eyes staring at Sayoni.

“You have to go to your home today. Why aren’t you leaving for it? It’s already gone late,” said Sayoni with her slower spaced words.

“And where were you from the time being?” he asked getting himself back to actuality, rubbing his head with palm.

“I was looking after Nani, as much I could spare her from knowing what’s happening here. She saw all this lastly and gone faint over the door of her room. She can’t tolerate such mental pressure at this age. I meant her to get conscious, laid down along her, then consoled and stayed till the time she slept,” she answered.

“So, is she slept now?” asked Mark, trying getting up of his place.

“Yes, she slept but you please relax don’t exert yourself much. Relax, be seated if you can’t stand,” said Sayoni pulling his hand down to sit.

“Yes Miss,” he smiled getting back on his place, gaping towards time in his watch.

“Aah… Why I hadn’t believed it’s been done deliberately,” said Mark picking his head up keeping hand behind over floor to support head facing roof while exhaling out air off the mouth, giving mental repose.

“What? And who did it purposely,” queried Sayoni getting bewildered.

“You don’t think much, just give me the commitment to travelling with me today”.

“Mark, you are going with Tamanna. Don’t you think it isn’t good of asking me as well,” she replied.

“It’s not just both of us, Maunik either coming with us?”

“Yeah, I know but …?,” she said before getting lost in reasoning.

Swiftly without enlightening anyone of her appearance. That Fowl came and settled taking space aside to Mark towards his left. Being Ignorant, these both stayed engulfed listening to each other’s concern. No one is in the belief of her presence. That unforeseen voice coming out next meant their consciousness to fluctuate. Waver is to realise chirp sound adjacent to them.

“See... she is sitting next to you,” said Sayoni in esteemed zest.

“Where?” asked Mark before he turned and realised the actuality of bird in his thought, sitting next to him.

“You can take it,” voice evoked from bird beak.

“You can speak as well,” stunned Sayoni spoke with her opened mouth covered by her fingers.

“I did what I wanted to,” said the bird, pointing towards Mark’s face.

“You said again,” said Sayoni.

“I just go aware, as it’s not a usual act. it’s completely intentional,” said Mark pressurising his body to get up.

“But you have no authorities to play with nature’s rule, Mark,” said bird before it flue to settle over his shoulder.

“What the hell is going Mark, can you tell me. What you are doing against nature,” asked Sayoni being furious carrying extreme perturb on her face.

“Please don’t get annoyed, will let you know everything. leave everything over me from here, as of now,” said Mark fastening his steps behind the bird that raised above into the sky disappearing inside clouds.

“Sorry Mark, that bird gone missed after so long struggle behind her,” said Ashish who halted, with his uncontrolled heavy breaths as he just interrupted running.

“Hey Ashish it’s good you came. I got those papers, could you please hand it over to those hooligans” said Mark passing the rolled sheet of paper towards him.

“You found those. But I question how, what you did to get them? They seem the same that bird duct along,” asked Ashish.

“Yes, everything you said is true. But I am extremely sorry can’t answer you those right now,” said Mark.

“Please carry them and hand over it to those,” said Mark while rushing holding Sayoni’s hand to pick his car.

“Mark, nani is inside and she’s not well ... understand,” she said snatching her hand off Mark.

“Ok wait,” said Mark while opening up his wallet and finding something.

“Ashish I want one more favour from you, I know am asking more but I will keep this help in my knowledge for life,” said Mark as he said turned back to face him carrying delight over the face.

“Am glad to help dear, you just say,” replied Ashish.

“Sometimes I feel, things are not as they’re meant to be before. You came as a treasure to my life,” said Mark lending both Ashish and Sayoni to be in perplex of digging into his words.

"Sayoni's nani is inside and she needs care. Can you look over her health till we come back," asked Mark.

"This would be a prospect of humanities, you can accept me yes for it," he replied.

"My positivity towards life gets doubled, whenever I meet a person like you," said Mark.

"You please settle down the remaining task in your bucket," said Ashish thumping Mark's back stronger, cheering his moral.

Mark lastly crimped his eyes, bowed his head once facing Ashish, before he kept hold of Sayoni's hand and stepped ahead. Mark consolidating breaths and his strengthened belief of settling down life with its best output. He ran holding Sayoni's hand to reach out place, where he left his car.

"We are late Sayoni... Maunik would be waiting over airport," said Mark holding Sayoni's hand running together.

"I know you are late, but why you're carrying such fear over face?," she asked while running being a Milano or each other.

"Fear is time only, I can't lose the chance of getting back what I lost due to time," he replied.

"Your word is crimped from long, making me a way of knowing the truth behind," said Sayoni gaping Mark's flexed face.

"I want to reveal all that upfront you, but this running time isn't allowing to," be said and tighten up their joined hand.

Sayoni's ardour said inside gazing his face, while legs functioning to console his time crucifying desire.

She was in astray peering Mark's face outflowing with eager. That what she doesn't know and either not wanting to clear. Her stole she carried, flowing analogous to his shirt. Flowing such into his emotions, wanting blindly to follow even if it's any of his flirts.

Acute impressions took place inside her. Emotion wanting her to fly opening every feather. Her eye kept over Mark as they both settled inside the car. Mark hassled face and sniffing hands making her bother. She didn't ask him, regardless started finding a point of relief. Though she kept her hand over his head and asked him to strengthen his belief.

While he geared up the car with accelerating speed. Sayoni rolled her finger into his hair, peering his face that's trying to heed.

Nothing much is required, to make me believe on you.
Your emotions are ever enough for my heart, to stay in awareness of you.
You were never asked to justify your point you say.
As your words and wish had already come into my prayer.
You don't have to find a reason to give a justification, behind actions you do.
Your concerned eyes, makes me believe in whatever you do.
Those breaks in your tone, when something wanting you to get hone.
Your smile tells me everything about your path and the way it's dealing stone.
Clarification was never a path required between us, to travel any distance.
My faith will ever be like a moon, not a star, so wouldn't fall maintaining persistence.
Those bulging difficulties will lessen ever, crossing them with you.
My life ever asks God to give a chance, for showing what all I can do for you.
Sometimes giving your blood isn't also enough, to prove what you aspire to do.
But I believe my prays for you over my all sleepless night, will serve you everything that you wanted to.

Final Escape

Rushing up and down, crossing every road.

Mark drove the car so rush, which he never allowed anyone nor ever himself afford.

Nothing he spoke, while juggling with his steep growing and destroying stress.

Sayoni without asking anything, trying not to let him get depressed.

Carrying water to drink passed from her to him, after every couple of minutes.

While carrying he stares her eyes, whose not asking a question

After getting answers in peanuts.

Her devotion without queries meant his heart to give away everything.

The way she makes positive reasons, from empty words of mean-less meaning.

Whenever his broken soul, collected energy to reveal.

He wondered of running time staring at his smile, wanting to steal.

Gearing his car, accelerating its speed.

He wanted to give those corrections to his life that it needs.

Rubbing his eyes, he wants to retain sharp vision over his way.

Above time build cracks going deeper, making life hard to stay.

"Easy Mark! What would if that child came in between?," said Sayoni as Mark passed his car very next attached with the footpath.

"Am driving on-road track only," he replied noticing the slower moving traffic ahead.

"But can't you ....," she stopped while saying.

"Yes please, yes ... I already realised my mistake, but don't say more so that I'll start feeling guilty. As there is no space of any other emotion left in me right now," he said picking a U-turn heading back over the same track.

"You can drive easier as well if you have enough time to ride twice over the same track," she said turning her face opposite to him.

"This way will kill our time, can't you see the movement over traffic ahead," he said pressing his leg heavily over accelerator with exceeding gears.

"Can you call Maunik once, to know where he's waiting presently," he said taking his last right turn to reach the airport.

"He's not picking my phone, he texted back that he's waiting for you since hours sitting inside the canteen next to airport waiting for area," she replied.

"Why can't he talk?" asked Mark.

"He texted for this, that two commandos are standing his sides holding stain gun," she replied.

"So what? He's not a terrorist," Mark said with an intrinsic partial smile coming onto his face.

"I wanted him to come over ring road track, so could we'd saved half an hour. But don't know in which mood he is, after waiting for hours there," said Mark pointing Sayoni's eyes that were directed towards frontal track being astray of something.

"Huh! Are you even listening to me?" he asked.

"Yes ... Yes I am," she said.

"Why ever if am trying to fix everything, nothing is ready to fall on its place," crooned Mark as he exhaled air out of his mouth peering ahead, handling steering.

Time passed and track to the airport came to an end. Mark's heart repeatedly stayed repeatedly wishing to find no check-post over its entrance gate. Sayoni like ever crushed her sorrow developed by Mark, of not listening to her suggestion over his wills. Mark entered airport premises, feeling of catching the right decision of changing over the way in the middle.

Unfortunately, he has to stop his car behind a long queue of approx. 20 cars.

"For What? Why this queue is maintained and blocking way?" asked Mark, putting his head out of side window, stopping a traveller walking out with his luggage.

"There's a check-post ahead," the traveller replied pointing finger towards the way.

"Oh... damn!" said Mark, smacked staring in anger.

"Though I said you to be on the same track," said Sayoni.

"You didn't say it," he replied with low voice staring ahead.

"Don't pretend such. You know Mark, I meant that only," she replied facing Mark.

"Am losing it all, how could I control it," he said with face getting into vain and distress of capturing numbness.

"Hey... Mark What happened? Please don't get such low," she said in angst pushing him to face towards, by her fingers, with a sort of plea on her face.

"What should I do now? am already late..." he said rubbing his closed eyelids and brows.

"Nobody gets late for anything. All happens in a way, God decides," she said peering into his eyes.

"And if God is wrong in doing something, then," he asked.

"God is never wrong in doing anything. It's we his concealed slaves, who realise positivity in his acts later," she replied.

"How could his act be counted in good stake, if he takes someone's life?," he asked getting conscious to generalise her reaction with an answer she'll convey after it.

"I will not answer it ," she said getting very silent and being lost kenning intention hidden in his words.

"Why so!" he asked getting more attentive discerning towards her face, which she pointed upfront.

"Till you won't reveal for what you are worried and whose life is in stake," she replied.

"There is nothing like such. I asked to know about the biggest decision God takes so sudden, without letting a person reap fruits of life," he asked in stress, with stretch Mark getting deeper over the head.

"Nothing happens suddenly, as the count of days a person will live is already decided before birth. It's we humans who forget this while going ahead in our life. That our life can leave us anytime and we should be ready for it.," she replied.

"No... no... that couldn't happen. Am not agreed to your words," he said and left the car, getting out with his eyes gazing around to find out away.

"Hey... Mark! Mark look here... see see," said Maunik showing out higher his hand from a distance.

"Why isn't he's hearing me," Maunik said coming closer to their car.

"What the hell Maunik, where were you," said Mark, as his eyes encounter him, the second he reached next to him and meant him tuned his gaze.

"Come get in first, then convey anything," said Mark stopping Maunik to say anything, keeping his palm over his lips.

"Aah... God... Wow Maunik you came, Mark was in immense stress due to your absence," she said and stopped her giggling through her hand.

"For what? I haven't died," asked Maunik.

"Of getting late to pick you, buddy," replied Mark.

"That is the usual thing you do. So I am in complete concoct of this," Maunik replied.

"Forget it, you tell me Maunik, why you aren't picking my calls, nor replying accurately over text," she asked being furious.

"I misplaced my passport somewhere on Australia airport itself," answered Maunik.

"Misplaced? And how the fuck it's related in not replying to us," she queried facing back seated Mark inside the car, keeping the face in force.

"I don't know how come austere checking is going on. They are enquiring out due to some predicted terrorist attack," said Maunik controlling breath pause in delivering.

"And you mean, they kept hold of you?" she asked.

"Huh... how come you realised such?" Maunik replied with an amazed mouth.

"Because you have jinx of calling trouble towards you," said Mark while trying to pull back the car and leave airport space.

"Mark please, let me know what exactly happened. Look his face, he's still not normal," she said anxiously.

"Tell me Maunik what they did with you then?" Sayoni's inevitably flowing concern.

"When you're calling me, I was sitting on the bench under two giant trooper surveillance. My details are getting checked to get known about my identity," said Maunik.

"Why such tragic pictures are shown now. If these things hadn't occurred before," murmered Mark after hearing Maunik and letting the car get turned out of such a small alley road track.

"You said something Mark?" asked Sayoni.

"No I haven't," he answered.

"So why exactly has all this happened?" Sayoni asked Maunik.

"They were treating me as a terrorist. As I don't have a passport and no such other document to display my identity," Maunik replied.

"Carry more such heavy beards, tattoo and long hair kind of

terrorist look," crooned Mark.

"You said something again Mark?," she pinched.

"No I haven't, but what you both started. Hope we are heading for concern and somebody else either waiting for us," Mark replied both.

"Yes, I brought something for her," said Maunik, spying something in his bag with his both hand into.

"Nothing for me Maunik," said Sayoni.

"What for you my buddy, for my true bond of friendship is enough," he replied.

"I don't ask anything, doesn't mean I don't want anything," said Sayoni.

"Oh seems you developed wrath for me," Maunik said over her pout face,

"Then who will have these now," he added building smile over the face, bringing his hand carrying a box filled with her loved doughnuts.

"Aww.. lovely .... love you Maunik !!," she said turning towards him as her eyes stole what was kept inside it.

"Now, show me what you brought for her," she asked.

"Yes, for her I brought this," he said putting the pendent of the thin box is kept.

"Aw... such a beautiful, she will love it," said Sayoni.

"Yes, she loves; such things," he replied.

"See... a person is giving such a costly pendant to a girl in front of her male guy," said Mark with a smile below pushed up eyebrows.

"It's not like that .... hey man !!, it's only you who give me the knowledge of money, as being a materialistic thing in life" Maunik replied in the intense will of conveying.

"Why you took it so seriously? I didn't mean it," said Mark driving in speed turning car over every crook at the end of an alley.

"Mark you are not following the right route," pinched Sayoni.

“I know, was wrong before but this time it isn’t,” Mark smiled and raised gear boosting speed.

“Yes, the last cut and a turn after it, we will be at Mark’s home,” said Maunik pushing himself a little closer to both, looking ahead.

“But I guess we are heading to pick Tamanna?” she asked, intervening conversation.

“Her home is not farther from mine, whether we talk of here or over Lansdowne,” said Mark facing Sayoni, broadening his cheeks.

“Why you said in Lansdowne as well?” she asked.

“Tamanna is Mrs. Sinha aunties real daughter,” Maunik pinched in between.

“Mark, the same Sinha aunty who’s the best buddy of your mother?” asked Sayoni.

“And how you know about it, Maunik?” asked Mark, placing his car over Tamanna’s out-yard garden gate.

“Aah… Huh! You only told me once,” replied Maunik placing his right foot on the ground opening cars gate.

“Is there no one at her home?” Sayoni asked gazing Mark’s face whose still lost thinking something, looking towards Maunik through the rear mirror.

“What happen Mark, aren’t you getting late now?,” she asked budging his body to get him back conscious and attentive to her words.

“What?,” she asked above his amazed face opening her hands wider, as Mark starred.

“Nothing …. Yeah, Nothing !!! .. what I started thinking… move outcome, let’s move out,” said Mark opening his door to step out.

“I either don’t know, as what mess her spirit would have created inside,” crooned Mark, walking towards the door.

“Why your eyes so intensely peering that right corner of the house,” asked Sayoni walking behind Mark towards the already opened gate by Maunik.

"That was her room, see how silent it is right now," said Mark with extreme swiftness in his voice, with his eyes consistently beaming towards that space.

"I can't get a reason behind such a change in flavour of our voice," Sayoni said with rising confusing marks while keeping her hand over Mark's shoulder.

"Maunik, seems am unable to handle these mysterious reactions of Mark. Can you please talk to him once," said Sayoni pointing her eyes over the space where he saw Maunik standing last.

"Where is he," asked Mark facing Sayoni's faced way.

"Why he's reacting so suspicious today?" said Mark compressing his eyes staring towards his mind, fighting together with some unwanted thoughts.

"He didn't answer my any question, I raised over the way," said Mark walking back towards the car, checking back gate.

"See, it isn't locked either. He missed checking the door, one thing which Maunik takes immense care off," said Mark noticing his backdoor being partially locked.

"Do nobody stays across her house?" asked Sayoni noticing immense silence on the street and surrounding aside Tamanna's home.

"Even am trying to notice, as of where these people are lost, whoever makes these tracks to stay loaded with sellers," replied Mark in a slight steer.

"Is today Sunday?," he reverted facing Sayoni.

"Yeah, it's Sunday Mark," she replied.

"Might that would be the reason," he said moving towards the door getting in.

"Do Maunik's aware of her house," asked Sayoni.

"No..." replied Mark.

"Then where he is?" she asked.

"My mind isn't able to get! Oh... See he's sitting there, crossing his legs over bench," he said while turned with his confused reaction becoming attentive heeding Maunik.

Mark followed by Sayoni, ran closer to Maunik. Where he's sitting siding opposite to them with his straight back and pointed face without anybody move except slight shivering. Mark dealing many things, hadn't given concern to this never seen the attitude of Maunik. Mark ran closer, calling his name. The situation became more awkward when after calling thrice he didn't look towards them. He kept sitting in his dumbstruck fashion conceding Sayoni to build fear. Those distressed face which was masked with delight to make things easy for others. They broke there tense that they kept hidden, as Maunik turned and clubbed Mark tightly with his face sweating in fear.

"Hey what happened? What happened damid, would you say?" asked Mark, while pouring his hand of severity over Maunik's head.

"Ok, calm down… Now tell me what exactly happened?" he asked again putting his face above by holding his both ears with hand to interact his eyes.

"Am not in me, the way I am. Seem like someone is capturing my body, controlling my actions," said Maunik with his fearsome reactions.

"What the hell, you are saying. Are you even realising what you just said?" she asked pulling him away of Mark, faced in anger holding his both arms.

"God, I can't even convey them the reality. It's for everyone's saviour," Mark crooned looking down toward grass, while Sayoni's trying to let things get out of Maunik.

"How could it happen, Maunik please don't make a mess over here. It's already been late for Mark to go," said Sayoni shagging Maunik's arms below the horrified face.

"Why aren't you telling him to stop all this. I'd encountered time fear in you, Mark. Aren't you getting late now?" Sayoni said to Mark's numb standing face.

"Can anyone from you both, tell me what exactly happened here? Please, I am getting completely distraught now," she screeched with her stressed face pushing her hair lying on the face to go back pushing fingers over them.

“Mark, how can you stay quiet? Can’t you discern my woes over the concern,” she said shaking Mark’s arms.

“Relax… Calm down. Nothing went wrong here, things are all accustomed,” said Mark making her revive of her distress.

“Why you aren’t listening to me?” asked Mark holding her more dense.

“I can’t handle it more. You have to tell me the story behind,” she asked with tear sprout in her eyes, as her dread settles down.

These three had gone entangled in each other. Forgetting the reason and place they just came to. Maunik reaction isn’t getting healed with that developed dismay and trepidation he encountered and haven’t revealed yet. Maunik voice took cease getting adrift through, what he encountered. Sayoni hitherto came out of her hushed behaviour of being hostile one. Making hard for Mark to handle those queries raised by her every new second. Where Mark’s eyes are discerning fear coated over Maunik’s face. He has to solace developed angst of Sayoni, whose head placed over his chest. With his hand patting her back. With evoking desire of telling them both everything, Which he’s commencing with. Wanting to settle down trepidation of both after revealing the truth.

I would have conveyed if it’s so easy to be delivered.
I could have told with willingness, getting out of the way that makes you bewildered.
If its that simple to get understood.
My devotion has already revealed it very descriptively, which I easily could.
My soul either wants you to walk along.
Strength getting weaker to run a race, that could be so long.
My plea wants to settle down your dismay, your fear.
Understand am blocked, at this time can’t make anything go clear.

I know, your tears are in need to grasp, wanting to take part in my strain.
But whenever I start to convey, it gets blocked by my brain.
Your hand over my shelter is the only thing I want.
But see at present I can't have it, even if theirs none of my fault
Am dried of bearing such pain from a long time continuously.
But felt reliable, as your eyes poured my shirt through
tear of care, so deliberately.

"Sharpen my awareness Mark, if am unaware of anything. Can easily encountering you capturing my chagrin in your eyes," said Maunik staring a point with his same menacing face.

"What the hell, he's speaking !! Why aren't you telling me," asked Sayoni clouting Mark's chest with that tight fist.

"Hey Sayoni… you either came! What a surprise," a voice stood out of house indoor entrance gate.

"Huh… Yea," said Sayoni looking towards the door.

"You come here, these guys will keep on teasing you with such things," replied Tamanna staring Sayoni hanging stretching her hand over door.

"Come on! Come here … seen you after so long !!," said Tamanna.

"I haven't met her before, why she's saying such," Sayoni murmered gazing Mark spiking her brows.

"At least her consideration got changed somehow to other thing," crooned Mark.

"Why aren't you answering me. Had you meant any vow of not answering my raised queries," Sayoni asked in anger from Mark.

"Hey come on… come in faster," Tamanna shouted restlessly with her dozed body draping over the door.

"She's drunken? see," said Sayoni shaking Mark face holding his chin.

"How could I know," replied Mark peering towards Tamanna.

Tamanna with her wobbling feet stepped ahead. Covering

distance slower. The way her abruptly evoking smile settles down while she controls herself of falling down. Mark and Sayoni stood numb gaping toward her and the way she was a backlash. Mark unable to fathom those changes. Tamanna came, perching upfront Sayoni, holding her hand. Shocked and stunned Sayoni gazed Tamanna's mysterious face keeping dread on the corner of her too and forth reactions. Tamanna guffaws louder putting up her clenched hand into her palm and said.

"Why are you getting so cold?" asked Tamanna with her same unstopped nickering.

"Nothing it's just due to these cursory cold breezes," replied Sayoni with a stammer.

"Seems, my home is much coldest," Tamanna replied with her intoxicated moves.

"All is good with you dear," asked Sayoni.

"Yes! What do you feel?" replied Tamanna with her raised brows.

"Aah... about this you're saying ... oh yea, I felt of having a couple of packs before we leave," added Tammana in her same forty winks flying in the air.

"You didn't tell such thing about her," murmered Sayoni pressing Mark's palm harder.

"Come on!! let get settle for a while," Tamanna said while hauling Sayoni's hand towards to carry her along inside before her other hand was kept hold tightly by Mark to say :

"We had already gone far late".

"Leave my hand, am not worried about it," said Tamanna facing Mark's with those vexed eyes.

"But I am... can't afford to waste time," said Mark with his nervous gone voice, before she pushed him off from his chest to go aside.

Tamanna meant her way clear, taking Sayoni along holding her hand. Mark setting himself reliable after her push. Maunik getting floored peering all. Present pictures were all beyond his realisation. Atlas, Maunik ran towards Mark in hassle.

"How come she became such, she wasn't like that. Either your words revealed any such near thing of her," asked Maunik stumping Mark's arm, with eyes directed towards those steps of Tamanna and Sayoni entering the house.

"How come you turn into so restlessness by her only push. What happened to her? Why aren't you conveying, Mark?" asked Maunik above his extreme agitation.

"It wasn't a normal push," Mark replied, still lost encountering their last moves before they disappear.

"Hope you could generalise devastation over my face. Then why aren't you letting my doubts, go clear," said Maunik keeping hold of Mark.

"You know, I don't know when I checked out and carried away from the airport to this place. I don't have any clue what exactly happened in-between," said Maunik.

"I carried you from the Airport in my car, how can you forget?," said Mark ring in dismay of reality.

"I don't know!!!... I don't know please clarify?" Maunik asked in extreme steer, upholding face above his heavy breaths.

"Then who carried your body, it was totally you," said Mark getting bewildered rubbing his forehead and thumping his feet over grass.

"Hey! Hey ... listen ... and tell me very clearly as what you saw here, what made you react such daunting?" asked Mark making his face go closer with eyes staring into his eyes for brief.

"I don't know, which force pushed me and brought here. But whatever it's persuading me repeatedly, is telling to not go along you today. And when I denied, it had shown me the cruellest behaviour of mystifying power," said Maunik with his fearsome voice, sweat dropping off his face.

"Convey me clearer Maunik. What exactly you say?," asked Mark.

"I saw the cruelty over the animal. Saw such things which makes me hard to say Tamanna, a human. Those red-blooded lips and mouth speaking besides blood need. Those chunks of animal steaks hanging next to her face. That smile she took showing out such a wildest stake. Like a ghost staring behind her face. She wasn't what you said and which I met before. She was something ethereal," said Maunik breathing out his fear, of which he couldn't only heal nor exactly state.

"What are you thinking, could you convey?" shouted Maunik, wanting Mark to answer. Getting complete exhausted from Mark prolonged silence and suspicious adrift gazing around.

"You please calm down ... calm down ... you are right ... yes, you saw reality. Maunik I hitherto lived our today's date, which now we are living back," delivered Mark, throwing out words in a single shot, stuck in the mouth.

"Living back? What do you mean," he queried.

"I don't have time to clarify you, just believe in what I say, I need you," said Mark turning against Maunik with his bowed head.

"I travelled time and came to the past for saving the lives of my loved ones. And now I need your help, without any query, to settle this down stable," said Mark.

"What?" shocked Maunik.

"Yes, Tamanna you saw was in the capture of her futuristic black spirit. She died in future and her spirit travelled back with me, to block making a change to any.

"How could?" intensified Maunik stepped ahead with eager turning Mark toward peering his face.

"I took the help of Mr. Charles to build 'Time Machine' to travel time back. I lost everything in and 24-hour intervals and came back to secure what I can. So you please don't even ask any more question about what and how? as I won't be able to. Time is passing so rapidly, as I couldn't capture, even if I want," said Mark holding the face of Maunik between his both palm.

"Help me ... help me with this. I need you, my buddy.. I need you. Am broken such from the inside, that I can't even convey. Secure me from it, my chum ... secure me," said Mark getting broken and helpless in a way of plea, busted down sliding his hand from his hand to his base with slight coming tears in his eyes.

"I haven't ever seen you such Mark. Don't fall," Maunik picking him up to stand.

"Am not going to ask anything... Nor even going to say anything. But I feel you could convey how you're upto next?" asked Maunik making himself comfortable, floating strength to Mark.

"For now, let's we also follow her way," said Mark.

"What? What should we do?"

"You take Sayoni along with you in another car, following us."

"Would it be secure. Don't she'll get aware of it and could impact you?" he asked.

"She couldn't impact me, though even her own black spirit had empowered over," Mark told.

"So you want me and Sayoni to follow you both in another car?" asked Maunik in his still stammering voice.

"You can't help me before you get rid of your dread," said Mark keeping his palm over the right side of his neck.

"It's not that easy."

"I know, but I don't have the time nor I have any other way to save you all."

"Such a tragic chapter life had shown, I can't believe," said Maunik settling down over below lying bench.

"You stay there itself. Am getting worried of Sayoni, let check here first. Hope Tamanna hadn't harmed her anyhow," said Mark, putting down Maunik cell phone, before he ran back towards the home entrance door for getting in.

Headily Mark reached doorstep with his hurried legs flowing sideways in the air. Holding the doors job he balanced himself before it got opened by Sayoni. She stood amazed gazing Mark carrying such a wretched face, balancing his body to stand still. Mark with a stunned face after looking something he didn't expect. Sayoni giggled louder looking Mark, the way he all stood.

"What happen? what's so hurry? so you couldn't even control yourself," said Sayoni keeping a hand over the face to stop giggle.

"You had word with her," asked Mark.

"All's good?" Mark queried with his suspicious face.

"Nothing is normal in her, you never ever conveyed, her such behaviour," she replied with a smile on her face.

"What happened, she said anything to you?" asked Mark.

"What would she say... Man, she is such a darling! She treated me so well," Sayoni replied with her finest impression covering the face.

"Is it? And you had a drink as well," asked Mark.

"Yeah.... she served carrying such melody in her voice, that I unable to deny," replied Sayoni thumping his chest with her palm.

"Are you finding yourself alright?" queried Mark looking her same drowsy moves he noticed over Tamanna last.

"It's completely fine Mark. Why you're making it direr through your repeated questions," she asked being furious to know.

"Ok, don't panic. We are getting late, so could you take it quite rapid coordinating with Maunik," said Mark with a pleasing face.

"But where's he. I am not able to confront him," she said staring his back, peering above through his right shoulder.

"He's in your dot front, might get hidden through bench height," said Mark with his eyes trying to peer Tamanna inside.

"Got it, can perceive his hair upper layer. But why he's lying beneath," she replied smiling, gaping towards Maunik.

"Convey me first, where's she?," asked Mark footing on his toes higher encountering her around with his gaping eyeballs from one side to other.

"Move let me see him! She's inside only," said Sayoni giving him a thrust passing ahead.

Sayoni had crossed his way and Mark's eyes were still trying to heed Tamanna's glimpse inside. Those scrolling eyeballs with his slower steps taking lead to enter the room, finding her fragrance in that silence shaded with darkness.

"What happened inside, aren't there electricity," said Mark moving towards room switchboard with his creeping feet.

"Hey Tamanna... am already getting futile of being late. Please come out," said Mark sliding his finger over wall finding switch board and lastly switching it on. Light raised with a spark inside.

Her closer coming steps with such an intensifying desire. Wearing black gown partly spaced from bottom till top of her legs. Walking closer to Mark carrying an enlightened candle, she said some lines making this aura easy to handle.

I know am wrong in judging your aspiration.
As you brought a fruit along, that only grows with true love inspiration.
My severe behaviour would have broken you every day.
But believe, I wasn't aware of your true intentional pray.
It's not that I hadn't dreamed ever of a true person like you.
But those social calamities around had meant me ever to judge you.
The fault is mine, as for every wrong thing in my life you have nothing to do.
Still I don't know, how could I had blamed such a nice person like you.
Your senses can recall every single word you said to me.
Forgetting how hard it would stepping with some bad picture, carried to see.
Seems my desires had meant me more ambitious.
But your devotion towards me never acted suspiciously.
Yes, it's me, who killed that prosperous, fragrant growing bud inside you.
And you ever melted me, the way you get to hold my hand when I needed you.

"You'd been late to come, Mark," she asked whispering in this silenced hall.

"Aah... yes though am trying to make things quicker," he replied stabilising his fumbling tone, staring towards that sensual reaction on her face he confronted last night.

"But I wonder how could you get late?," she asked while getting seated over a sea-saw bench, folding her legs.

"I was... yea I was," Mark unable to reply.

"You were late for carrying Maunik as well," said Tammana playing with her bells.

"Yea, it was due to that repeated check-post," replied Mark.

"And what's before that?" she asked, sipping from her glass of whiskey, lying a hand full of distance towards the right side.

"Before that... what ... what would be before that," he replied continuing the same stammer in his voice.

"Do you feel, if you and Sayoni don't convey me I wouldn't get the picture?" she asked taking her second last sip.

"I said her over the way, to not talk about it with anyone," he replied.

"What anyone! Don't you'd been already aware that I know everything," she said with exceeding enrage, heading up from her bench.

"When we both came together from our present to past," she said taking her last sip of alcohol, throwing away glass impelling towards Mark with her swiftly stepping feet. After her catwalk she picked her gown little upwards from aside.

Shocked Mark peering her, hoisting dread over his face. Those inclined closer feet of her had generated so many negative myths in his mind. Settling present time hassle he's into. She came closer and raised his hand holding finger, giving them a kiss bowing her head a little. Her sensual eyes, still enclosed in Its last night flavour. Her desires came into their accurate picture when she slides her finger over Mark's face. From his eyes to nose and then to his lips.

"So you're aware of my instincts for you," asked Mark with his unnerving face and eyeballs trying to stare towards her, scrolling inside eye curvature.

"Yes... how could I've missed perceiving your knowledge of knowing me, that's dripping down from the corner of your eyes.

"Don't be scared Mark, this spirit wouldn't harm you," she before she roars loudly.

"Please stop, don't laugh... don't laugh like that," said Mark pressing his palm tighter above his both ear.

"Oh, now my laughter either vexing you," she said holding Mark sturdy of his waist with her arms covering back.

"No ... No .... nothing like such I thought for you before, nor any feeling against you fake to my mind ever. I don't know how you developed such misconceptions," Mark.

"I was shouting, tearing in front of you the time as well and you took Sayoni ruthlessly away off me," he said with a pressurised voice of conviction.

"So you are worried about Sayoni," she replied whispering into his ear, ferrying her lips closer.

"Again .... again you're conceding that black spirit overpowers your positivity. Why couldn't you're trying to generalise reality," said Mark, with developed thrust delivered provoking off his body.

"Listen ... I care for you... I aegis of you," said Mark turning around holding her cramped in his arms, peering into her eyes with stronger fling intentions.

"Huh... you aren't able to read my eyes and lips ever," said Mark composing his face off her, an unsorted sprite of emotions.

"I divulged already, before I asked you," her spirit said making him to face towards herself, pulling through her fingers.

"Hope you found enchanted me for you, behind my emotions," her spirit added.

"Are you just wanting to get me, not whole myself," asked Mark in chagrin.

"Wanting you Mark. What are you saying?" the spirit said getting more concerned, pulling his face closer applying pressure, making him encounter her glittering eyes.

"Ohh... Wait! Wait! We are getting late," he said with the agitation of her intensifies emotions of pulling and smelling his face.

"Calm down! Get mild, Nothing getting spoiled. I just want to be in you," said Tammana's fierce spirit pulling Mark to get wholly attached to her body, with her heavy going breaths of desperation.

"No... no we have to move early... getting late... why couldn't you understand," said Mark pulling his face off her curb pulling him.

"You have to answer me and fill my all desires," yelled Tamanna's spirit, making Mark go gaze her eyes pressurising for giving steer of his body towards herself.

"We are getting late," Mark reiterated his last word and got lost peering into her eyes, dipped in her hypnotism. Getting drowned with his face sliding from her neck to shoulder.

They both got lost in one another.
Like sound becoming inquisitive before interrupting, for spreading its feather.
Those hands getting rubbed over others palm.
Their desperation had chased with time and can't settle calm.
Passing out heavy breaths, getting out of one's mouth floating to other.
Everything started supporting, generating the best flavour of this weather.
Drifting over one another, with their gone senseless face.
Flowing heavily in love, forgetting about its pace.
Those ear hearing desperate whispering needs, of both finest grave.
Time not allowing them to miss anything, for receiving further blame.
Lending out each other sensual desire, over each other's shape.
Willing to cross limits, forgetting how hard it takes.

Hour passed of dipping into one another. Motioning body went humdrum. Lying flattening there back over bed, staring roof.

Smile on Tammana's face with Mark's staring at the roof gone concealed and thoughtful. Those unclear unwanted shadowed images letting mark eyes go disturbed. Sound of heavy breaths blowing out air into the aura.

"What are you thinking off?" she smiles and asked, same glancing towards the roof.

"We are getting late... why aren't you understand," said Mark with his head relaxing over his folded arm peeking up.

"What should I understand?" she queried.

"Guys were waiting outside for us," he said lying in his same studded posture.

"So what you want from me?" her spirit asked in a heavy tone.

"I don't know, how come I left my hassle of leaving this place and mixed up in you. We both know you are a spirit, with no beginning no end. I don't want to lose those things for what I travelled back my time, he said getting up from bed wearing a shirt.

"So you realised it," the spirit said.

"Aaaaah... no, it can't be... no," shouted Mark, his eyes still gaping wall watch.

"What happened now, I stood up on your will," said spirit with doziness, standing next to the bed.

"It's running closer to the timing, no .. I can't wait can't wait for a minute," said Mark as he rushed to pick his wallet fallen over the ground, impeded toeing his trouser up by tightening his belt.

"Don't make me feel panic now," the spirit said settling her wore gown above shoulders, carrying herself closer towards drinks counter out of bedroom over the right side of the hall.

"What you started again, please concede of my moves," said Mark tightening up his cloths wearing his shoes following her.

"Why should I?" she said making her pack out of whiskey bottle.

"You can't do this, I plead. Please move along," he requested as he ran to came out of the room and found the glass of whiskey in her hand.

"What you're trying to achieve, I sensed way beyond yours. Don't forget am a spirit inside Tamanna's body.

"But you can't kill the body which spaced you," requested Mark, walking closer towards her with his feeble face.

"Hahahahaha .... what a jest, I can do the worst I want to. I am a black spirit," sprit said in its intrepid fashion.

"Don't make a hell, I request you, please abide me," said Mark with ruined emotions down settling on the ground above knees.

"All happened in accordance with your will, till now. Please come along now," he said raising folded hands, bent on his knees, eyes filled with water.

"You'll get nothing crying in front of a spirit, who's emotionless".

"But somewhere you are a part of the person I loved madly," he replied in a steer.

"I meant from part of her negative emotion, I am far awayfrom heart-heartedness. Don't try ploughing seeds in me, you couldn't succeed," her spirit said bending below with her Insidious eyes staring closer Mark's face.

"I hope you are getting me and my desires," the spirit said.

"You have no rights to captivate your own living body," said Mark slower, adjacent coming face towards.

"Hmmmmm ... and you will tell me about my rights?," she replied upholding high pique over the face.

She raised before she turned around in extreme vexation to probe her power. Slashed her hand off bottles positioned over the counter shelf, lending to broke. Her eager to spoil erupts into the picture. The way she started throwing ornaments, spoiling them down into pieces. She kept on tossing her pique from one to another. Dumping whole room into a mess, in half a minute. Her enraged eyes peering Mark after every throughput dump she does, proceeding around the room. Setting hunch of what she can do after what she does. Her aggravation was out of control. Nothing was left unbroken and babble on the floor.

Feeble Mark was sitting on his place noticing her level of disappointment shown. Finding out the way to cut it from beneath, from wherever it's grown.

Entire aura got destroyed, by the way, she played 'Precipitating this destruction inside'. Like aura asking a favour to get spared of such cruelty. suddenly, the door started thumping from outside. Sayoni and Maunik voice in steer started approaching inside.

"What's happening inside? Are you both fine, Mark and Tamanna?" shouted Maunik bouncing over the door.

"Open the door, what happened? ... will somebody open the door?," screamed Sayoni hitting her hand stiffer over door.

"Coming," said Mark rushing towards the door, keeping his eyes over Tammana's violent gone spirit.

"Yes, what happened? Everything being ethical here, what you both panicking for?," asked Mark as he opened the door and peeped outside from small space, letting his head move out.

"We heard heavy sound artefacts shattering," said Sayoni being desperate to peer inside. Sayoni started jumping on her toe to spot from opened space of door above Mark's head.

"What… What... are you trying to? what you're encountering?" asked Mark putting his hand out barely, out of this small opened space, pushing her head down while she jumps.

"Why aren't you opening the door?" asked Sayoni.

"I already opened, am able to respond you both, can't you see," replied Mark.

"Why aren't you opening it up to complete?" she said putting thrust over door.

"Hey …. What, what you are doing wait… What?" said Mark with shuffled tone and feet dragging upholding door, handling thrust ahead.

Mark disguise his face, keeping him away from those raised question by both, after encountering the internal texture. He just left his ears to stay reactive for confronting whatever they convey.

"What is happening?" said Tamanna standing next to the door

staring Mark.

Tamanna standing next to Mark over to his left side. She's being well dressed with her complete outfits she wore for today. Carrying zero hunches over the face of what just happened between both.

"What?" said Mark facing shocked, as he realised her voice over to his back.

"Yes, same question. Why such an eerie reaction he's carrying?" added Sayoni.

"Tamanna... You and," Mark stopped as he spoke noticing Tamanna and a whole room with his those scrolling eyeballs in scare.

"Seems nothing happened inside, but that voice heard were conveying a mystifying picture," said Maunik with fumbling tone stoking Tamanna.

"How come the room transfigures accurate to its previous formation," crooned Mark.

"Can perceive things being sequestrate here. Guys tell me when are we leaving?" asked Sayoni going closer to Tamanna.

"We'll leave. Already we had crossed our time limits," said Mark pulling Sayoni away from Tamanna, making her stand next to him.

"Then what we are we waiting for?" asked Tamanna being point-blank reacting benighted.

"Yeah .. correct … perfectly asked," replied Mark peering everyone.

"Yes, why we are passing time here, at what we could have covered half a distance," said Sayoni.

"Huh… let's move as planned," said Mark ferrying bag above his shoulder, lying below.

"Like?," asked Maunik carrying patience over his nervous body.

"Like you and Sayoni will follow us in another car," said Mark upholding Tamanna's hand, leaving hall stepping out.

"Let me drive?" said Tamanna coming onto Mark's way putting

her hand forward asking for keys.

"No… Let me do," he replied dislodging her from his way and opening the door after unlocking pressing over a key.

"It's better I'll drive, from you getting lost while driving," said Tamanna's spirit holding his hand.

"In what I'll be getting lost," asked Mark turning back to face her.

"In your so-called versatile thoughts, that just wait or your mind to be ideal," Tamanna's spirit replied with her unstopped chuckling till the time Mark hadn't handed over keys to her.

"Huh… How could I give away this to her? How could I?" Mark asked himself repeatedly after he handed keys and she took her place over the driver seat.

"Now, how much time you need to get in?" she asked calling out Mark in vexation.

"I can't understand her spirit," Mark stressed out, thumped his head with fingers and stepped ahead with his manifestation towards Maunik to follow them.

"Aren't you feel, Mark started behaving weird?" asked Sayoni pinching Maunik's shoulder while both getting into their car.

"What am asking. You hitherto seems lost for him," replied Sayoni after not receiving a reply from him after seconds.

Both cars geared up, heading towards the destination. Those menacing hand of Maunik, scrolled car behind with his silenced face. Many queries took germination inside Sayoni's soul.

Those ways pretending to showcase difference, she's left herself getting rid of their presence.

Peering Maunik's sweating face, in such low temperature inside. Making Sayoni's query getting unanswered. Sayoni's prudent attitude helping to settle her anxiety quite easily. Giving space to time for reviling everything, the way they found much feasibly.

Storm with heavy rain started over their empty tracks. Those desolated roads seemed giving plenty of space for both cars to slide swiftly. Silent sitting Mark carrying niche of human over this aura. Looking outside, with his face touching window glass.

Mark's drowsy face below his mind lost in consolidated thought of things he encountered. Those deserted eyes, bare of emotions, asking to shut for a while. The gap between his words will remained unfilled. Finger wants to design muddled glass, as to how they want it to get filled. Hours went without any interaction between Mark and her spirit driving car. Things are not aligned, the way he wanted. Joining one word with others, he tried to write something over haze covered glass pane, before her spirit spoke and asked.

"Why you haven't felt yet? you are repeating a journey to save a person whose spirit has already overpowered her body?" she asked asserting towards Mark rushing car in extreme speed.

"Hey what the hell, can't you lessen it down little?" asked Mark with eyes peering ahead over the track.

"Don't you want to reach your destination soon?" she asked giggling.

"What? Which destination you're talking about?" he asked with a sinking heart.

"Don't stare me such," she replied.

"Wait stop the car, let me drive," he said gaping her through blunt open eyes.

"I am not going to get scared by you, although you need to feel scared of me," she replied.

"I can't understand what you want. Would you convey?" he insisted.

"For what such panic, Mark?" she pinched with her same continuous smile.

"I don't want to lose everything or my life," he replied purring out air off his mouth getting seated straight.

"And you find this as a saviour, of what you did," she asked.

"Are you not hearing my words. Stop it, I said just stop it," Mark's screeching voice getting converted to fill his eyes with tears.

"Hahaha, I wonder how could a normal being comrade a spirit."

"Don't show me yours tears, I don't contain heart," her spirit said.

"Have you ever loved me," he screamed.

"Yes, though I came after death to complete our alignment".

"This is not loving, it's called stubbornness," he said wiping his tears.

"I have to leave you. And I had," she said with her no change of emotion.

"See the sky outside. Look how that star severance from its world," she said pointing him to gaze up, heeding way of a falling star.

"What do you mean by that?" he asked observing a shine in dark black sky.

"You can't change anything which already meant," the spirit said and smiled, rushing down car over tracks.

"No, you can't spoil my life... No," he yelped badly.

"You can't play with Nature. Whomsoever time came to go, have to go".

"No.. !! No ..you can't be so cruel to take away everything of my life," Mark in adjuring.

"These words are from my mild heart Mark, it's me your Tamanna .. see," she said looking with her solitary eyes, over which Mark floated over their first meet.

Those eyes didn't contain any sword of slaying down.
Regardless, untold things they contained that are yet to be found.
Floating music settled right upfront one another.
Asking to believe someone and listen clearly what is said further.
Plane carrying memories took flight from its spot.
Will of reaping every bit of moisture in relation, they found once over that slot.
It's majestic or you can call mystifying.
Something that's lost, is found again to settle things fine.

Those eyes travelling their previous traversed path in each other eyes.

God gifted something back for which they are willing to pay any price.

Like a candle, her eyelids were falling and raising looking towards him.

His throat getting wet, believing something he saw in his dream.

The chapter whose last para was ended with elongated dots.

Those dots spoke a different melody, toeing their last beautiful nod.

"Lost where, Mark," she queried.

"I can't relate any word you said," he impeached ceasing.

"Then it's you who lacks in knowing my tenor," she replied.

"I can't dovetail your battled behaviours," he said being bemused self.

"Listen," she said with undoubted silence on her face pressing her toe hard over break.

She stopped the speedy roaring car abruptly. Mark balanced his body, taking the help of complete stretch over the seat belt. Mark stabilised himself, peering into the rear mirror of the car, there is no glimpse of Maunik and Sayoni the much his eyes can see far. Tamanna's spirit eyes tried recalling car of both following them. Her eyes aren't worried about Mark's thriving chapter whose last para was ended with elongated dots.

Those dots spoke a different melody, toeing their last beautiful nod.

disproportion, the time she applied break. But her eyes were despairing to encounter both. Maunik riding his car to catch their car which had gone lost from their mien. Sayoni wasn't scared of the situation they are in, as being unaware. But was in hassle on not confronting Mark's car roading ahead. She's pressing Maunik's shoulder repeatedly insisting to catch them soon.

"How far they had gone? See the meter, am riding on 120 km/h now," said Maunik.

"This you could have ridden previously as well, though we hadn't lost them".

"Are you in your conscious, aren't you seeing how dangerous it is now as well".

"Don't know how come this bitch is riding," said Maunik slowly looking ahead straight from the mirror.

"What? What you said just?" She intervened, like hearing something against her norms.

"Nope... Nothing! Nothing I said. What you heard?" he replied with his fumbling voice.

"Forget it... look ahead, just try to encounter them," she said moving his innocent face forwards through her hand, that's looking her.

"You bother worthlessly," he said giving a twist to his chin and accelerating.

"Can you monitor the glass wiper, I can't see ahead," he said bending his face to peer over the frontal way.

"There they are, see," Maunik pointed his finger forward after driving harsh for a couple of minutes.

"But why had they stopped in the middle of track? .. and that too when there's nothing around," inquired Sayoni being astray with her abduct eyeball inside enlarge opened eyes and hand place over Maunik's shoulder.

"How could I know?"

"Am in plight same like you," said Maunik noticing them both standing at a corner of the track on this hilltop. Car was also parked a meter distance from both of them.

"What are we doing inside? we should get out and see," Sayoni said and raised a hand to open her side door.

"No we shouldn't I feel," said Maunik while concessively looking towards both and ceasing Sayoni holding her hand.

"What? Why I can't go and check out what happened?" she petitioned Maunik whose staring towards both with his hushed face, discerning their action.

"See ahead what's happening, can you believe?" said Maunik.

Mark just stood evenness over his feet after hitting his feet with a rock. He was about to feel down which is stopped by the hand of brace through Tamanna's spirit. This is what Maunik saw and stopped Sayoni stepping out and wanted her to see.

"Aaaahhhh ..... he would have .. How these guys can be so remiss. God, she saved Mark, else my life would have finished," said Sayoni keeping a hand over her awe opened mouth. Her jolted reaction meant her loose pressure over her body, exhaling out thoughts she's into and lies down placing her back over the slanted seat.

"I believe to encounter this from a distance," said Maunik holding her hand.

Heavy brooks of air had taken this aura flowing out in their zest. Not even a single voice except the words spoke out of the two "Mark and Tamanna" could be heard around. Hanging Mark's arm in control of Tamanna's hand with no scare on his face. Mark budges his long lying hair with a strong stream that passes across. They kept in this pose for seconds and Tamanna said staring his face.

"You can't go from this world, as the time is not yours," she said while smiling.

"I had lost my hopes. And what could I do of life after loosing everyone important of it," said Mark still hanging with his slanted body and feet stuck over those corner of track buttress through her hand immobile.

"You hadn't realised yet from my words, only this pain I would be taking along with me," said Tamanna's spirit with those unseen wings opening their arms out of her back.

"Come... It's time for me to go," she said pulling Mark up to stand on his feet without her facilitation.

With his startled face, Mark set himself balanced gaping towards her just developed vans constantly. He stepped towards her and touched those to feel there significance.

“What was that, how could it? I am losing myself,” said Sayoni gazing Tamanna’s changing reckon being inhuman.

“This is what I was conveying you. As my existence and whatever I did after my life wasn’t a thing, a spirit like me can do. And you gave me a chance to rollback, the way you travelled time,” she said.

“I want you to listen to me clearly, as thee are my last words,” she said with a sober smile kept on her face and a cherish list sparkling in her eyes now.

“Time is passing now. Look around to this place and time at present,” she asked Mark, circulating out in all four directions with her spread wings and smile stood over the face.

“What happened?” she said looking his plunged face after looking up fro his watch.

“It’s all same as before,” he said swiftly being senile.

“Time had repeated itself and am happy to have a person like you in my life, for whatever time it would be,” she said before the fire started burning below her feet dismissing her body parts leisurely.

“You too had been the strongest beam to let me flow in the breeze of emotions I wanted to,” said Mark putting his hand forward with his pleasing face.

“You don’t have to worry Mark, everything will be perfect. Now nothing will happen against nature. And what all is happening, it’s required to occur,” she said with a smile while getting dismissed in the flame burning out below her.

Mark ran to touch her face as its last which is left before she vanishes off. His delighted body moves were anxious to express he gratitude towards her pure educate of soul. He’s wanted to ferry her about his aspirations towards before she vanishes off. Though he fastened his step towards her and left impotent to touch her face lastly. She left the space with a piece of very prosperous music drumming out in this aura. Mark shattered on his feet as she disappears. On the other hand, it’s Sayoni whose running to carry Mark in his arms with some tears in her eyes as he stood right now. Sayoni’s whispering footstep voice meant Mark to realise the presence, as his eyes floated towards her. That running feet and

Mark joint emotions are both clearly conveying of wriggle towards their alignment. Sayoni was already awestruck for what had already happened. She wanted to query every single thing that almighty weaponed.

Those questions are intact, with several untold incidences.

But their soul was relied on happiness, seeing one another presence.

The confused heart wants to solve the trajectory developed inside the heart.

Knowing what all happened in life and from where it started.

The end was good enough to tell them about there being for each other.

Their hand were telling everything, wiping out tears from the face of one another.